HOLY TERROR

HOLY TERROR

BARBARIAN PRINCESS™ SERIES BOOK 01

MICHAEL ANDERLE

DISRUPTIVE IMAGINATION

Copyright © 2021 LMBPN Publishing
Cover copyright © LMBPN Publishing
A Michael Anderle Production

LMBPN Publishing
PMB 196, 2540 South Maryland Pkwy
Las Vegas, NV 89109

Version 1.00 October 2021
ebook ISBN: 978-1-64971-961-4
Paperback ISBN: 978-1-64971-962-1

THE HOLY TERROR TEAM

Thanks to our JIT Team:

Diane L. Smith
Daryl McDaniel
Zacc Pelter
Rachel Beckford
Peter Manis
John Ashmore
Jackey Hankard-Brodie
Paul Westman
Kelly O'Donnell

If I've missed anyone, please let me know!

Editor
SkyHunter Editing Team

To Family, Friends and
Those Who Love
To Read.
May We All Enjoy Grace
To Live The Life We Are
Called.

— Michael

CHAPTER ONE

"I blame you for this."

Strider tossed his mane but showed no other response to her words.

"There must surely have been dozens of work opportunities to be found farther south," Cassandra muttered and settled a little deeper into the saddle as she studied their surroundings again.

She wasn't sure why she did that, except perhaps as a matter of instinct and habit. Hundreds of checks over the last few days had revealed nothing but trees and the odd squirrel. Aside from the road, of course, that had been so long neglected that it did not appear to have been repaired even once. After only a few more years, calling it a road would be an insult to all other proper roads.

"But no," she continued, even though she was sure Strider had no intention to speak to her. "I let Skharr go to Verenvan while I found myself a different calling. It seems my choice has me wandering the reaches of the north of the empire, looking for business that in no way befits a barbarian princess."

The damn horse still had nothing to say and she had begun to feel she was going mad from the lack of anything in the region. It had been ravaged by war and she had anticipated from the reports that it would be crawling with deserters and those criminals who generally plagued populated areas that had recently seen the effects of a sustained campaign.

By the time she reached one of the closest villages in the area, she realized that she was almost a year too late to help the folk in the region. Whether it was by soldiers—imperial or otherwise—or bandits of any kind, the village had been burned to the ground. All that remained was cold ashes and the signs of the living folk had made in the area.

The scene had repeated itself a few more times until she realized that she needed to travel farther north and away from the effects of the war. Or at least far enough away that it hadn't completely destroyed any chance at life.

"Fine, you don't need to say anything," Cassandra said and patted Strider on the neck. "I am happy for the company regardless of how engaging it might happen to be. I do wish we could have the rapport the other barbarian had with his horse but he never did say how he communicated with horses, only that he did. And I am still not sure whether he was lying or not."

Her instincts preferred to believe he hadn't lied. Perhaps it was merely the fact that he had been a barbarian for longer than she had. There were numerous reasons why a real barbarian would feel a little more in tune with animals than paladins.

She had thought about asking Skharr but in the end, it was likely that he would have simply fed her a handful of thoughts on the matter and left it to her to decide, given that he probably wasn't entirely sure himself.

It wasn't like Skharr to lie. Not as far as she knew him, anyway, and it made little difference. The only reason she considered it was because her mind was dulled and drained to the point of agony thanks to the unyielding boredom that prevailed over the landscape.

The only good thing to be attributed to the area was that the weather and temperatures were somewhat agreeable. The season was on the edge between summer and fall, which allowed her to camp comfortably without needing to build a shelter, and it hadn't rained for most of the journey aside from a little drizzle here and there. When it did, she surmised there would be real difficulty as the road she now traveled on would turn into a river of mud that would stick incessantly to her boots and Strider's hooves.

Cassandra knew her luck wouldn't last. Hell, she wasn't sure if she could call what was happening around them luck. Thankfully, water sources were plentiful in the area. They looked like they had once been drained dry by the armies that had marched through but had since recovered.

In fact, through the lack of any human presence, the whole region had begun to revert to wilderness. It would make the Northeastern Pass almost unreachable if something wasn't done. Perhaps the Emperor could turn his attention to the necessary repairs to the roads across his empire.

They approached another bridge across a small river and she slid off the saddle.

"I suppose you'll understand if I tell you to stay still and not run off anywhere?" she asked and patted Strider's neck again. "If you were to run and take all my supplies with you, that would truly be the end of the world. For me, at least."

Not that she had many supplies for the beast to run off with. She'd managed to stave off using them by gathering roots and berries and added the odd creature she managed to trap or fish for. She was the veteran of many a campaign and had collected skills that allowed her to survive in the wilderness without needing to rely on rations.

The bridge—possibly erected by a passing army—looked relatively intact and it appeared to be strong enough to take the weight of Strider and herself, but there was no point in putting that assumption to the test without making sure of it.

She advanced on the planks and watched the river below carefully. It didn't move too quickly, nor did it appear too deep to ford, but this close to the mountains, she could assume the water was ice-cold.

It looked clear enough for her to see the rocks below. This was certainly a good place for her to refill her water skins and maybe try a little fishing before she moved on.

Once she was on the other side.

"All right, I think it'll hold our weight," she muttered once she'd tested the strength of the beams a few times by jumping on them before she returned to where Strider waited for her and browsed a few scant patches of grass. "And if it doesn't, we'll have ourselves a nice refreshing bath. From the smell of you, I would say you need it."

Cassandra might have been losing her mind but it almost felt like the beast had rolled his eyes at her.

The thought made her smile even if it was a little far-fetched. She took him by the reins and began to lead him across the bridge. The timber below them groaned a few times when the horse put his weight on the structure but gave no sign that it would splinter and collapse as they continued.

"I've wondered if it might be time to call on Theros for a little help," she muttered to distract her mind from the noises the wood was making. "Probably not. He isn't the kind of god to appear when I need something to do and if he were, he would give me the kind of work that we would most certainly regret. This isn't what I planned but by Janus' puckered hairy ass, I'll take anything at this point. Even a glorious death."

Strider snorted although she wasn't sure if it was simply a noise he made or if he had laughed derisively at her comment.

She chose to believe it was the latter as they reached the other side of the bridge.

Before she could unhook the saddlebags and start setting up a small camp, she was interrupted by the sounds of fighting from over the next hill. She hadn't heard it over the rushing water but once she had moved past the river, she immediately recognized the noise made by those locked in some kind of conflict. Not much else in the world would produce the sounds of clashing steel and wood, along with cries from what she could only assume were humans at this point.

Not many elves or dwarves were left in the region, but she always ran into one or the other during her travels so she didn't discount them.

"I didn't pray but maybe the old bastard heard me anyway." Cassandra chuckled as she mounted quickly. Strider could feel her excitement and perhaps the gelding shared it at the prospect of something—anything—to break the boredom that had plagued them for too long.

Either way, he was more than willing to surge into a gallop at the slightest encouragement and raced over the hill to where the sounds were coming from.

This wasn't what she had thought the problem in the region would be. Ideas of scouts and armies had stuck in her mind but all she saw was a group of folk on foot under attack by brigands. None of the beleaguered travelers were warriors save one, a massive man with a thick, bushy black beard. His only weapon appeared to be a quarterstaff but he used it effectively to prevent the half-dozen or so mounted raiders from attacking the rest of their group.

He wouldn't last long, however. She could already see his arms dripping red from the many wounds they had inflicted on him. The raiders didn't appear to take the challenge very seriously and laughed when he pushed them back. One swiped a cut across his shoulder that made him stumble.

"Son of a whore," Cassandra whispered and shook off the miles of travel that had brought her to this road, She heeled Strider into motion and drew her sword from its scabbard on her saddle. They would hear the sound of it as well as the galloping horse. Even though it sacrificed any surprise she might take advantage of, it was worthwhile as long as it kept the raiders from hurting anyone else.

They turned their horses when they heard a new arrival but did not appear to be overly concerned. It was only one rider and not one who was heavily armed or armored for that matter, and they simply chuckled and trotted their horses forward.

Cassandra made a point to not meet them with overconfidence. Skharr could walk around like nothing in the world could hurt him, but the moment her focus waned was the moment when something stabbed her in the back.

She shifted in the saddle and a lance sailed past her chest, and her blade flicked outward. The speed and power from her and Strider allowed the sword to cut cleanly through the attacker's neck and his head thumped on the road. His horse advanced a few more steps and neighed nervously when its headless rider dropped lifelessly from the saddle.

Another lance was thrust toward her chest and Cassandra moved again, this time to parry it and push it upward. She twisted her wrist and the raider fell back with a scream, his hand suddenly no longer connected to his arm. Without so much as a second thought, the former paladin leaned in and sliced the blade of her sword across the raider's unprotected neck. A warm spray of blood caught her on her arms and shoulders and the man dropped from his saddle, clutching a wound that was too deep to stem the bleeding.

The other brigands immediately realized that they had made a mistake. A rough-sounding order was issued and they reined their mounts in, unsure of what to make of the woman who had appeared from nowhere and killed two of their men.

Taking advantage of their hesitation was necessary, but probably not in the way they anticipated. Cassandra brought Strider around, clicked her tongue, and let him trot to where the folk were watching, unsure of what to make of her as well.

She slid her sword into its scabbard and slipped smoothly from the saddle. The beast came to a halt on his own as she approached the man who now leaned on his quarterstaff.

"You're rather handy with that, aren't you?" she asked, her steps slow and cautious.

"Not as handy as you are with that sword," he answered in a deep, rumbling voice. "Who sent you?"

"Would you believe me if I told you I was merely traveling the road?"

"No one travels this road," the man answered.

Cassandra looked to where the raiders had gathered closer together and tried to decide what to do. If they attacked as one, there would be no way for her to counter them.

"Have a care," she said and placed her hands on his shoulder over the wound. "This might sting a little."

"What might—ah!"

The man growled as the magic slipped from her fingers and into his body and immediately began to heal the wounds he had suffered. He knew how to keep the horsemen at bay, which was something she would need in this fight.

"Are...are you a mage?" he asked and attempted to look at where his shoulders were healing.

"Of a kind. I used to be a paladin."

"To what god?"

She opened her mouth to reply but moved back quickly and drew her sword. "Now might not be the time for introductions."

He turned and scowled at the raiders, who had decided not to wait any longer and now began to push their horses forward again. Cassandra wished she'd thought to take one of the lances or had mounted Strider again.

Her eyes narrowed, she watched the brigands as they advanced on the travelers but instead of rushing to where Cassandra and the warrior stood, they rode to where the others were unguarded. It appeared they were no longer in the mood to fight and instead, approached the defenseless travelers, who quickly backed away with terrified screams.

"No," she whispered and raced forward. "No, no, no!"

They ignored her, grasped Strider's reins, and pulled him with them. The beast did not put up much of a fight and merely snorted and tossed his mane before he acquiesced and joined them as they rode away.

"Those shit-stains!" Cassandra shouted, hurled her sword ahead, and grimaced as it spun and sank into the ground well short of where she had aimed it. If there was ever a time to have a massive barbarian with a damned bow that could pick the shits off from a distance, it was now.

She could only glower at their backs as they rode away with all her food, supplies, and her portion of the dragon's treasure. The worst part was that they didn't yet know how lucky they were to find such extraordinary spoils.

"They are gone," the warrior said and joined her as she trudged frustratedly to retrieve her sword, almost the only possession she still had in the world. She had the armor of a barbarian princess under her leathers, of course, plus her clothes and the weapons she had strapped onto her person.

All else was gone.

There was a time when material possessions didn't mean much to her. Now, however, she was traveling and stuck in the middle of nowhere and had no idea whether she would be able to survive with a sword and her wits.

"Well, we have our lives," the warrior said with a firm nod. "For a moment before you arrived, we feared we would not have those."

Unfortunately, the raiders had taken the horses of their dead comrades as well, although they had left the bodies. She moved to where they lay and searched them quickly. There was little in the way of coin or food but their weapons were of good quality at least. They were probably deserters or perhaps they'd managed to steal weapons and armor from soldiers.

The warrior followed her and helped to hold the bodies. "You still haven't told us your name."

Cassandra looked up and realized that the other travelers had moved closer as well. They appeared a little unsure of her and whispered amongst themselves as they shook their heads.

"You've not told me yours," she answered and took a dagger from a brigand's belt as well as his lance, along with a small purse that had a few coppers in it.

"I am Caephas. These folk have been without a home and I offered to show them means and opportunity in these lands that have been mostly abandoned."

"A soldier?"

"Aye. A lifetime ago, I fought under the emperor's banner. I fulfilled my oath but abandoned all I had to help those in need as penance for my misdeeds."

She glanced at the man and his silver eyes locked onto her for a moment. "Not many soldiers feel guilt over what they do for lord and land."

"Not many soldiers did what I did."

"Fair enough." She offered him her hand and he took it at the wrist in a warrior's grip. "I am Cassandra."

"Cassandra. The Paladin of Theros?"

"No longer." She hefted one of the lances. "I strongly recommend you teach the folk to use these. You'd be surprised how effective a spear is against mounted warriors, even with little training."

Caephas took the weapon she offered. "And yet you are here, protecting the people who worship him."

"By chance, I assure you," she insisted but she could tell that her assurances fell on deaf ears. The men, women, and children were already whispering about how a servant of Theros had been sent to assist them.

They were half-right, at least. Technically, she was a barbarian to the god but she doubted that these people would understand the significance of that.

"You'll have to allow us to thank you for your help at least," Caephas stated once she had finished searching the bodies. "We don't have much but what supplies we can spare are yours. And a warm meal besides, I think."

As much as Cassandra wanted to pursue the assholes who took Strider, she knew running after them wouldn't bring anything worthwhile and she would likely simply find herself tired and dying of hunger and thirst after a few days.

"I won't decline a warm meal," she answered with a smile. "Although it should be said that I didn't ask for Theros' help, whatever the reason. And who the fuck helps by having a horse laden with treasure stolen?"

The people began to head to the river to set up camp for the night.

"He might have a plan that rewards you with more than you lost," Caephas suggested with a shrug.

"I won't wager my life on that," Cassandra answered and looked around suddenly. Either the madness had touched her again or maybe soft laughter drifted on the wind for some other reason.

The voice was difficult to ignore, however, and she was sure it said, "You're welcome."

"Maybe Janus isn't the only ass in the family," she muttered and resisted the urge to shudder as she moved to join the rest of her newfound companions.

"How many do you think we'll lose?"

Adrian shrugged and held his spear a little closer. "You know how the Herald likes to work. If she does things her way, we won't have to fight at all."

"It hasn't worked the last two times."

"Which is why the last two towns were burned to the ground." He turned and smirked at the man who stood next to him. "Once word spreads through the settlements about how every man, woman, and child was burned in the taking of their towns, those who have no desire to meet the same fate will be very willing to avoid it by any means necessary."

"Not every man, woman, and child. She always makes us spare one."

"How do you think the word is spread?"

Yaleh had reason to be concerned. As towns went, this one was not the worst he'd ever seen. A dozen or so homes had been constructed around a long central hall at the top of a hill. All appeared to have been built recently but showed the definitive signs of having been lived in.

The most interesting part of the town, of course, was the wall. Made of palisades, it held up the packed earth that the rest of the town was built on. This would put even the most vigorous of attackers on the defensive if the wall were breached since they would likely be buried under the dirt.

It even had a moat, although not the kind filled with water. They'd filled it with spikes so the only way to safely approach the wall was the narrow bridge across it that led directly to the gate. There, two towers allowed archers to rain death on any who might attempt the approach.

Someone with a keen mind for battle had designed all this, prepared for the possibility that someone would try to kill them and take what was theirs. An army was needed to break through those gates.

Thankfully, an army was what the Herald had at her disposal.

Adrian looked over his shoulder at the rest of the troop,

already organized and in formation with their shields facing ahead while they waited for the order to attack.

The cavalry would be ready at the back like they always were. Archers assumed their positions along the lines, ready to provide covering fire for the poor bastards ordered to charge the town with the means to traverse the moat and climb the walls. They would forge ahead of the engineers who would bring their battering ram up to the gates.

The mercenaries who would take the front lines were those who were paid the most, given that not all of them survived. Adrian counted himself among those. He'd been warring and battling for years. Generally speaking, he would avoid entanglement with folk like the Herald, but when someone like Belladonna called, men like him answered. It was in their blood.

They were being paid and offered enough coin with the spoils that it made the whole situation worthwhile for a man like him, but there was something about how she carried herself that naturally made him avoid folk like her. Even watching her ride to the front of her troops was unnerving and he returned his attention quickly to the walls.

"You have a problem with our fearless leader then?" Yaleh asked and nudged him with his elbow.

"No problems. The woman unsettles me, is all."

"I'm not sure why. A beautiful, powerful woman always did have my attention."

Adrian rolled his eyes as her horse advanced. The man was right, at least in terms of power. It seemed to radiate from the woman as she rode with marked nonchalance. She returned the stares of the archers she was within range of and almost dared them to attack first.

None of them did, not when the cool blaze of her green eyes leeched the courage from every man and woman on the walls and made them doubt their strength. While they looked at an army ready to ravage their homes, they truly feared the Herald above all else.

She remained seated in the saddle, leaned back, and studied the walls for a moment as soft gusts of wind touched the long black hair that was loosely braided down her back. Although she carried no weapons and her attire included no armor, something about her still unsettled the defenders on the walls. A few of them appeared to discuss whether they should simply shoot her.

He felt a little uncomfortable as well. Their army was silent and waiting but he could hear the orcs and goblins muttering in their own language. None of it was understandable as he'd never learned the language himself, nor the hand-speak they used to communicate. He didn't like fighting alongside them either given that about half of his adult life had been spent fighting against them.

Still, they followed the Herald's word as if it were from one of their chieftains. Perhaps it was. He'd never seen the like before in his life.

"Citizens of Torsburch!" she called and it carried to the walls and likely across them as well as even her horse was startled when her voice suddenly exploded outward. "Your choices are clear! You may send your leaders out to negotiate peace with me or you will see your city burn and every living thing inside your walls put to the stake, and to flame, and to cross."

Her statement was about as dry as could be for a situation like this, but there was more to the words. He'd seen her manipulate folk merely by speaking to them. Magic or no, it was the kind of power she could have used to make the other cities surrender if she had wanted them to.

Which either meant she reveled in the violence inflicted or it had been carried out on the orders of another.

It appeared as though they were ready to negotiate. Walls like theirs didn't need many men to defend effectively, but whoever had built them would be able to tell that they were overwhelmingly and desperately outnumbered.

The gates opened slowly and a small group rode out from inside. The Herald looked back and motioned for a few of the mercenaries to approach as well. He could understand why, of course. With a group that large, they would be able to kill her and ride back to their walls if they were so inclined. Or they would think they could. Either way, it would interfere with any attempt at a peaceful resolution.

Adrian joined her and remained on his feet even though most of the others were mounted. He was a larger fellow and had never quite felt comfortable atop a horse. Nor had he ever quite trusted the mad beasts either.

Still, none of them believed that the Herald would need their help if it came down to violence. They were simply a show of the force that carried a message no one could ignore.

The kind of show that was required by those who approached them on horseback. They were barbarians, by the looks of them, although the fact that they rode their horses instead of walking next to them indicated that they were from the deserts in the east. He had only learned this fact because they had a handful of the barbarians among their ranks and they liked to brag and boast about their fighting prowess and that of their kin.

It was never clear whether it was all barbarians or only those of their clan, given that they grew angry when he referred to the famed DeathEater clan that had produced some of the most renowned warriors.

They were odd bastards.

The chieftain of the town was tall and powerful and looked comfortable on the massive warhorse he rode. He grasped the hilt of the sword at his hip and was followed closely by a younger lad who was cut from the same cloth. If Adrian had to guess, it was his son, and both appeared to lead the small troop of warriors to meet with the Herald.

"We are a small town," the barbarian stated once they were all present. "We have no great treasures. Our fighting force is no threat to those who have come and gone through this land. We owe our allegiance to none and if you pass us by, we will not make any attempt to impede your progress."

"I am the Herald of Grimm the Cruel," she answered, almost like she hadn't paid any attention to what the man said. "Son of Karthelon. Everything you have and everything you are belongs to him. Give it willingly and you will live. Fight and your deaths will serve as an example to others who think of resisting."

"We will not surrender our city," the youth snapped and pushed his horse forward. "Not without a fight. If that is what you seek, your men will be piled outside our walls by the hundreds before the gate is breached."

"That can be arranged," the Herald answered with a disarmingly charming smile. "But I tire of endless bloodshed. I am sure both our armies would appreciate it if their leaders put themselves on the line instead of ordering folk to die for them. A duel, I think—myself pitted against your finest warriors and the winner will hold the city. There will be a fight but one that does not end in the destruction of your homes."

The barbarians looked around and muttered amongst themselves. Adrian could understand their surprise since he felt it as well. The invaders held the clear majority over those in the city and a dedicated push could take it before the sun reached its peak.

But there would be no questioning the Herald, at least not openly. If she wanted to fight, far be it from him to tell her she couldn't.

A doubtful expression had settled on the chieftain's face and was mirrored in some of his men. "How can we trust that your men will honor this agreement?"

"I am the one who commands them. Without me here to do so, they have no reason to throw themselves to their deaths at your walls." She slipped from her saddle and advanced on the group on foot. "Do you agree to my terms?"

He laughed, dismounted, and patted his saddle. "I do. I am my finest fighter, although my son almost matches me, and I would pit him against you or any of your men."

"Fight with him against me," she answered. "There is no denying that it would give your position more weight."

Both men exchanged a glance as the son slid from his saddle and drew the ax he carried at his hip. "What of your weapons?"

"They will be provided should I need them."

Adrian didn't like the response but as much as he felt as though their leader was being unnecessarily reckless with her own life, something in her words made him wonder if her recklessness was merely confidence instead.

The mercenaries appeared a little confused but both sides formed up into half-circles that created the ring the fighters would use. He still wasn't sure what they were expected to do if she lost. An organized army like this would inevitably attack something even if the leader was killed.

The chieftain drew his sword, looked at the Herald, and tried to decide if this was a trick of some kind before he lunged forward and bellowed some kind of battle cry of his people as he swung his blade.

She watched him advance and moved like a dancer might have to sidestep the first strike and slip around him as he tried to contain her. He was a large man and if he managed to grapple her, he would win, especially with his spawn close and ready to strike.

His son launched his attack and showed some skill as he feinted to the right before he twisted and attacked from the left. This forced her to take a step back and dance around him as though he were standing still.

Adrian hadn't seen her fight before and he had to stop himself from staring at her movements with a slack jaw as she carefully watched the two barbarians who prepared themselves for another attack.

Absolute calm radiated from her face as she plucked a few strands of hair from her scalp and winced slightly at the sting before she refocused on the two men.

She smiled but not a word was said and he realized that the strands of hair had begun to take on a blue light. In moments, they burst into flames of a similar color. The fire bit into her hands and scorched the skin but if anything, it made her smile turn even more manic as the son charged at her first and showed no fear of the flames that came from her hands.

His father, on the other hand, was immediately afraid and backed away but tried to not let his rising panic dictate his actions. Either the man was truly brave or he did not want to show cowardice in front of his men.

The damn barbarians had an odd fear of magic that was unique to their breed. He would never understand it. Magic was dangerous, yes, but no more than a spear to the chest or gangrene.

The Herald was laughing now and the flame had engulfed her hand and burned it thoroughly. She ignored this and lashed it out to slash it like a blade across the face of the younger man and he fell back, screaming. A thick, black burn appeared and sizzled and boiled before their eyes.

There was no time to tell if the lad was still alive as the father's fear was suddenly overcome with rage at seeing his boy injured or even killed. He attacked his adversary and raised his sword for a massive swipe across her body.

She was waiting for him and uttered her manic laugh as the flames flickered forward, burning hot enough that Adrian could feel them from a dozen paces away. They wound around the chieftain's torso, climbed higher, and immediately gave him a crown of fire. He screamed and fell to his knees.

The shrieks didn't last very long and the fire burned intensely to the point where little more than a pile of ashes remained. A handful of charred bones still smoldered amongst them but little else.

Almost immediately, the flames went out and the Herald finally showed a sign of the pain she had controlled while wielding the fire. She dropped to her haunches, her eyes closed, and ran her fingers over the cracked and blackened skin as she whispered softly. The charred flesh fell away to reveal fresh pink skin beneath.

Adrian had always known she was a powerful mage but seeing her able to inflict damage as well as heal it with equal amounts of competence showed exactly how powerful she was.

Finally recovered, the Herald turned to the men who stared in abject horror at their chieftain in a pile of ashes and his son who had not risen after falling with the wound to his face.

It was unlikely that he would again given the condition of his wounds and the way she turned her attention away from him.

"This is what happens to all who oppose the Herald of Grimm the Cruel, son of Karthelon!" she announced. Her voice carried again and reverberated so forcefully that the horses flinched and backed away. "All you have and all you are belongs to him. Return now and see to it that your gates are open when we approach."

Sending them away might not have been the wisest decision but there was fear in the eyes of the men as they swung their horses around and returned to the town. With the power she wielded, they might not need to bring the battering ram to bear at all. The Herald could simply burn the gates down if she wished to.

She would probably make them do all the work, however. What was the point of having an army if they didn't work for you?

CHAPTER TWO

It couldn't be a coincidence. She had gone to the north to find herself something to do, something to work her way through that would allow her to build her name away from Theros.

Despite all that, she was entangled with a group that held the god as their own. Not only were they devout followers but as the night she spent with them revealed, she traveled not only with stout believers but members of the clergy.

It explained why the pilgrims were so quick to recognize her. Cassandra hadn't thought she was so well-known that all the followers of Theros would recognize her name, but the clergy would know the names of the paladins they could call on when needed.

"Why do you travel with these people?" she asked in an attempt to distract herself from the fact that she wasn't riding. She hated walking over long distances and she had become a little too used to having a horse to at least help carry some of the load.

Caephas turned to look at her and shrugged. "I already told you."

"Penance for sins of a past life. I understand that." She

shrugged and shifted her pack to the other shoulder. "But I would imagine there are other ways to find penance. Many make a pilgrimage to some holy place or another. There are even orders of knights pledged to defend them. I would imagine someone of your skills would fit in well with a group like that."

"I thought of joining such a group but these appealed to me a little more. They do not seek any holy place to pray to some god or another who might or might not be listening. They are the kinds of skilled hands—carpenters, blacksmiths, and the like—who can help civilize the area after it has seen the ravages of war. I felt that would be a better use of my talents."

She could understand that, at least. And there was the fact that he chose the more difficult challenge as penance as well, which she could respect.

"It does make you wonder how the barbarian clans will respond to having these people arrive," Cassandra commented as they started moving again.

"Do you think they would have something against these people?"

"I wouldn't," she admitted. They had been nothing but kind, respectful, and even generous to her, gladly sharing what supplies they could spare. "But there is something unpredictable about the clans, especially in this region. Closer to the mountains, they would be a little more protected but out here, the clans have a tendency to be raiders more than anything else, especially a little farther south and east, closer to the desert. A soldier who fought in these lands would know this."

His head snapped around and she smiled at the hint of panic in the man's eyes. She had suspected it for a while but it now felt like it had been confirmed. He grasped his staff like he was afraid of what she would do now that he was caught in a lie, but she raised her hand.

"I won't say as much to the other folk here but I would suggest speaking the truth over lies."

She could tell he was not convinced by the way the massive hands still clutched the quarterstaff almost like he was considering scampering into the wilderness and away from her. It did raise the question of where he was planning to go but she stood by her word.

"You won't tell them?"

"Your secrets are yours to tell as you please." She pulled the water skin from her hip and took a sip. "Whatever your reasons might be, you do appear to be doing these people a good deed, although I would prefer to know it if you plan to lead them to any harm."

"Of course not."

Cassandra smiled and patted him on the shoulder. "Then keep or share your secrets as you will."

The rest of the group had paused in their travel for a short rest under the blazing midday sun. She had begun to get used to the patterns the pilgrims followed after a few days traveling with them, but it would take her a little longer to get used to trudging everywhere on her own two feet.

Caephas sighed deeply and his broad shoulders sagged as he sat on a nearby rock. "The truth, then. I suppose there is no real reason to hide it."

She remained silent and let him find the words he was looking for on his own. One of the skills she had learned as a paladin was to listen to people and allow them to come to the resolution of their problems without her needing to interfere.

"I was once trained in the temples," he stated finally and shook his head, "to be a paladin like you. Words about Cassandra the Paladin as the mightiest among those who were so elevated were shared quickly and eagerly. But circumstances arose that saw me dismissed in disgrace."

That certainly seemed like the kind of story that needed to be told, although Cassandra again chose to wait and let the man tell it at his own pace.

"My mother was dying and needed me to be at her side in her final hours. The priest in charge of our training saw to it that I was removed. If I were to forsake my calling for my mother, how could I expect the temple to stand at my side?"

Cassandra narrowed her eyes. There would have been a time when she agreed with the priest's words and even added a few of her own to the matter. Paladins were meant to forsake all in the name of serving the Lord High God and his will, which meant that any attempt to change that would be going back on the oath they made to Theros or whichever god they served.

As she grew farther and farther from the teachings she'd espoused so deeply when she had been a paladin, however, the more she realized how horrifying the implications were.

"I knew your magic from when it was taught to me," he continued and lowered his head into his hands. "From there, it was easy to make the leap from your name to your reputation even if you do not dress as you once did."

She looked at her garb. It wasn't quite the barbarian princess attire she was starting to get used to. The chainmail undergarments were still worn beneath but she was dressed in a pale gray shirt and leggings that fit a little more snugly than a paladin would usually wear, although they did match the color of her riding boots.

It had taken her a while to find proper clothes for herself and for quite some time, she rode around in the undergarments. She had grown to revel in the horrified expressions of those she came in contact with.

The people had begun to arrange their camp near a small stream. The sources of water were becoming more scarce, which meant that even though it was in the middle of the day, they would probably remain in the area until the next day to make use of the water before they moved on.

She couldn't entirely disagree with the idea. Traveling in the wilderness like this had a way of making people want to push themselves to reach their destination as quickly as possible to avoid being stranded without food or water in a foreign land.

It was more common than people realized. Even powerful and skilled generals had stranded their troops while moving a little too eagerly when caution would have been better.

"You haven't said anything."

Cassandra looked up and realized that she had let her mind wander from the conversation at hand.

"Do you believe my actions to be that horrible?"

"Was it wrong to care for your mother in her time of need?" she asked and raised an eyebrow.

"Wha…what?"

"Your mother. She needed you. Did you think it wrong to attend to her in that time and be at her side before she left this world?"

It was his turn to narrow his eyes a little defensively over her question. "No. No, of course not."

"Then what do you have to be ashamed of?"

He paused, tilted his head, and looked at the folk they were protecting. "Not much, I suppose."

"If you could go back, would you change your actions?"

"No."

"Then you stand by what you did."

Caephas nodded slowly and drew a deep breath. "I suppose I do. But still, my promise was made."

"I don't remember much of the first oath of a paladin." Cassandra shrugged. "It has been many years since I recited it as a child but from what I recall, it is an oath to help those in need in the name of Theros."

"Well, yes, but—"

"And so you did."

He nodded. "I suppose you are right."

"But you went back, didn't you? You made the attempt to rejoin once your mother had passed?"

"Of course."

She smiled. "Then the only one who should feel shame is that priest. He would need a woodsman to help pull that tree-sized stick from his ass and allow him to realize that he has no idea what he is doing."

That brought a laugh from Caephas, who shook his head. "Well, I am glad you see it that way."

"And in the end, you are doing precisely what paladins are meant to do—watching over the innocent and protecting them as well as you can manage to the best of your abilities. I am sure that all those who consider such things will take note of that and of your efforts in performing your duties as a paladin, whether you were sworn in and took your oaths or not."

"I…hadn't thought of it as such. All I wanted to do was make up for the shame."

"And in so doing, you became what a paladin should be." Cassandra patted him on the shoulder. "Helping those in need should always be considered a noble effort, no matter the reason why one chose to do so."

CHAPTER THREE

A handful of civilization centers remained in the region and allowed the people she was traveling with to settle for a moment and decide whether they wanted to stay there or move on.

Cassandra had a feeling that they would prefer to move on. The devout were a very particular group and Edge's Rest was not where she pictured them for a longer period of time. From the looks of the settlement, it was a trading post that had flourished beyond the intended purpose.

She had already parted from the small group as they continued to the port at the river, likely looking for passage or those who might need their skilled work. Instead, she headed up the plateau to where the city was situated. The high elevation meant that it looked over the whole region without too much difficulty, and it was immediately apparent why it had grown so quickly.

It was on the border of the empire and connected it to the various city-states and smaller kingdoms to the east, and its position allowed it to operate without interference from the empire as a whole. There was no sign of flags or any soldiers wearing imperial colors as she entered.

Soldiers were present but it was immediately apparent that they were not there to keep the peace. The sight of a couple of men swinging their fists in the middle of the road while the soldiers appeared to be betting on the outcome was an interesting one that would probably not happen anywhere else in the world.

Or maybe there were pockets here and there that allowed for this kind of lawful lawlessness to occur. She simply hadn't seen any of them before.

"Skharr would like this place," she muttered, folded her arms, and watched the fight as well.

Both men appeared to be fighters in their own right, powerfully built and covered in the kinds of scars that came from living their lives on the ragged edge. They also seemed experienced in fighting but showed that they needed some instruction on defense and the other technical aspects of combat.

Then again, maybe that was why it was so much fun to watch.

The one on the right—who sported long, flowing red locks— roared, threw himself forward, and drove his fist into the other man's jaw. The second man was bald but wore a thick beard in a tight braid that the other fighter caught hold of to hold him still as he hammered another punch that cracked the skin over his eyebrow.

Blood flowed from a deep cut over the man's eye, although he showed no sign of slowing and immediately grasped his taller opponent by the back of his neck as he snapped his head forward and pounded his forehead into the other man's mouth and nose.

It drew a roar of approval from the small crowd that had gathered, although it didn't look like either of the fighters paid attention to what was happening around them. Both men were now covered in blood and staggered somewhat. The redhead moved forward and delivered a hard fist into his opponent's gut. It was answered immediately by the bald man, who tackled him to the cobblestones, straddled him around the waist, and screamed as he rained punches on him.

He stopped barely short of killing the man given the way he coughed blood, but the swelling showed that he would need attention from a local healer. If Edge's Rest had one of their own. It seemed like the odd kind of place for a healer but if one were present, they would likely be protected by the rest of the ruffians who wanted to make sure someone was there to care for them should they happen to need it.

Finally, the sounds of fists beating flesh stopped and the bald man drew a deep breath, leaned back, and paused to wipe some of the blood from his face. There was a great deal of it—both his and that of his opponent—but there was no doubt as to who the winner of the impromptu bout was.

"All right then, Beeru, Sacha, that's enough of that," one of the guards ordered and motioned for the others to join him. "One of these days, you two will kill each other and all I can say is that I hope you do it at the river. That way, at least the blood will be washed away on its own."

Beeru, the bald man, was helped to his feet and led away while Sacha, the redhead, needed to be hefted by two of them and dragged away. The man who appeared to be the captain laughed and shook his head as he followed the group.

The rest of the local inhabitants appeared to be equally as amused but quickly returned to their business of drinking, fucking, and whatever else was on their minds.

One fellow, taller than Cassandra and with broad shoulders and a thick mop of brown hair, wandered down the street with a pleased smile on his face and without a single thread of clothing on his body.

"My cock is magic." He uttered a high-pitched laugh when he realized she was staring.

It was of a decent size, she was willing to admit, but she'd seen bigger in the past.

"Prove it," she answered with a smirk. "And see it disappeared from my sight."

The man laughed again, clearly under the influence of something stronger than the typical liquors or spirits that could be found in the area, and wandered off again.

It was an odd city. The guards were more than willing to partake in the debauchery that filled the streets as well as the dozen or so taverns, inns, and sand dens within the walls. They also appeared to be enthusiastic in defending the proprietors and employees of the establishments in question. It was likely that whoever paid them profited a great deal from the businesses and merchants who made their living inside the walls, so any who did business there were under the protection of the man or woman.

The kinds of illegalities that would have most other law-abiding citizens of the world shocked were allowed but if anything interfered in the flow of coin into the city, it would be punished severely.

It was odd that none of them so much as cast her a second glance. Cassandra was almost tempted to pull her clothes off and walk around with her armored undergarments on display but for the moment, she had more important business to deal with. Finding supplies and possibly a horse with the meager coin she could scrape together would not be an easy task.

Her gaze settled on three guards seated on barrels while they threw dice on the fourth. It was an odd choice but she needed to start somewhere.

"Apologies," she said as she approached. Their attention settled on her immediately although none of them so much as bothered to stand. "I find myself in need of supplies. Where might one find a market in this town?"

"A new arrival, eh?" One of the guards chuckled and rolled his neck. "I suppose we do have the time to search you."

"Unless you'd like your comrades to know what your body

looks like without any hands, I wouldn't," she answered with a smirk.

The trio laughed and the one who spoke immediately turned his attention to the dice they were throwing.

"Where have you come from, violent stranger?" another asked and took a swig from a nearby skin that she doubted held any water.

"Far from these lands and I intend to move farther still."

He nodded. "You can find a handful of merchant stalls and buildings at the cliff overlooking the river. Those tend to sell the wares you are searching for."

"Your assistance is appreciated." She bowed her head in thanks, knowing the trio would watch her as she wandered off.

She had no idea where the cliff side of the city was but it didn't seem like the kind of town she could be lost in for long. Despite the endless variety of activities, it was still smaller than most towns she had been in. A handful of people looked at her but most of the eyes were drawn to the young men and women who were scantily clad outside the brothels, calling for those on the road to come in and sample their wares.

Cassandra imagined that this was some kind of punishment for those tasked to call and shout at the people on the street while the others were involved inside making coin.

She wondered what the condition of the people working in this city was. Many folk said that whores chose the profession, but she knew better. Even if it had been chosen, it was out of desperation for most of them. Her instincts as a paladin told her that she needed to act and help these people somehow. There had to be some way for her to make their lives better.

But the reality of it was that any change would be resisted. In the end, she was only one woman going up against the will of an entire city. There wasn't much she could do.

After a moment of watching, she gritted her teeth and her fingers held her sword hilt a little tighter before she moved on. A handful of youths stood near her and looked away like their attention was elsewhere, but they were inching in her direction. They no doubt had long, nimble fingers anxious and waiting to slip into her pockets and relieve her of what little she still had.

The chances were that if she remained where she was, she would have to spend the night in whatever cells they had available after she'd rearranged a few faces for the amusement of the guards. As interesting as the idea was, Cassandra simply did not have the time for it.

One seemed a little more insistent than the others. He stepped in front of her with an intense look on his face as he reached for a dagger he carried inside his cloak.

There would be no time to teach him a proper lesson and she had better places to be and more important things to do. Instead, she acted before he could even broach the subject of whatever reason he had to stop her. She imagined that a speech about donating was imminent but she didn't wait for him to finish it.

Quickly, she unhooked her sheath from her belt and snapped her sword forward, still sheathed. The hilt thudded into the lad's mouth. His lip split and a couple of teeth came loose with the impact as he fell back with a soft cry. He let his dagger fall as he clutched his mouth.

"I'm sorry about that," she muttered, unsure why she apologized as she hooked her sword into her belt and moved away from the scene.

A hint of gratification followed when she realized the other pickpockets immediately backed away to look for easier targets. She could have scared them off easier and quicker with a quick display of her magical abilities, but that would have garnered her a little too much attention. As it stood, there was one lad—still very much alive although now missing a handful of teeth—who knew better than to get in her way.

Hopefully, the word would spread as she moved toward the market. There were a few sights to see still and she noted that a man was being lowered slowly into a massive vat of water with his hands bound above his head.

"A punishment?" Cassandra asked aloud.

The man heard her and laughed. "I've been a bad boy. Would you care to join the punishment?"

She shuddered and moved on hastily. While she wouldn't judge the vices folk enjoyed, there were certain things she simply could not understand, no matter how hard she tried.

With that thought in mind, it certainly seemed like a place that Skharr would enjoy visiting. Hell, if he stuck around for long enough, she assumed he could probably make himself king of the little town.

Now there was an idea.

The market was as described with a view overlooking the river, the port, and the landscape for miles. It was a genuinely impressive view as long as one didn't mind the various human stenches that filled the streets. She wasn't one to complain over-much about that kind of thing but she assumed they waited for the rains to wash the streets instead of doing it themselves.

The merchants at least put some effort into cleaning the area in front of their stalls and stores, and more guards were present there than anywhere else in the city.

These were better-armed and armored than those she'd seen at the gate. Perhaps they were paid by the merchants to protect their businesses and it was likely a good investment too, given how infested the city was with all kinds of criminals. Even those stupid enough to try to steal from those under the protection of the guard.

"Welcome, weary traveler," the owner of the shop called when she entered and approached as he cleaned his hands on a white cloth hanging from his belt. "It's always good to see new folk coming through our little Rest. We have many of the foul kind about here but you look like you're a step above most of them."

"I would not hold myself over any man," Cassandra

commented. "And if you expect me to buy your finest and spend with your richest customers, I am sorry to say you are destined for disappointment."

"For the heavens above, there is always the muck below," the merchant answered with a laugh. "I am accustomed to dealing with all kinds and those who possess both weighty or light purses. My wares are good quality, both the cheap and the expensive, but you'll have to manage your expectations on the former."

Cassandra had expected him to say something like that but in the end, she didn't need much—some rope, flint, and what food couldn't be acquired in the wilderness. If she had more coin, she would try to find a decent horse to ride but at this point, she would settle for a mule.

Theros would have a laugh at that, no doubt.

As she inspected those wares that were in the range of her meager purse, a massive shoulder pushed her to the side. She spun to look at the new arrivals, ready to give them a piece of her mind.

But for some reason, she paused. The two of them were both head and shoulders taller than she was and from their garb, she felt it safe to assume they were barbarians. With that said, the lack of any bows told her they probably were not DeathEaters, although she wasn't sure how she could tell. Maybe it was the energy they exuded.

Then again, Skharr did seem something of an outlier. To measure the whole clan based on one example was poor form and she wouldn't make that mistake.

"We need food—for us and our horses," one of the men snapped. "Camp equipment as well, the best that you can provide."

The shopkeeper raised an eyebrow. "I think not. But if you'll look at my other wares—"

"Do you think your cheap shite will do for DrakeHunters?" the other one demanded. "Your finest wares and at a fair price.

There are too many gougers in this city thinking to prey on the desperate."

"Which…you are?" Cassandra asked and raised an eyebrow. From the worn state of their clothes, it looked like it had been a while since they'd seen any care.

"That is none of your concern," the first one replied. "Step aside before I make you."

"I'll have to ask you to avoid antagonizing those of my customers who intend to pay," the shopkeeper protested and a couple of the guards began to approach, their hands on their weapons and ready for trouble.

"We'll take what we need and at a fair price," the barbarian insisted.

There would be a fight, and as much as she did not want to be involved, if something happened and she could have prevented it, she would have a problem with herself.

And that was not acceptable. She drew a deep breath and took a step forward before the guards could decide to intervene and give the barbarians an excuse to draw their weapons.

If she knew anything about them, it would turn messy and it would happen quickly.

"Hold your men back for a moment," Cassandra stated and spoke in as commanding a voice as she could muster. It had taken a fair amount of work but her time as a paladin had taught her how to speak with authority. "I speak for these men. I am the Barbarian Princess and any negotiations they might need performed, I can carry out on their behalf."

A moment of silence settled over the shop and even the guards looked like they were uncertain as to what to do. Their hands remained on their weapons but they glanced at the shop owner as if waiting for some kind of order or action that would tell them who needed to be punished, if anyone.

The proprietor seemed a little confused as well, but nowhere near as confounded as the two barbarians, who appeared to be brothers given their similar appearance.

"I wasn't aware that we had—"

"No, I don't know if...but if she says—"

They were trying to make sense of her, that much she could tell, but neither of them was in a position to question her claim. That was all the indication she needed to hold her ground, even if they decided they needed convincing. Both barbarians were large and strong but were also young and inexperienced.

It was an odd combination but she felt something like a kinship to them. While full of bravado, piss, and vinegar, they were in need of a little guidance and a hand to show them the way.

The fact remained, however, that both were headstrong and from the looks they exchanged, she suddenly realized that they intended to challenge her claim.

One of them extended his hand to push her aside and continue with their original purpose, a choice that would lead to them fighting a dozen guards who would likely kill them both.

It would not be an easy fight but if she could manage it, there would be little else to say. Barbarians respected physical strength more than almost anything else.

As the hand touched her shoulder, she caught it, grasped the thumb and forefinger, and twisted until the man was off-balance. With that in mind, she was already moving in to drive her heel down on his instep, then waited for him to bunch up and lower his head to where her elbow could hammer into his cheekbone. It had enough power behind it that it removed what little balance he had left and he tumbled heavily. He looked a little stunned and a bruise appeared on his cheek that would likely swell into his eye too.

Despite these minor injuries, he was none the worse for wear. His brother, on the other hand, immediately joined the fight and lunged directly at her without so much as making a sound. It was a trick she'd seen other barbarians perform on occasion and so expected it and pretended that her focus was still on the one on the floor. She glided out of the way as smoothly as she could manage but left a foot out to catch him as he passed.

He tripped but caught himself before he fell and turned to find a fist waiting for him. It met his jaw with a hard crack and stunned him for a moment. It provided the time she needed to snap her hand forward and hit him in the gut with all the power she could muster to drive the breath from his lungs and double him over.

Cassandra raised her elbow and hammered it on his back to finally drop him next to his brother. She felt a little out of breath as she regarded them warily. They hadn't expected such a quick and effective reaction from her and were both powerful warriors who would most likely not be caught by surprise again.

For the moment, however, her point was made and neither man would question her authority again. At least not for a day or so.

"Now then," she stated and extended her hands to both men. "Should we get back to the business of seeing you two outfitted or do you want me to show you how royalty defends itself again? I am sure I could toss the two of you over the cliff behind me and you'd survive as long as you landed on those thick fucking skulls."

It looked for a moment like both were in the mood to continue the fight but they paused and exchanged a glance before they took the hands she offered to them.

"Where did you get that scar?" one of them asked and indicated the one that was visible on her forearm.

She looked at it, narrowed her eyes, and ran her fingers over where she remembered the searing heat marking her. It was still a little tender and the scar still had an angry red welt look to it, which told her she needed to reapply the salve that had softened the skin and allowed it to heal.

"It's from a dragon, stupid." The other one grunted and shook his head.

"I know that," the first retorted before he turned to her again. "What I am asking is how she managed to receive a burn from a dragon and live to tell the tale."

Cassandra raised an eyebrow. "What are your names?"

"I am Tandir," the first answered with a chuckle. "The ilk you see beside me is my brother Bandir. Of the—"

"The DrakeHunter clan," she finished for him. "I heard."

"The ilk is the one who was dropped first," Bander muttered and pulled some of his long brown hair from his face as he rubbed his back where she had struck him. "How did you survive getting close enough to a dragon for it to burn you?"

She looked at the shopkeeper and the guards, all of whom had been ready to jump into action in her defense but held back when they realized she required no aid. They too appeared to be interested in finding out how a princess survived being burned by dragonfire.

"I killed it," she stated simply and honestly.

"Bollocks," Tandir muttered. "No being in the world can stand alone against a fucking dragon, not even the most powerful mage."

"I was not alone," she answered with a small smile. "I was joined in battle by a fellow barbarian by the name of Skharr DeathEater. Between the two of us and a great deal of luck, we managed to fell the beast."

Both laughed and exchanged a look before they turned to face her. "You…you fought alongside Skharr DeathEater?"

"Do you doubt my word?" Cassandra raised an eyebrow and watched their expressions.

"Why…no," Tandir answered with a small shrug. "He might not be of our clan but the stories… Are they true?"

"Some of them. Depending on which stories you heard."

"That was the second dragon he killed then?" Bandir asked and took a step forward as if eager to find out.

"Second?"

"The stories of how he brought the emperor to his throne. He slew a dragon there too."

"He survived a dragon there," Cassandra corrected. "By his word, they managed to sneak past the dragon and in the last moment before they entered that particular dungeon, it saw them and attacked as the doors were closing. The fire caught them but he protected both with a shield. It was destroyed and his arm was burned, but a vial of healing potion was enough to keep him alive and his arm ready for a fight."

Both shared a look that told her they had more than simply heard the stories. They held them to heart and certainly looked up to the barbarian.

"Have you more tales of Skharr?" Tandir asked.

"I'll tell you what," she answered with a smile. "Buy me a drink and I'll tell you all I know."

They looked at each other again and she laughed.

"All right, you sad sacks. I suppose I can buy the drinks myself."

The horse was tiring and she could feel its strength starting to wane. Verda had heard of horses being pushed to the point where their hearts gave out but she couldn't do that, not when the beast had carried her so far.

By now, she was as tired as her rider was. The heat radiated from the gray mare and sweat soaked the saddle. She needed to consider how they could continue. Torsburch had been taken and she'd only managed to escape with her life, a horse, and what supplies had been in the saddlebags when they slipped away.

The hope was that she could hire some mercenaries to liberate the city with the coin she had found in the saddlebags, but she doubted that enough would come at so low a price.

Still, she had to try. There was no telling if the forces who had taken her home were following or if there was anything she could do about it. All she could do was continue to run and push the mare until they reached Edge's Rest. It was a community of criminals and a seething pit of villainy, to hear her father describe it, but if she had even a remote chance of finding the warriors to reclaim her home, it would be there.

For all she knew, they were already punishing her family for her escape.

The walls of the trade outpost rose in the distance before she was finally able to bring herself to stop. Verda looked at the road behind her and tried to discern any movement that would indicate that she was being followed, but none appeared. She pulled a few strands of black hair back from her face.

It took a few attempts as the strands clung to the rivulets of sweat that trickled over her face.

"Gods…" The word slipped from her mouth almost thoughtlessly as her body relaxed. The fire in her blood had begun to dissipate and all that took its place was the fatigue that came from however long the ride had been.

The mare snorted and pranced, anxious to continue moving. Maybe the horse knew better than she did and her pursuers were only minutes away. She let the mare move toward the walls ahead. Walls were safe—or they were supposed to be. They hadn't done much to keep her home safe.

Maybe these would be different. She would have to lie to any mercenaries willing to take her coin. Aside from the massive army they would have to contend with none would want to face the Herald willingly.

But the townsfolk needed help and they needed it desperately. If it meant she had to lie on both counts, she would do it willingly. All she had to do was get them there and trust that the terrible reality would overcome any anger or resentment her dishonesty might cause.

CHAPTER FOUR

There wasn't much to be said regarding the quality of the drink they could afford, but Cassandra had long since allowed herself to have an open palate when it came to food and drink. The ale that was presented had a slightly bitter taste but she assumed it would be better than the wine, which smelled sour from across the room.

Still, beggars could not be choosers, and what little coin she had paid for a jug the trio could share.

"I still have no idea how the hell a dragon can speak or why it would be so attached to a fucking doll of all things," she continued and sipped her ale. The empty room allowed them at least a little privacy. "All I do know is that the dragon was angry that we'd taken the doll. Hell, it looked like it had been repaired during the decades since the beast had been trapped in that gods-bedammed place, which meant it went out and snatched folk who knew how to repair it."

Tandir chuckled and shook his head. "A mad dragon is the kind of thing one hopes they will never have to encounter. Those that wander the mountains are horrid enough. But...didn't you say the elf gave you a potion that allowed you to understand what it was saying?"

Cassandra frowned and nodded. "Correct. Still, how would it know how to communicate in a way that would allow us to understand it? I don't know, maybe it was the potion that somehow taught us how to speak to it. Anyway, when it returned to the pile, it began to rant and rave about the godsbedammed doll and after a moment of conversation, we started fighting. The monster poured fire into the whole fucking chamber, which made it difficult to stand our ground, but Skharr managed to deflect its blast with a mystical shield."

"You would think the dragon would be immune to its own power," Bandir commented.

"It was. But it wasn't immune to him dropping the damn roof on its head. With it pinned down, I managed to retrieve the spear I told you about and stabbed it through the neck. In the end, the creature only wanted freedom and the bonds it had been put in had left it in a great deal of pain as well. I can't even imagine how mad I would be if I were bound and restricted to a painful situation like that."

She shook her head and sipped from her mug again.

"Dragons aren't the hateful beasts they would appear," Tandir agreed and sounded a little wistful. "But a beast like that couldn't be allowed to roam free, especially if it wanted to wreak vengeance on the world at large."

Cassandra raised an eyebrow. "It's an odd thing to feel bad over killing a creature that deranged, but yes. I've had fewer qualms about killing humans if I'm honest."

"What happened to the spear you used to kill it? You must have kept it, at least as a souvenir."

She wasn't sure which one asked. They looked similar enough that she had a difficult time telling the two apart, which made her think they were more than brothers—twins, surely. Not quite identical, but similar enough, both with scraggly beards that hadn't quite come in properly, their hair shorn at the sides and the rest in a braid a little past shoulder length. They had warm blue eyes and their grins showed their canines that looked a little like fangs.

One had a scar on his right cheek and the other appeared to have had his jaw broken in the past, which made it look a little asymmetrical, but for the life of her, she couldn't make out which was which. Maybe they would say each other's names again and she would be able to determine one from the other.

"I did have the spear," she answered and shook her head. "I carried it on the saddle of the horse I was riding—a horse that was stolen from me, along with most of the treasures I took from the dragon's hoard. I've been gathering supplies so I might go and find the bastards who took it."

She could almost hear the laughter in the air again, although perhaps it was only the sound of the wind whipping through the holes in the building's walls. She felt as though something was speaking below what she could hear but she could discern the voice, at least, buzzing in her ear like a gnat.

In that moment, the door to the tavern swung open and a group entered, speaking loudly, laughing, and sounding like they were already deep in their cups. From the looks of them, they had likely already been forcibly removed from another establishment, and perhaps also the one after that, which compelled them to find somewhere that would allow them to continue drinking without interruption.

The laughter suddenly made sense. Cassandra was already well on the way to drunk but she would remember the armor the men wore like it was yesterday. These were the same godsbedammed bandits who took Strider.

Coincidences like this simply weren't possible. Or perhaps they were. This was the only town in a thousand miles that would allow men like them to indulge in their vices and spend stolen coin without questions being raised, so it made sense that they came to Edge's Rest.

And the chances were that once they found the treasures in Strider's saddlebags, they would take the time to enjoy the profits of their thievery. There was certainly enough of it to allow them to continue enjoying those profits for the days it would take for her to reach them.

Still, she couldn't help the feeling that another's hand was at work and she wouldn't miss the opportunity. It might well be that while she had taken the time to offer Theros all the insults she could muster for putting her through the trouble of having to trek all the way on foot, they had likely spent her treasure on drink, food, gambling, and all the other pleasures and comforts that the city provided.

Not much of it would be left, depending on how long it had been since they'd arrived—and it did appear as though they had been enjoying themselves for a while—but they were still wearing their armor. It offered a sliver of hope that some of the treasure remained and at least Strider was still among them.

"Speak of the devils," Cassandra muttered. "I have a new story."

"But I wasn't done," Tandir said, confused.

"Quiet," she admonished and made sure they hadn't attracted attention from the raiders who were ordering about as much drink as they could stomach for the moment. "The story is of a princess who rode to the aid of innocent craftsmen being attacked on the road, only for the bandits to steal her treasure-laden horse after she dismounted and tried to help their wounded. And, as luck would have it, as the princess was drinking her sorrows away with two barbarians, those same bandits came in to spend their ill-gotten treasure."

Bandir narrowed his eyes. "That is a story. One that seems like the barbarians who joined our princess could help to continue and even finish it if she has a mind for it. Are those the bastards who robbed you?"

"Wait, what is happening?" Tandir asked, clearly distracted by something else and not following the conversation.

"The assholes who wandered in now are those who stole from Cassandra," his brother explained, clearly not concerned about his confusion. "I think we should be able to make them pay for their audacity in stealing from our royalty."

His brother looked over his shoulder as the bandits began to sing a song in a language she couldn't understand—either that or they were so drunk there was no understanding it, no matter the language—and the trio turned quickly to their table again.

"So we rip their throats out, then?" Bandir asked and raised an eyebrow.

"We can't kill them." Cassandra shook her head. "I need them alive so they can tell me where my horse and what remains of the treasure is. They can't do that with their throats slit."

"Not without a necromancer." Tandir chuckled but his brother elbowed him in the ribs.

"Not even as a joke." He turned his attention to the barbarian princess. "No weapons then. How do we do this?"

She scowled and tipped her mug back to drain the last of the foul liquid inside. "I'll need to know a way to tell the two of you apart. For the life of me, I can't remember which of you is Bandir and which is Tandir."

"I'm Bandir," the one to her right muttered. "He's Tandir."

"That does not help me in the slightest."

"My eyes are green going to blue at the center," Bandir answered.

"Mine are blue going to green at the center," his brother finished.

It sounded like something they had to explain often but it still didn't help. In her condition, she couldn't tell one from the other and she couldn't waste time and effort to stare into their eyes for a few minutes every time she needed one and not the other.

"Right, a simple solution then." She growled, stretched over the table, and hammered her fist into the nose of the one who called himself Tandir.

"Fuck!" he shouted and immediately covered his nose where she'd struck it. "What in the hells was that for?"

"Now I'll be able to tell the two of you apart a little easier," she answered with a grin.

He offered her his middle finger in response and clutched his nose with the other hand before he turned to his brother. "Does it look bad?"

"That's not what I would say," Bandir answered and shook his head. "If anything, improvements were made."

"Fuck you."

Cassandra chose not to point out that the man had insulted his own looks given how alike the two of them were and instead, moved the conversation forward.

"You're both fucking wildly handsome. Now, shall we fight or do you want to braid each other's beards as well?"

Neither man appeared to be in the mood to do any braiding and immediately turned their gazes on the group that still sung their song off-key without making any sense.

"We should beat them merely for singing that godsbedammed song," Bandir commented as they stood from their table.

"What song is it?" she asked.

"It's the language spoken down south, past all the deserts. It's about sailors finding mermaids and... Well, I suppose you can imagine the content by judging their character, but even barbarians find it foul. A few of our clans consider the sirens of the sea to be holy to some extent."

Cassandra narrowed her eyes. As much as she could guess what the content of the song was, she was still curious to find out in full so there was no room for misinterpretation.

Tandir interpreted her hesitation correctly. "The song is about pirates finding a tribe of mermaids sunning in the open. They proceed to fuck, kill, and eat them, and they are discussing the precise manner in which they go about all three."

She scowled and drew a deep breath. "I did not need another reason to crush the bastards, but damned if they did not provide me with one."

The brothers chuckled as they turned and the innkeeper could immediately tell what they had in their minds as they began to advance on the brigands, rolling their shoulders and ready for a fight.

He did what she didn't expect from him and quickly closed himself in the back as though he was ready to call the guards but only once the fighting had stopped. She wondered if she would have to take after Skharr and start handing out a few coins to make sure they didn't end up in a cell. Covering the damages that could be caused by a fight would help keep them on the innkeeper's good side.

Then again, the proprietor did not appear too fearful. It was almost as though this was an everyday occurrence for him, the kind of thing he accounted for every morning when he was opening shop.

The bandits appeared to realize that something was happening as well and they were already on their feet when Bandir uttered a shout and rushed in to swing his fist into the jaw of the man closest to him.

They were quick to react and pushed to their feet, ready for a fight as the second barbarian roared and dove directly into them. He landed feet-first in the chest of one of the bandits and the man careened back into one of the tables and flipped over it.

Tandir landed on his back but in a move Cassandra hadn't seen before, flicked his feet up, launched them forward, and used the momentum to jump back to his feet as two of the bandits rushed in to tackle him.

It was her turn to join the brawl and she threw a hard punch to knock one of the men off her barbarian friend with a hard blow to the ribs. There was enough behind it to hear bones cracking inside as he fell back, tried to take a deep breath, and failed. She caught him by the collar of his shirt and dragged him close to swipe her elbow across his jaw and he fell with a thud.

Another of the bandits rushed in to tackle her as well but she grinned, took a step back, and waited for him. As soon as he reached her, she hooked her arms under his shoulders and twisted to use his momentum to flip him over her hip. He landed in a slide and knocked a couple of chairs over as well.

There was nothing quite like a good brawl. Cassandra could feel heat in her chest and a smile touched her lips as she snapped around in time to crack her elbow on the skull of an opponent who had hoped to catch her unawares. She stamped her boot on the one who was on the floor to ensure that he would not be up and ready to rejoin the fight when she turned to look at the others.

A few were already down, groaning and struggling to regain their feet. Those who remained, however, were drawing their weapons—mostly daggers as the lances had been left behind but one of them did have a cavalry saber as well.

"I suppose you have a plan for this as well?" Tandir asked and stepped back. His nose was still bleeding from where she had struck him but he did not appear to have taken any further damage. His brother had a cracked lip and a little swelling over his eye but both seemed to want more of a fight from the bandits.

"It's not very different from the previous plan," Cassandra commented. "You were already trying to not get hit with mixed success. Now, the consequences are a little more dire. On the other hand, there are fewer of them."

She was right on that count. There had been ten when the fight started and only four were still on their feet. Despite their drawn weapons, they looked around as if trying to decide whether they would remain or would make a break for it.

There seemed to be no real consensus among them. Two began to rush toward the doors. A third moved to join them but the one with the sword stopped him when he grasped him savagely by the neck. "Run, and I swear to all the gods that I will run you through myself, you useless shit!"

That seemed to put a little more courage in him but not the other two.

"Stop them," Cassandra snapped and rolled her shoulders. "I'll take these two myself."

"Are you sure?" Bandir asked but nodded when she turned to look at him. "Never mind, then."

The brothers rushed to intercept the escapees before they could reach the door and left her with the two who remained.

"So you're sending your friends off so you can face us alone?" the man with the saber asked and twisted it deftly to loosen his wrist. "How gutless."

"Is that so?"

"Suicide is the coward's way out."

Cassandra grinned. "Has the sight of your men on the ground not given you a clear indicator of how this will end for you? I would suggest that you lay your weapons down and I might allow you to live but in all honesty, I have ached to tear into all of you since you ran off with my horse."

The man's eyes widened and she laughed.

"Yes, I did kill two of your boys but at this point, after you made me walk for miles, I will put you through every ache and every pain you caused me, you miserable shit crapped from a whore!"

The saber-wielder took a step back as she lunged forward, swept one of the nearby chairs up, and swung it violently. She had aimed for the man with the sword but he pushed his comrade into the way instead and a shock rushed through her hands from the impact that broke the chair. It was a little painful but far from what the man she had struck had to endure.

He fell immediately and left her with nothing but the chunks of the chair in her hand as the other bandit decided he would show a little courage after all.

The saber attacked in a careful swing from the side and Cassandra slipped away from it and noted when he arced his wrist and brought the strike back to aim for her head.

She ducked under it and held one chair leg between herself and the blade at all times. He tried to press his advantage but it was an unwieldy blade for the enclosed space—usually put to better use on the back of a horse—and rushing at her would not get him what he wanted. She had to commend him for having a sound tactical mind in using one of his men as a shield and not charging at her despite a perceived advantage.

Which meant she would have to press her advantage. Cassandra stood her ground, smiled, and watched and waited for the man to attack and the saber to flick around. When it happened, she raised the chair leg to stop it.

They met violently and the sharp blade bit deep into the wood and stuck for the moment. She leapt forward and swung the second leg to hammer it into his wrist. He screamed, dropped his sword, and fell back as he tried a desperate overhanded strike at her before she swiped the chair leg in a vicious thrust into his jaw.

The sickening impact brought the man to his knees. He toppled and muttered and coughed as he clutched his face.

She shook the saber carefully from where it was caught in the chair leg before she turned to look where the brothers were still engaging the other two.

It appeared that the brawl was continuing. Tandir still held one of the men by the collar and dragged him to a nearby wall while the bandit threw weak punches in an attempt to dislodge him. Bandir showed considerably more energy, lifted his man off the floor, and with a roar of effort, hurled him across the room.

The trajectory launched him into the other barbarian and all three sprawled in a heap amidst groans and curses.

"What in the blazes are you doing?" Tandir roared as his brother approached to help him up.

"I aimed for the other one."

"Why?"

"I thought it would be fun for them to knock each other out."

Cassandra smirked and checked her knuckles where bruising was starting to show. It felt like the skin had split around her elbow as well but there wasn't much more than a stinging sensation in the area. It would be more painful as time went on but she would be able to heal herself soon enough.

Both barbarians were standing but their bandit counterparts were a little slower to regain their feet. They looked stunned and like they still wanted to run, but all avenues of escape were cut off.

"Try not to kill them," she called, ran her fingers over the cut on her elbow, and winced as the skin began to mend and left only a smear of blood with no source.

"Yes, yes, we already know," Bandir muttered as one of the bandits lunged and brandished his dagger.

Tandir tripped him before he could step in to swing and his brother finished it with a firm punch to the jaw to send both man and dagger to the floor without so much as a whimper.

The last one staggered away and attempted to reach the room where the innkeeper had hidden, hoping he would find some refuge there.

Cassandra stepped in his way and tilted her head. "I suppose if I want something done right, I must do it myself."

"Is she insulting our fighting skills?" Tandir asked.

"We weren't going to let him go," Bandir added. "We were

toying with the bastard. Drawing a dagger in a brawl is shit manners and how are we to teach him better manners?"

"You—" The bandit hissed in fury and jerked his dagger from one of them to the next. "You attacked us without provocation."

"You robbed innocent travelers on the road," Cassandra pointed out.

"So do half the population of this fucking town."

"In your particular case, you happened to take what was mine." She stepped in when he was distracted and hammered her fist into his face with sufficient force to fell him immediately. With a grimace, she cradled her fist in her hand for a few seconds to heal anything the strike had broken.

CHAPTER FIVE

All the godsbedammed cretins were on the floor and appeared to have trouble regaining their feet, although Cassandra judged that roughly half of them were at least in some state of consciousness. It wasn't the standard she wished to achieve while working as a barbarian but time for corrections would come later.

For now, there was business to attend to.

"Make sure that none of them leave, Bandir," she instructed and directed the order to the more physically powerful of the two, at least by her estimation. Tandir appeared to be the smarter brother. "Make sure the innkeeper is well and that he knows all damages will be paid for, one way or the other."

"They will?"

"He'll involve the city guard otherwise and we can do without such entanglements. Just see it done. Even if I do not recover all that is owed to me, these bastards should still have something in their collective purses to cover what is owed."

The saber at least would prove to be more than enough to ensure that the guard was not involved over a few broken tables, chairs, and jugs.

For her part, however, she intended to ensure that violence

was not all that resulted from her encountering the bastards again. She turned her attention to the man who had been the better-armed of the group and who she assumed was the leader among them. He was one who had recovered consciousness, although from the stunned look on his face, it did not appear as though he would regain his feet without assistance for a while yet.

It was about time she helped him in that regard.

Cassandra grasped him by the collar and lifted him off the floor. He was a little shorter than he'd appeared when holding a sword. Then again, he was a cavalryman and they tended to be shorter or at least shorter than her, which meant she was able to lift him completely off his feet to put him at eye level with her.

"I think it's about time you and I have a talk," she said coldly. His eyes widened and he made feeble attempts to fight her off before she deposited him on a nearby table. He was left seated but still swaying as her blow had left him feeling a little woozy.

"What...why?"

"Because you owe me my treasure, my spear, and my horse," she answered and patted his cheek. "And I'll take it out of you bastards one way or another. Bandir, search them all and see to it that they're left with nothing but the clothes on their backs."

The barbarian nodded and complied immediately. Tandir knocked on the door to the back room and after a few attempts, the innkeeper peeked out of a small slot he'd made in the door.

"You'll have to pay for the damages!" he declared loudly, likely putting up a good appearance since Cassandra could make out the whites of his eyes even through the slots.

"Aye, we will," Tandir answered. "State your price and I'm sure these bastards will be happy to pay it. Come on out."

The slot closed and after a moment, they heard the sound of a bolt being pulled and the door opened. The innkeeper had a look about him that suggested he would run at the smallest sign of trouble, but he hadn't done so yet. Bandir worked quickly and took everything but the brigands' clothes and their boots.

While boots were the kind of thing folk often disregarded, Cassandra had known soldiers to kill for a good pair of boots after marching for months.

Maybe it was for the best. Men on horseback tended to not care much for their boots. There were raiders in the Northwest away from the oceans and in the open plains who made their living on ponies and were noted for riding barefoot.

"Right, then," she said and slapped the raider on the cheek to ensure that his attention was on her and not what was happening around him. "You clearly remembered me when I told you of my action against your shit-eating comrades who are rotting in whatever semblance of hells you happen to believe in. You remember me, yes?"

"You...yes," he whispered and nodded slowly and exaggeratedly like he had difficulty controlling himself. "You came when we were attacking those *bateri* on the road."

"Ba...what?"

"*Bateri*," Tandir interjected as he helped to relieve the rest of the raiders of their possessions. "Cattle. I would assume his people use the same term for innocent folk on the road they choose to attack."

A surge of heat rushed through her body as she held the man's collar a little tighter. She resisted the urge to snap his neck and managed to regain control of herself before she stared into his eyes again.

"You remember how easily I killed your comrades, yes?"

He nodded.

"Do you want me to kill you in a similar fashion?"

A shake of the head confirmed the negative.

"Then you will tell me where my horse is and assuming you dumb bastards have any sense in you, where you left the treasure that was on my horse's saddle."

He looked at the barbarians, who were finished collecting what could be taken and now negotiated what was owed for the damages caused by the fight. She could hear them explaining that the raiders had robbed their princess and this was merely their way of taking what was owed for that misdeed.

The innkeeper agreed that there was no need to call the guard, although the barbarians did suggest that he made sure the bandits were removed from his premises and maybe a night in cells would teach them better manners for the future so he wouldn't have to worry about them taking any vengeance for what happened.

She slapped the leader in the face again. "Focus, you miserable excuse for a sentient creature. Your life is in the balance based on your answer."

"We...the horse...we still have the horse. And most of the treasure." He nodded, suddenly talkative now that he was reminded that she might well kill him. "All our horses are kept in the Edge Stables. They will protect the beasts and you need to present a key that opens the section where our horses are kept."

That was all the answer she needed and she smiled and pushed him back onto the table. He groaned and rolled off to land with a solid thud.

"Did you find a key on them?" she asked.

"No. It might be on that bastard, though."

Tandir made a good point and she patted him down quickly and found a small copper key, along with a small purse that was filled to bursting, mostly with silver coins.

"How much do we owe for the mess?" Cassandra asked.

"The guards will need some convincing as well—"

She handed the innkeeper the whole purse and patted him on the shoulder. "I am sure you will settle on an honest price with them. For ourselves, we cannot tarry. Might we consider the matter resolved?"

The proprietor's eyes widened. Even a jug of the ale they had bought had only been worth half a copper, which meant the purse of silvers was likely more than he would make over three or four days.

"The matter is resolved."

"Excellent." She smiled and gestured for the other two to join her as she headed out onto the streets. "Where is this…Edge Stables that he mentioned?"

"Most horses are stabled near the gate," Bandir informed her. "The city guard keeps them under lock and key. For those who can pay the fee, of course."

It sounded like their bandits could, in fact, pay the fee, and she motioned for them to follow her.

"You found what you needed, I take it?" Bandir asked and jogged a little to keep up with her.

She had begun to get used to the twists and turns in the streets of the small town and soon judged where the gate was and how quickly it would take them to get there.

"He said their horses were stabled in a place in those very same stables, along with my horse and most of the treasure."

"Perfect." Tandir chuckled although he also needed to increase his pace to keep up with her. "Why the hurry then? I doubt that horse or treasure will go anywhere anytime soon."

"I don't know if those bastards are their full number," Cassandra answered as she located the gate and continued to walk purposefully toward it. "Assuming there are more, those who remain might realize that the others were attacked and move to defend their possessions. Or they might simply decide to leave and take everything with them, leaving me with nothing. Again."

"I wouldn't say nothing," Bandir commented and hefted one of the coin purses he was carrying. "They might not have spent much of the treasure but they carried enough coin to outfit the three of us for whatever journey we might have to undertake, within reason. It might be enough for a horse or two as well."

"I'll tell you what," she said as they approached the stables—she could identify them simply from the smell that emanated from the building. "If I recover my horse and any of my possessions, I would say you earned all the coin and possessions you took from the bastards."

A handful of guards were already rushing to the inn they'd left. She wasn't sure how the word had reached them so quickly but it didn't matter. If the bandit had told the truth, she would not want to remain in the city for long. Not only would she be in possession of treasure that most would kill for, but the knowledge would spread quickly given that the bandits had no reason to keep it to themselves.

It was the kind of treasure that would make even the guards willing to kill.

Her father had not been lying. Edge's Rest immediately brought the term "hive" to mind, although maybe that had more to do with her time spent tending to the hives their meadery maintained.

It buzzed with activity and most of those she saw immediately made her feel as though they were sizing her up with the intention of slitting her throat and taking everything she owned. Verda was not sure how she could even fight an attempt on her life at this point, given how deadened her limbs felt. She wasn't even sure if she could walk and her mare was acting the same way.

The poor beast would carry her onward, but her hooves clipped and tripped gently on the cobbles that had begun to pave the road on the approach to the walls.

All eyes were on her and she wondered if she had chosen the wrong place to come to. There were a handful of outposts belonging to some army or another about fifty miles farther.

Her father would have died before coming under imperial control but they were now subjugated by someone who was infinitely worse and it felt as though there was nothing else to do.

Perhaps the imperial troops wouldn't even take her coin and would be content to simply retake her home.

Her numb fingers tightened around the reins and she couldn't bring herself to turn her horse and ride away. She doubted that she would survive another day in the saddle.

Even climbing out of it felt like a titanic effort that she was uncertain she could accomplish without mishap. She would surely lose all her strength, fall with a thud, and would be unable to pull herself to her feet again after that.

But she would do it because she had to. Someone had to help and Verda growled her determination, pushed up a little, and drew her leg slowly over the saddle to slide off carefully.

"There's a good girl," she whispered and patted her mare on the neck. "I'll have to get you some carrots—or apples or whatever you enjoy as a treat. Once…once we've found some mercenaries who have a willingness for danger."

"Mer…mercenaries?" The man's voice was altogether too close for her liking and she almost jumped away, especially as it was followed immediately by the heavy smell of spirits on his breath. He was taller than she was and displayed clear signs of being completely and utterly inebriated along with what smelled like cheap wine dripping from his scraggly beard.

She stood her ground and straightened her back as well as she could manage before she answered. "I am in need of a mercenary company. Would…would you know where I could find them? A place where they convene, perhaps?"

"I might know if you had the time to wet my mouth with ale or…other bits."

"Why would you want me to wet other bits of you with ale?"

He paused and narrowed his eyes almost as though he was

trying to make sense of what he'd said as well, but he shook it off quickly.

"There's...a place. By...near the gate. Mercs are assholes. Don't need...don't need to spend time with them."

Verda could tell he was building to something in particular but she didn't realize it until he lunged forward. As drunk as he was, she couldn't be sure if he attempted to take hold of her or the purse of coins she carried at her hip but in the end, he was not able to complete his intention.

The mare was already shifting as the man lunged, and either she was intent on keeping her rider safe or maybe she was startled. Her hind legs lashed out and caught the man in the ribs and he sprawled onto the street.

"Heavens." Verda gasped and patted the mare carefully on her rump. "Do you suppose... Is he still alive?"

The question was answered when the man, who lay with his belly on the cobbles, exhaled a thunderous snore. She wasn't sure why she felt committed to ensuring that he was alive given that he had tried to rob her blind or worse.

Having a life on her hands was not something she felt comfortable with, even if it wasn't precisely an innocent life.

Still, he had directed her more or less to where she could find a few mercenaries who might take her coin and find a way to help. It wasn't like she had a choice and it did not appear as though anyone would step in to help the drunken man, who continued to snore on the street.

They likely would not have made any attempt to help her if he had been successful in attacking her. But that was a matter for another time, if that. Hopefully, she would not need to return to this place at all.

So many people were packed into the city—more than in any town she had been to—and she struggled to not get lost. It was comforting to know that the mare followed her obediently and also looked a little less tired than she had been before.

Verda decided she would have to come up with a name for the beast. She was the only reason they were still alive and she wouldn't forget it.

"What are you doing here?"

Her mind had wandered and she flipped her hair out of her face and settled her attention on a man in padded armor with a sword at his hip who stood in front of her.

"I…what?"

"This area is reserved for mercenaries," the man told her and placed a heavy hand on her shoulder. "You need to leave."

She could hear something happening on the other side of the square she had entered almost without thinking and she realized there were more gazes on her.

"Mercenary business is conducted here," another stated. "It is time for you to leave."

"Before we remove you."

"No, you don't understand," she insisted and pushed past the stammer that tried to seize her jaw. "I…I need help. I am here for…for help!"

"It doesn't matter why you are here. Leave!"

Hands began to push her away and all the fury she'd pent up inside her over her time in the saddle—fueled by her worry about being intercepted or attacked by those who had raided and taken her home—began to bubble up despite the exhaustion that filled her limbs.

"Let me go!" she screamed. "I'm here to hire someone to help —let me go!"

The captain's look told her all she needed to see. Cassandra could almost feel the doubt oozing from the woman as she studied the key that had been handed to her and then the three barbarians before her.

"You are the owners of those horses?" she asked.

"We have the key, don't we?" Tandir countered with a shrug.

"Holding the key doesn't mean you own what is inside," the officer snapped but it was easy to tell that she couldn't prove they didn't own the horses. More importantly, the troop that left them behind likely had many members, some of whom might not have been present when the horses were brought in.

"Is there a problem?" Cassandra asked and stepped forward.

It was clear that while the captain had her doubts, she was not overly interested in seeing them to fruition and she shook her head. "Head on into the barn. That key opens the section to the far left and they were on deposit for three more days. See to it that they are removed before then or all possessions left behind will be forfeit."

The real issue, the barbarian princess felt, was that the other mercenaries in the area were watching the interaction. Perhaps they knew better or were interested in trying to acquire what was being protected inside and would wait for them to step outside to steal it.

She didn't care and was willing to bet her skills against those of any in the city. Besides, she intended to leave as soon as she had Strider with her again. She approached the door in question, slipped the copper key into the lock, and opened the door slowly.

At least a dozen horses were inside and watched the three new arrivals as they moved along the hallway at the center.

The barbarian brothers both paused, looked around the stables, and whispered something to one another that she couldn't make out, but she knew what they were thinking regardless.

"If you were to ask my opinion," she said and placed her hand on one of the stable doors, "I would say the trouble you went through to deal with the raiding bastards was enough to justify you taking their horses if you needed them."

"Is that so?" Tandir already had his eye on a stallion in one of the stalls.

"My only question is why you were asking for feed for your horses when we first met if you didn't have horses in the first place."

They looked at each other for a moment, and she realized that she had touched on a raw nerve. Her guess was that they didn't like to admit they were short on coin and preferred to not discuss the decisions that had to be made because of it.

"Never mind."

"No, it's—"

"I understand," she stated quickly. "Horse feed, oats, and the like, is cheaper to buy and yet still edible for humans and can even be made into decent meals if someone has the right spices and a creative mind. I've been in need more times than you might know and I understand the idea better than you might think."

Both men chuckled and shook their heads and she left them without saying anything more. She wandered to the back of the stable where she could hear the familiar whinnying of a horse she recognized.

"You dumb bastard," Cassandra muttered and pulled the stable door open as it appeared that Strider recognized her too. "I suppose it would have been too much trouble for you to put up a fight before—"

Her tangent was cut off when the beast moved close to her and pressed his forehead into her shoulder.

"You're right," she whispered and patted his neck. "Blaming the victim never does anyone any good. Know that I missed you and not only because I don't appreciate having to trudge across creation on my own two feet."

A soft snort from the beast was all the answer she needed as her attention was drawn toward the saddlebags stored in the corner of the room.

They took up a great deal of space and a quick check

confirmed that it was because most of the treasure was still in place. Some of it was missing, likely already spent by the bastards, but given that they intended to take their horses and probably their supplies as well, she would call it even. Anything lost by the brigands would be counted against the effort that had gone into recovering her stolen property.

Cassandra chose not to wait around for the end of the world and saddled Strider quickly, loaded what remained of the treasure, and smiled when she discovered that they hadn't discarded the spear she'd used to kill the dragon. Her barbarians were right when they said that it was a fine piece of her history that she did not want to have stolen from her.

Strider followed her as she walked toward the door again and her barbarian friends fell in behind. They had chosen their horses, collected what supplies had been left in the saddlebags, and even taken a couple of the weapons that had been stored there. The bandits would not be left with nothing but a few of them would have to walk out.

Trouble awaited them, however, the moment she stepped out of the door with Strider. A handful of mercenaries had gathered, led by one who wore plate armor. If not for where he stood, she might have wondered if he was a knight from some obscure order or another.

"Where are you taking those horses?" he asked as he stepped forward.

"They belong to us," she answered, utterly lacking the patience to deal with these mercenaries with anything resembling diplomacy.

"You were not seen riding in with them."

"They were stolen from me on the road," she retorted. "I am taking back what is mine, regardless of who might have brought them in."

Her claim appeared to fall on deaf ears and the reason why was clear as more gazes settled on Strider and the contents of his saddlebags. There was a tenuous alliance of the mercenaries in this town, but she had a feeling that any semblance of loyalty disappeared when they found a reason to steal from each other, no matter what the reason.

"You won't leave here with them," the knight stated.

Cassandra looked around and couldn't help a small smile. "I will. Whether it will be with your blood covering them or not is a decision you have to make for yourself."

It was about time she put her spear to use again and it seemed like an opportunity would be created for her to do exactly that. The gathered group merely waited for the knight to indicate what the plan of action would be.

Before any of them could make that decision, noise from the entrance drew their attention and she narrowed her eyes and tried to identify the source.

A handful of mercenaries attempted to restrain someone and it wasn't long before a woman's voice rang through the small courtyard.

"I'm here to hire someone to help—let me go!"

CHAPTER SIX

Neither she nor the merc leader knew how to proceed. The group still wanted her treasure and were more than willing to use the excuse that they thought she was stealing it to take it from her. Their demeanor told her there would be no reasoning with them but at the same time, they showed no inclination to attack while something else was happening.

The woman continued to shout, her agitation evident as she pushed through the mercenaries. The knight was as curious about what was happening as Cassandra was. As the guard was nowhere to be found—likely having melted away at the slightest sign of trouble— they would have to find out what was happening themselves.

"We'll continue this later, then?" he asked.

She nodded. "Fair enough. I'm happy to kill you all another time."

That drew a chuckle from the man as he removed his hand from the arming sword at his hip. "Your confidence is noted."

They would have to address that comment another time. She turned away from him and approached the source of the commotion—a young woman barely out of her teens by the looks of her. Her thick, curling black hair was in a mess and not only as the result of being manhandled by the mercs who had tried to push her out. They backed away to give Cassandra space and their apparent leader strode toward them.

The newcomer's dark-brown eyes were as wide as saucers and everything about her, from the dark circles under her eyes to the way her shoulders sagged, spoke of exhaustion.

And not only of the body but of the mind as well. She had the look of someone who had been pushed for too long to the edge by events that made her fear for her life and she wasn't sure how to turn it off again.

"I am Langven," the mercenary leader stated as he approached. "I am captain to a company of mercenaries here and if you have need of our services, tell us about it and we will see if there are any takers."

She calmed a little, steadied herself, and straightened her back as she looked around as if to determine what was happening. Staring at Langven didn't appear to help her unsettled nature and when she looked at Cassandra, she looked even more confused. The mercenaries around her seemed to give the barbarian princess a wide berth, even though she did not appear to be much of a fighter.

"My home," she said finally and shook her head. "My name is Verda, and my home...it was taken from me by a group of bandits—about a dozen of them. Fewer now, I suppose. Some died while taking it—Torsburch. They managed to kill our chieftain and his son. I...I have coin and a few gemstones to offer in payment for any who would be willing to take the work. It should prove to be easy but I cannot do it alone."

Something seemed odd about the girl. She genuinely needed help but she hadn't told the truth about what they would face. It was in the way her fingers flashed through her hair and away from the purse of coins she'd clutched with a vice-like grip from the moment Cassandra had laid eyes on her.

"Show us what you can pay," Langven answered firmly.

"What? Why would I hand over—"

"You are asking us to walk into the jaws of danger," he insisted. "We deserve to know that the payment justifies this."

"They won't steal it," the barbarian princess assured her. "Not unless they want all the others to take their heads off. The guards do not appreciate thievery either, not while inside the walls."

The mercenaries exchanged a glance and seemed to realize that she was right, which likely meant they had fully intended to steal the riches from the woman and hadn't thought it through.

Verda paused, sensed their hesitation, and touched the purse again before she took it from her belt and handed it to the man. True to his word, he inspected the contents—three gold coins and six silvers, along with three emeralds, a ruby, and a diamond —and returned them to the purse when he was satisfied that the treasures were as described.

It wasn't a fortune by any means but enough in the form of riches to hire a small mercenary group if needed or to allow a man to live in a town like Edge's Rest and enjoy everything it had to offer for at least a couple of months.

"This is only to retain your services," the woman said and looked a little calmer once she accepted that those around her wouldn't rob her outright. "There are more treasures to be paid when the work is finished as well as any loot you take from the bodies of the dead."

The mercenaries muttered amongst themselves, and Cassandra could see that while Langven had said he was the captain of his company, it did not include the entire group assembled. In fact, if she read the crowd correctly, it appeared that more of them were rivals who were as willing to stab him in the back as work with him.

She cast a look at the two barbarians beside her and they appeared to know where her mind was. Each nodded gently without so much as consulting with each other.

"If you won't take the work, me and my crew will," she stated firmly and gestured to her two companions. "Clearing a few brigands is exactly the kind of work we like."

Langven studied her carefully and she could almost see how his mind was processing the situation. He was experienced enough to know that she was a strong fighter, and by the looks of the barbarians with her, they would not be slouches either.

If he was the captain of all the mercenaries present in the depot, he might have been able to overwhelm the three of them but he was limited with only his own men.

Finally, he returned his gaze to the young woman. "If it's not too far, those coins will be enough to pay me and my men to kill a few bandits on your behalf. Where did you say your home was?"

"Only a few days' ride away, in Torsburch," Verda explained and pushed her hair out of her face again—which still caught Cassandra's attention, no matter how innocent the girl appeared to be. The last time she had been taken in by something like that, a goddess had been hidden in a halfling's body.

It had worked out well for them in the long run but simply because it hadn't killed her once didn't mean she would assume that her luck in such matters would hold.

"I've never heard of this town." Langven narrowed his eyes. "Torsburch, did you say?"

"Many small hamlets have been established in the areas left barren by the war," Cassandra interjected and repeated what had been told to her by the pilgrims before they'd parted ways. "Folk appear all over and start their little towns and even cities. I wouldn't be surprised if a dozen or so appeared before official mapmakers were able to properly document their existence."

He nodded with a smirk. "Very well, then. Show us the way

and we'll tear these bandits a few new holes before we send them to whichever afterlife awaits them."

"We'll come along as well," Cassandra asserted. "Call me paranoid but I don't trust you and your cronies to not kill the girl on the road and take her coin for yourselves."

"There is not enough coin in it for all of us." He shook his head. "I would not share what little there is to be had."

"I and my men will be happy with what spoils we earn through killing the bastards," she responded in a no-nonsense tone. "Your gods smile on acts of charity, do they not? Well, some of them do."

The mercenaries didn't quite know how to answer that and she assumed it was because they held to different gods. Or maybe the same but with different names. Then again, perhaps they came from different parts of the world that had different gods who were equally as real and their power waxed and waned depending on where they were.

Many of the truths she'd held to for most of her life were being questioned at this point, and she wouldn't take anything for granted.

"I'll take her word to keep you from robbing me on the road," Verda cut in and latched onto the idea of having some protection, even though she seemed bright enough to know better than to trust anyone in this city. "As long as you all decide how to divide the pay, I would not mind other parties coming to keep each other honest."

Cassandra raised an eyebrow at the man. He'd been outmaneuvered and any further objections he had to the barbarian princess and her two companions would be interpreted as his intention to rob the young Verda of what riches she still had to her name.

"Very well," Langven answered but didn't look particularly happy at the concession. "As long as it is known that we will not divide any of the rewards with you or your two oafs."

"Oafs?" Tandir snapped.

"We'll show you oafs," Bandir warned.

"You would prove his point then, wouldn't you?" she asked and tilted her head.

"Well, yes, but—"

"So, in order to defend yourselves against being called oafs, you would act the part of oafs?"

Neither barbarian liked the point she was making, although it was certainly a good one. She turned her attention to Langven.

"Tandir, Bandir, and I will take what loot we claim from those bandits we kill," she stated firmly and folded her arms. "And should you attempt anything like taking the coin before the work is done, I'll slit your throat myself and hang you by the heels with hooks until you bleed out like a stuck pig, then earn the coin you attempted to steal. Is that utterly and completely clear?"

The mercenary leader's eyes narrowed but a small smile touched his lips as he took a step forward. The fact that all of them seem to have lost any interest in the treasures Strider carried was probably the best part of the whole situation.

Either that or the bastard was more than happy to kill her, the two barbarians, and Verda and take all their coin in one fell swoop. She couldn't tell which option was on his mind but at the moment, she decided to assume the worst of the folk of Edge's Rest until proven otherwise.

Of course, this meant sleeping with one eye open at all times but she could manage that. Maybe Verda couldn't given that the girl appeared to be a step away from collapsing for some much-needed rest, but she could.

"Agreed," Langven answered and extended a hand for her to shake. She made a point of keeping a hand on her sword in case it was a ruse before she took it.

There were no unpleasant surprises and all she felt was the man's firm grasp before he brushed a few strands of bright red hair from his face and turned to the rest of the men.

"Right then, gather your shit and meet us at the gates," he snapped. "We leave as the sun rises."

Verda appeared to be relieved by the statement and Cassandra would make a point of finding somewhere for the girl to rest before they left. But there were matters that needed to be attended to first.

She turned to face the barbarians beside her, who both seemed determined to make sure that none of the mercenaries were interested in what was carried in Strider's packs.

"Apologies." She shook her head and patted Strider's neck. "Volunteering you both for work without giving you a say in the matter was probably not fair. I would understand completely if you have no interest in accompanying me."

They exchanged a look, which made Cassandra wonder if there was any truth to the myth that twins were able to communicate with nothing but their minds. The reality, though, was likely closer to twins knowing each other so well that non-verbal communication became akin to a first language, the kind they learned before they even learned how to speak or read.

"Fighting alongside a barbarian princess feels like the kind of thing folk will write epics about in the future," Tandir said with a shrug. "Besides, it would be better than simply sitting here, getting into fights and trying to scrape by on our wits."

"Wits aren't quite the word," Bandir quipped with a chuckle. "We were sent from our clan to gain some experience and to see the world, although I suppose the need for us to direct our troublesome natures was another reason."

They studied Cassandra's confused expression.

"What?"

She paused, unsure of precisely what to say. "I knew you were trouble. I merely wasn't sure you were aware of it yourselves."

"We can be aware of it and still be determined to cause as much trouble as we can manage," Bandir muttered. "Still, the experience and seeing the world was the real attraction. It's certainly better than having a controlling clan elder looking over our shoulders for every waking hour of every day. All we've done so far is lose our coin and ourselves in the world. It's about time we find ourselves in trouble under someone else's guidance."

"Aye," Tandir agreed. "And about time we had deserving heads to crack with good coin to be made on top of it."

CHAPTER SEVEN

There was no more debate as to whether they would keep their horses or the treasures they carried, although Cassandra wasn't comfortable riding across the countryside with all that had been earned.

Then again, she didn't trust any who might say they could store the treasure for her. There would be nothing to prevent them from taking the coin and fucking off to parts unknown.

Still, she did manage to trade a few of the larger pieces she'd carried to the local merchants and was able to purchase all the supplies any of the three would ever need for the journey there and back. With this done, a hefty amount of coin and other precious items remained that could be used for trade elsewhere.

She didn't doubt that she was giving them the better side of the bargain but there was the matter of them helping her to liquidate the treasure instead of carrying it around.

The rest could be passed on to the two barbarian brothers, who could help to guard and carry it.

"Are you not afraid that we'll simply run off with what you've given us in the night?" Tandir asked.

"That is a risk, I'll admit." Cassandra smiled and patted his muscular arm. "But I know that you know I'll track you down and beat the ever-loving shit out of you for it and leave you with naught but the clothes on your back for your efforts. If I'm in a forgiving mood."

The brothers chuckled but decided that they weren't sure if she was joking and were not in the mood to test her patience with any more jokes.

The barbarian princess paused as they approached the stable area again. It appeared that the raiders had managed to talk their way out of trouble with the guard, although they still showed signs of the fight. They paused in gathering their horses when they saw Cassandra and the two barbarians approaching.

"Are you all right, lads?" she asked, feeling a little cheeky. "It looks like you've all been through a proper wringer. Do you think you might have the time or the coin to spend on one of the local healers?"

They understood her but offered no response. None of them were interested in the prospect of an honest fight with them, although she had a feeling they wouldn't mind finding the group on a dark night when knives could be stabbed into backs without resistance.

But the option wasn't offered and as the three of them joined the group that Langven had gathered, they decided that the opportunity wouldn't come along soon. Still, they would do well to watch their backs as they traveled. As she turned away from them, she could hear a handful of mutterings directed at her. They were speaking their own tongue and not one she understood, but she assumed that it involved a great deal of foul language.

Looking back at the barbarians confirmed that suspicion.

"What did they say?" Cassandra asked.

"A few comments regarding your...well, your outfit," Bandir answered. "I suppose they don't trust themselves against our fighting prowess and so think that they would be able to…well, drive you to humiliation using other means."

"You can tell them they appear to enjoy the prospect of my boot on their necks," she snapped in reply. "There's no accounting for taste when it comes to that kind of thing, but it is an odd fancy that seems to excite men of their type."

The barbarians chuckled.

"Go on, tell them that."

"I think they understood you," Tandir noted.

"Well, then?" She growled and opened her arms wide. "Who wants to test himself against me? I've a mood to see you out of town and if you press me, that is what you'll get. Now fuck off, all of you! Go on!"

They complied without argument and those who had horses mounted quickly. Two of them needed to climb behind their comrades, which made her laugh as they pushed their mounts to leave the city as quickly as possible.

"You know they'll likely be lying in wait to try to ambush us when we leave, right?" Tandir asked once they were out of earshot.

"I am aware of the possibility," she answered with a small smile. "I would not bet on the intelligence of any man among them, so they might do something as incredibly stupid as trying to attack us, which means we will need to be alert for them."

There was no point in assuming that people would know what was in their own best interests, and it was likely that the bastards would try to recover what she took back from them. The treasure was the kind of riches that encouraged folk to make bad decisions.

They proceeded to where Langven was organizing his men. He appeared to be a good commander and made sure that they were all properly equipped and carried a fair weight. It was more impressive when one took into account that he wore full plate armor that she assumed was unbearably hot to be in all the time.

Still, it didn't look like he was inconvenienced in any way, aside from a hint of sweat on his neck and the way he habitually forced his bright red hair into a bun on the back of his head.

The man was a devious, callous shit but he had the skills to command his troops, she would give him that much.

"Why aren't we leaving immediately?" Verda asked him as Cassandra and her team approached.

"There is a great deal of wilderness between here and where you say your home is located," Langven answered shortly and sounded like he wasn't in the mood to answer her questions at this point. "There is no telling if there will be enough food, water, and other supplies for myself, my men, and you for that matter. All things need to be considered carefully, supplies bought, and plans made. Charging directly into battle with your head in your ass is a good way to have it removed."

"From the ass?"

"Well, that too, I suppose."

The twins, she realized, carried the weapons they had taken from the raiders. They had been armed with simple arming swords before but both had collected throwing spears that were stowed in saddlebags. Tandir had also taken what appeared to be a bearded ax and his brother held a flanged mace that reached almost to his chest with a heavy steel spike at the top. If used properly, it looked like it could be handled like a small spear.

Neither had chosen any shields. Cassandra would have suggested it given how light their armor was—merely a little padding between an attacking blade and flesh—but she wouldn't tell them how to fight.

They did appear to like their new weapons and once their horses were secured to hitching posts, they moved to an open section of the depot where they began to spar and test their acquisitions.

"Ah, the bodyguards have arrived." Langven's voice was more condescending than she thought was necessary, although she once again attributed it to one who did not know any better. "I suppose you were able to acquire proper supplies for your journey?"

"The merchants were rather helpful with that," she answered and glanced at their charge, who was practically falling asleep on her feet. It wouldn't be long until she would have to rest. "She'll need food and sleep before we leave, you know."

"I've tried to tell her to find an inn but she insists that we leave immediately."

Cassandra smiled and approached the young girl who was watching the barbarians.

"Do you think it's safe for them to fight like that?" she asked as the barbarian princess stepped beside her.

"Safe? Probably not. Although I would say they will hopefully not attempt to injure each other."

Verda winced as Bandir swung a little too close with his mace, barely missed his brother's head, and arced it quickly in a sweep that almost cut with the spike as well, which prompted a loud laugh from Tandir.

"Your men are skilled, I'll say that." The girl forced back a yawn and looked at her. "When do we leave?"

"In the morning," she insisted. "You've been in the saddle for days, have you not?"

"Well, I—"

"You'll be no good to anyone if you're unable to stand on your own two feet. You need food and rest. If you don't trust any of the inns, I think your horse has a pack with a few blankets and supplies for a quick meal and then some sleep. I have a feeling it will make the time pass a great deal faster as well."

The girl looked like she was ready with another argument but she was interrupted by another massive yawn that only served to prove the point.

"Go on. I'll be around to keep watch for you and I'll wake you when it's time to leave."

"You promise?"

"Aye. Rest now."

Cassandra placed a hand on her shoulder, felt her tiredness, and drew a little of it away, enough to ensure that her sleep would be dreamless and restful.

The girl made no further protest, approached her horse, and opened one of the saddlebags to retrieve a loaf of bread. She proceeded to bite into it while she set up a bed for herself near the rest of the group.

"You have some magical talent then?" Langven asked, having watched their charge.

"A little."

"I suppose that explains how you put those raiders on their asses." He turned to look at her as more of his men gathered to watch the barbarians sparring. "A little magic never hurt anyone."

"Barbarian legends say otherwise," Cassandra answered.

"They do. Which begs the question of how a barbarian princess has magical talent."

"Royalty is afforded certain privileges."

"I was not aware that barbarians had any royalty."

"Your ignorance is not my concern," she answered with a wry smile.

"It might be that of the Ebon Pack's," Langven stated and raised an eyebrow as one of his men tangled with Bandir, only to be tossed on the ground, which elicited a roar of laughter from the others.

"Ebon Pack?"

"A name for our troop. Since the early days, we carry a black fang into battle that allows us to know which fighter is on our side, either on a necklace, bracelet, earring, or anything else, as long as it is easily visible. It resulted in the nickname, and from there...well, a good name was forged."

With this explanation, she studied each man and confirmed that they carried the black fang their leader had mentioned, although most wore it on a necklace. There wasn't much to it, all things considered, but he was right. Having a name folk recognized was important in work like theirs.

"A good name might be up for debate," she answered.

"This coming from the princess who needs magic to win any fight she happens to find herself in."

Cassandra turned to face the man and regarded him steadily. "Magic does have its uses. But I didn't need it to defeat the bandits and I wouldn't need it to leave any of your pack on the ground and wondering how they ended up on their back."

"That sounds like a challenge," Langven commented.

"A warning, rather, but I suppose it makes sense that you would see it that way."

The warning—or challenge—was heard by a handful of the men who watched as she walked to where Strider stood and looked like he was also interested in some sleep before they left in the morning. The saddlebags were off and set down beside him in clear view so she would be alerted to any who might attempt thievery.

She drew the spear from where it was hooked into the saddle. Although she'd only used it once, it was a magnificent weapon. It was perfectly balanced and light in the hand and she was aware of exactly how deadly it could be when handled correctly. Most of her experience with weapons had to do with swords and shields, but she had been trained in the use of a spear. It was about time she started breaking those skills out for the world to see.

One of the Pack stepped out in front of her with a falchion in hand and grinned as though he expected the fight to be quick and easy. They anticipated that she would need the use of her magical abilities and therefore would count any use of it as a failure on her part. It was about time for them to learn that the skills of a former paladin were not only magical.

They didn't know she was a paladin, though. Perhaps they

would notice the skills and connect the two, but she doubted it. These mercenaries would have trained locally and across the continent and would not be quite as skilled as those soldiers who were trained in battle.

Not that them identifying the source of her training would be a terrible thing.

The challenger flicked his falchion to the side, feinted at first, and lunged forward. Cassandra already had the spear raised to block the strike and reversed it quickly to bring the butt in, rapped the inside of his left knee, and circled it to place the blade of the spear at his neck.

It had been a while but the skills were still there.

"I have no desire to injure or kill any of you," she stated and forced him to take a step back when she put a little more pressure on his neck with the spearhead. "Should you attempt either with me, that will change. Understood?"

The man nodded, took another step back, and swished his weapon, the annoying grin gone from his lips. It appeared that he would take the sparring match a little more seriously. He drew a deep breath before he attacked again and showed a little more care with his strike, then defended himself better as he feinted to his right and jumped back. Anticipating her counterstrike, he arced his weapon in from the left.

He was deft and fast with good footwork, and with a little more training, could prove to be a skilled fighter of some repute. His disadvantage was that he was slow to pull back and showed his intentions a little too obviously. Cassandra did not bite at the feint and instead, moved in to intercept where the strike came from as she slipped the haft between his legs, hooking it down under his heel, and pushed him to trip over it. He landed hard with a grunt.

"How did I defeat you?" she asked as she offered him a hand to help him up.

"By being inhumanly fast?" the man asked, took her hand, and climbed to his feet.

"Anticipation. Your shoulders betray you and reveal your feints and where you will attack next. You're fast but if you tell your opponent where you are coming from, that won't matter."

"How can I better myself?"

She shrugged. "Train in bursts. Teach your body to go from inaction to action from one moment to another. Improve your feet and allow them to power your strikes instead of your shoulders."

The man nodded, rolled his shoulders, and looked a little unsettled as another of the Pack stepped forward. He carried a saber and flicked it from left to right before he pointed the tip at her.

He was waiting for her to attack and she paused to watch his movements and tried to get a better idea of how he would defend himself if she struck first. She took a step forward and he immediately inched away, knowing she had a better range with her spear.

Cassandra lashed out first, shuffled her steps forward, and thrust the spear directly into where his sword was. He flicked his saber to deflect the strike, and with both hands on the haft, she withdrew it quickly and thrust again. She altered the speed and point of attack and each time, took a shuffling step forward that forced him back until he could retreat no more.

Her next thrust toward his head missed and thunked into the stone wall behind him. He took that as a sign that he had an advantage and slapped her spear to the side with the flat of his blade before he charged forward and aimed a swing at her neck.

It appeared that her warning about no harm being done in sparring matches would not be heeded, but it didn't matter. She had the haft of the spear raised like a shield and pushed his swing to the side as she wrapped her arm around it, spun it deftly as he rushed past her, and tapped the back of his head with the butt in passing.

The strike was enough to make him stumble to his knees and lose his hold on his sword as he collided hard with the ground. There wasn't much that she could suggest for the man. His skill and defense were all about as good as could be expected but he rushed in like a crazed goat. Experience would teach him better, provided he survived.

"Not bad," Langven finally admitted as he stepped into the sparring area. That was enough to quiet the rest of the Pack, who paused to watch their leader get to know their new comrade in arms. "No magic and still a handful as a fighter."

"I haven't used a spear in some years but I suppose the training does return when used," Cassandra answered and twirled the weapon around herself in smooth circles before she tucked it into her arm and smiled.

The barbarians weren't as interested in watching and with their new playmates distracted, began to spar with one another again.

She didn't much mind. They'd seen her fight already and there was no need to teach them any kind of lesson regarding what they would be dealing with, even a scantily clad barbarian princess. Although, if the battles began to rage, she would be clad in even less. The armor granted by her amulet did not extend to the clothes she wore.

Langven drew his longsword and grasped it with both hands. He stepped out in front of her and leaned the blade on his shoulder. It appeared to be a passive stance at first glance but the fact that he held the weapon with both hands told her it was likely some variation of the Gates of Wrath, especially from his footwork. He was watching and waiting for her to attack.

Given that even with his longsword, she still had a longer reach, he would wait for her to attack before he countered.

If she simply waited, the chances were that they would be

stuck circling each other all damn day and she had no desire to waste that kind of time.

She darted forward, jumped from one foot to the other, and flicked her left hand over her shoulder to twist the spear and attack close to where his sword rested on his shoulder. Years spent drilling through the motions had begun to come back to her, and she almost felt like there was something in the spear itself that made it easier to tap into the skills she'd thought were long forgotten.

Perhaps there was a little magic helping her after all, although they could not hold the use of a mystical weapon against her.

He parried the strike and immediately lunged forward and slashed his blade out to catch her, although he did not jump close enough for her to wrap him in a tight grapple. She reversed her grip, blocked his swing, and brought the butt around to catch him in the ribs before he could recover.

It was a good blow but the clang of wood on plate armor told her that it did little damage.

Langven ignored the strike, switched the side of his blade, and swung it to try to catch her in the neck as well. His movements were calculated and he maintained his composure, resisting the urge to rush in when he had some kind of advantage. Instead of attacking when she parried again, he backed away and changed his stance to a higher guard held over his head.

She recognized that he'd been classically trained. It was odd for him to lead a tiny mercenary group when he could make far more coin as a knight or a front-line mercenary for any one of the armies that required them these days.

It was a question for another time but she wouldn't make a fuss about it. With his more aggressive stance, he hoped to press her back. He swung his blade in a smooth figure-eight, which she evaded by stepping back and retaliated quickly with another strike from the side, only to see him deflect it with a smooth motion of his sword.

It had been a long day. Traveling on foot, taking the brothers on, facing the bandits, and still buying the supplies, and her body began to warn her that all was not well. She wasn't quite exhausted but her arms and legs begged for rest and screamed with fatigue that would slow her and give her opponent an advantage she had no intention to provide him with.

She needed to end the fight and she needed to do it quickly.

Cassandra drew a deep breath and let her mouth drop open as they circled again to indicate that her tiredness was worse than it was. Carefully, she watched the man's reaction and noted that he grew more aggressive with his strikes to force her back. She saw the twins now a little more attentive to the fight and guessed that they must have noticed her lagging and on the defensive, able to keep his sword from cutting her by only the barest of margins as he pressed his advantage. It was no longer clear if it was a feint or not as she now defended against his almost constant attacks, unable to answer with any of her own.

In that moment, she saw her opening. With the wall against her back and he pressed too close, his balance was off as he tried to find a way through her defenses.

The barbarian princess caught a swing and pushed her foot against the wall to launch herself forward and drive the spear haft into his chest with enough force to send them both sprawling. She rolled onto her shoulder and was on her knees before he could react, the tip of her spear pressed into his neck.

Langven remained very still, and she could see that he thought she might simply use the opportunity to kill him and call it an accident. These people had a way of projecting their ideas onto others but she wouldn't tease him over it.

She could hear the twins hooting and hollering in the back and they were more than happy to offer a little mockery to the man who was flat on his back.

"Are you sure he's the one you want leading your company?"

"If he's the best, I suppose we can't count on much in the way of help from the rest of you bastards."

Cassandra wasn't even sure which barbarian had said what and it didn't matter. She pulled her spear away and planted it in the dirt before she extended a hand to help the man up. In all honesty, she was more tired than she was willing to admit and no longer needed to pretend to be breathing hard as she helped Langven to his feet again.

"I might have deserved that," he admitted with a chuckle and retrieved his sword.

"You might have."

"I thought you would call on your magic for an edge toward the end there."

"If I feared that you were trying to kill me, I might have."

He moved away to rejoin his men and she pulled a rag from her belt to wipe the sweat from her brow as her gaze found Verda, who was still awake and appeared to have been watching the fight with wide eyes as she continued to eat. In that moment, it struck her how young the girl was. Her time would have been better spent doing the kinds of things youths her age tended to do.

For the life of her, she could not think of what those might be. Her youth had been spent training and perusing old scrolls, taking exams, and learning how to be a bright and proper paladin.

She'd unleashed all the energy that had been pent up over those years during her time on sabbatical.

Cassandra sat next to the girl and watched the two barbarians still testing their new weapons as the Ebon Pack returned to the work of preparing to leave at first light. She assumed there was not much more fight left in them for the moment.

"You're much better than I thought you would be," Verda commented and took a sip of water from a skin before she bit into the bread again. "I wasn't sure what kind of fighters I would find here, but this was the closest town where I could find any. There are imperial outposts nearby, but it would take...maybe two or three more days to reach them on horseback. I wasn't sure if I had that kind of time. I wasn't sure if the folks in my home had...that much time."

The girl leaned against her pack in an effort to get comfortable now that she was fed. It did beg the question of whether or not an imperial outpost would commit their troops to handle a mere handful of bandits, but there were already holes in the girl's story. Cassandra was sure the truth would become clear before too long.

"It is good to know that fighters like you are coming," Verda whispered, her eyes already drooping as she made herself comfortable. "With you, we might have a chance."

The barbarian princess smiled and patted the girl on the shoulder. "Rest, young one. We shall wake you when the time comes."

It didn't appear that the girl needed much encouragement as she was already slipping into a dreamless sleep.

It could be a little frustrating to deal with these independent types. They had problems with authority, every single one of them, which meant there would be an issue that needed to be addressed every damn day without fail.

"Do you think they know we're doing this for their benefit?"

Adrian shrugged. He wasn't allowed a moment's rest. Every time there was trouble, he and Yaleh and the rest of the frontliners were brought in to handle the rabble.

They were being paid the most so it did make sense that they did most of the work, but it was still a fucking annoyance. He had joined the army with the intention of fighting and winning battles, not corralling the conquered townsfolk.

There was no looting to be had in corralling townsfolk. Not much of it, at least. They would grow poor even while being gainfully employed, all because the damn Herald wanted them to maintain order in the city she'd taken by beating two men in combat and nothing else.

He paused barely short of kicking in the next door. "Wait, what did you say?"

"That these girls would work well as whores?"

"No, before that."

Yahleh had a habit of running his mouth without thinking about what was coming out. Adrian had long since learned to zone out when he was off on one of his tangents.

"Oh. I merely said that we're here for the benefit of the bastards. The least they could do is show a little appreciation for our efforts, don't you think?"

He tilted his head and studied his comrade in arms while he tried to understand the thinking that had brought the man to that conclusion.

No explanation came.

"You're a dumb bastard, aren't you?"

"What? Why?"

"Do you honestly think that kicking in doors and harassing the townsfolk is for their benefit?"

"Well, no." Yahleh shook his head. "This is only because they aren't following our commands. Examples need to be made as well as finding the fucking shits who ran off, them and their horses."

"Only one dumb shit and only one horse. But what part of our occupation here do you think is being done for their benefit?"

"The Herald said it. Bringing civilization to these places ravaged by war."

"You do realize that we are bringing more war to ravage the area, right?" Adrian shook his head. The kinds of people he had been saddled with never ceased to cause him trouble, yet Yahleh was somehow the most insufferable ass of them all.

"Well, yes, I suppose. But you know what they say about making omelets, don't you?"

"It doesn't fucking matter. Do you think they're doing any real farming, hunting, and trapping around these parts with us constantly breaking into their houses? No, this is for our benefit. I would say you're taking a little too much of what the Herald says to heart."

He knew better than to call her by any other name, especially a derogatory one. She did not appear to be the kind who would forgive that kind of insubordination.

But they had no time to discuss it now. Adrian took a step forward and put his boot through the door. It was not terribly difficult to break and the guilty looks of those inside were enough to tell him that something was afoot—something they were there to stop.

It was the way they seemed to have all paused. They had evidently heard guards talking outside and rushed to hide whatever incriminating evidence remained in their home.

He was quick to intercept the woman. She was older and not altogether foul-looking with a few wrinkles under her eyes but still no sign of gray in her thick black hair. Selah was right. The women in this town would certainly make a great deal of coin if they offered their bodies up.

She had been heading toward one of the windows with something heavy in her hands. He caught hold of her but turned as a fist collided with the side of his head. Just his luck too. He'd been called out in such a rush that he hadn't thought to bring his helm and the blow was almost enough to level him, although he kept a firm hold on the woman.

They both sprawled into a nearby table, upended it, and brought the chairs down on them as well.

"It wouldn't have happened if I'd brought my fucking helm,"

he muttered under his breath as he made sure the woman was still in his grasp before he turned to where Selah had tackled the man who had thrown the punch. Unlike the woman, his head was bald in contrast to a thick, bushy beard, and he had the look of a woodsman. Which explained the power behind the strike. Adrian was still seeing stars.

But Yahleh was not a small man and he handily took the woodsman down, pushed him to the floor, and kicked him in the teeth. It knocked a few of them out and another kick into his gut made the man double over to shield himself up from the assault.

"No!" the woman shouted and still struggled to pull herself free. "Leave him alone! He's done nothing!"

"I beg to differ," Adrian snapped and rubbed the place where he'd been hit. "Keep struggling and your husband will suffer more. Now tell me—what are you hiding in this house?"

It was their fifth house and he'd had enough of folk trying to resist their efforts. The whole situation wasn't ideal for the locals, but their resistance wasn't exactly helping them either. It was like they wanted their situation to worsen.

But he wouldn't comment on that. Not for the moment.

"Fine, we won't resist anymore," she whispered and fixed her gaze on the floor.

"No...you...can—"

"Shut it!" Yahleh immediately cut the man's protests off with a hard boot to his back, which forced a groan out of him.

"Please...please, don't hurt him." The woman displayed the pouch she held, smiled, and tried to make their attackers less angry.

He wasn't sure how that was supposed to work but as long as it got them what they wanted, he honestly didn't care.

Adrian took the pouch and opened it to reveal a small stash of gold and silver coins—twenty of each, more or less, and a handful of gemstones. It wasn't quite a fortune but not an amount to scoff at either.

"It would appear that someone has not paid all their riches into the coffers of the Herald," Adrian said and attempted to not show that the punch still throbbed. "Given the penalties involved, I would say you were gathering these riches with a purpose in mind. Tell us what that is and no more injury will be required."

She hesitated then and Yahleh was quick to remind her of the consequences of not cooperating. He sank his boot into her husband again and elicited another groan from him.

"It...it was to pay the mercenaries coming to help us," the woman admitted.

"It's not the kind of coin they would have been able to gather all on their own either," Yahleh pointed out, picked up one of the chairs that had been knocked over, and sat on it. "I would assume that the rest of the town had contributed their coin."

"I suppose the girl who went missing was sent to find these mercenaries." Adrian sighed and shook his head. "You had better hope she cannot find anyone stupid enough to come here. Otherwise, when they appear, we will have to make an example—the kind that will see you burning along with your miserable hovel. Come on."

Yahleh growled in protest but grasped the fallen, battered man and dragged him out after his comrade, who did the same to the woman. Both made sure that the rest of the town could see.

The chieftain's son was a tough bastard, Adrian had to admit. Not many men would have survived what the Herald had done to him but he stood there like nothing had happened. Well, not quite like nothing had happened. He was covered in bandages and needed the help of a crutch to keep himself upright as he watched them drag the two out of their hut.

"Are you truly going to scourge the whole town?" the boy asked, his voice muffled through the bandages.

"If we have to," Adrian answered in a cheerful tone. "But if you keep proving yourself to be problematic, you won't live to see it. Consider that as you take another healing potion."

Given the paltry sum that had been gathered, he doubted it would be much of a fight anyway, even if the girl returned. Mercenaries were in high demand and short supply in the region, and that amount of coin would be well short of what was required to gather enough men to pose anything resembling a threat. Still, it would be best to have a surprise prepared for any who would approach Torsburch, just in case. There was no need to be too arrogant.

They would still have to make an example. He had caught a glimpse into the mind of the Herald by now, having seen her operate for a few months. She had her ways of handling such issues and they generally did not leave many survivors.

Hopefully, it would mean they could move on again from this wretched place.

CHAPTER EIGHT

She'd had a feeling that something like this would happen. Verda had told them that the journey was a few days' ride from the Rest, but with the sun rising on the fourth day, there was no sign of any village or town anywhere along the road.

The girl was adamant that it had taken her a few days to ride from Torsburch to Edge's Rest, but that was because she had been alone and had pushed her horse to exhaustion. Unless Cassandra missed her guess, it was more likely that they would need five days to reach her home. The confusion was what could be expected from a young woman who rode through the night without any rest.

It was amazing that she survived the journey. The barbarian princess had spent almost a week on the march without rest and only a brief pause for a quick meal and a bite to eat from time to time, and it had left her almost dead as well. Then again, she was trained for it and experienced in those kinds of rigors. The young woman was not.

"What do you know?" Langven asked as their party began to pack their camp up. "Nothing to see as morning light illuminates the landscape either. For all we know, the girl might have simply brought us out here to be murdered and robbed."

"It would be the most convoluted robbery in history," she answered and took a sip of water before she refilled her skin in the small stream they had camped close to. "And not one that would make anyone rich. It would make more sense as an assassination, but who the hell would want to go through so much trouble simply to murder you?"

"About…two dozen people, although only five of them would have the means for this kind of effort."

Cassandra wasn't sure what she had expected from the answer. It made sense that people would want him dead and given his skills and the quality of his weapons and armor, it stood to reason that he hadn't always been a low-level mercenary.

More questions raised their heads but she was not interested in engaging the man any more than she already had. All she wanted from him was to silence his incessant whining about how the journey was taking longer than it should have. Her work was done and she had nothing else to say on the matter.

She moved on immediately before he thought she was someone he could continue to complain to. With her saddlebags in hand, she approached Strider where he had spent the night.

"You look well-rested," she said and patted his neck. "Then again, you did spend a few days in a comfortable stable with nice, sweet hay and grains for you to get fat on. For myself, only one good night's sleep and it was on the road again. I'm sore, my back is killing me, and there is no other way for me to express how jealous I am. Of a horse."

A quick shake of the head was his only reply and it didn't seem like he had anything else to say. Perhaps he wanted a few more hours of sleep like she did.

"Do you generally speak to your horse?" Bandir asked. He looked like he had taken a sharp knife to his beard and trimmed it a little.

"I would have thought you were able to have better conversations," Tandir answered and looked at the people around them.

"Better conversations, perhaps, but not among the present company," Cassandra answered with a small smirk. "Then again, it is a barbarian custom to speak to horses, although I suppose it depends on the skill of the speaker whether or not they are able to understand the beast's responses. I've never been able to claim such but it is comforting to have good company to share a long journey with. In fact, it is customary in the DeathEater clan to avoid riding their horses altogether."

The twins exchanged a confused look. "Why have horses if they won't ride them?"

"Horses can still carry heavy loads but they regard them as their brothers and think it would be insulting for them to ride them, even in the harshest of circumstances. Skharr refused to call his horse anything other than Horse and considered it to be a royal enough name to rise above all others."

Bandir chuckled and shook his head. "I always knew those damn DeathEaters were mad. I suppose this is all the proof we need."

"You can't say they do not produce powerful warriors," she responded and wondered if that sounded a little too defensive, although she had no idea why. Skharr did not need her to defend him or his name. And from what he'd told her, he had cut all ties with his clan, which meant he was likely no longer a DeathEater in anything but name.

"Strong fighters, yes, but there's a reason why they live up in the mountains away from everyone else," Tandir explained as they readied their horses. "They had a history of antagonizing the other clans and insisted that they were the only true barbarians in the region and started skirmishes and even battles over it."

"They tried to take over the other clans?" Cassandra asked as she mounted Strider.

"Not take over, at least that isn't what the stories tell us,"

Bandir answered. "It seems they considered the rest of the clans in the region to be an insult. Assimilation was not what they wanted. They wanted the rest of the clans dead or removed from the region. Eventually, the fighting reached the point where peace had to be forced and a decision was made. The DeathE-aters could establish themselves in the mountains where they need not be insulted by the rest of the clans and all the hostilities could cease."

"One clan was that much of a nuisance for so many others that they had to be the ones who sued for peace?" She raised an eyebrow. "How many clans are there?"

"Dozens as of this moment." Bandir joined her as the other mercenaries were still a little slow and not ready to ride out. Perhaps they also needed a little more rest, but it looked like Verda was anxious to be on the move again. "As you said, they make fine warriors. Great cooks as well, as legend tells it, but not fantastic in the realm of coexistence."

That did sound rather like Skharr when she considered it. There would be no denying that the man liked to work on his own and appeared to only take on company when he needed it.

"Come on," Cassandra muttered and nudged Strider forward as the rest of their party mounted and were finally ready to leave their campsite behind for the moment. They would continue to ride until late in the night, assuming they hadn't arrived at the town yet.

In truth, it did not appear as though there were too many travelers through these parts. She would not make herself mad with insane theories over what they might face but there were questions that needed to be answered.

"Still nothing," Langven commented as they approached a dip in the road that led them into a small canyon carved by an underground stream that she could hear flowing below.

The fact that the road led to the river probably meant that most travelers stopped in the area to get away from the heat that glared above them. The farther east and south they traveled, the more intense the heat became during the day.

And, oddly enough, the nights were a sharp contrast, much cooler than the day was. Someone told her that it was because the air was dry but she couldn't find any meaning in that. Folk who understood that kind of thing probably had a great deal of information and papers to support the thought but in the end, the why never mattered to her as much as it did to them.

In the end, the air was dry, which led to hot days and cool nights. That was that. She was far more interested in the studies into magic, which had to do with her upbringing. It made more sense to her for some reason.

Cassandra paused when Strider twitched beneath her. Something was unsettling the beast. They were almost a hundred paces into the ravine and if something affected her horse, she wanted to know what it was. This was the kind of place where monsters enjoyed spending their time creating their lairs and lying in wait for animals and other sources of food to come to the water.

But this was something else. She noted the two brothers had also sensed something and spoke quickly in suppressed voices. While she couldn't hear what they were saying, they scanned the edges of the ravine above them. It made her wonder if all barbarians had better senses regarding danger and when it was approaching.

From the looks of it, the other horses showed the same unsettled signs and she brought Strider to a halt and raised her hand to stop the mercenaries. Some of the Ebon Pack didn't see her and began to grow annoyed with their horses. They tried to determine what was happening amidst crude jokes and laughter.

Langven, unlike his men, did stop. He hadn't sensed anything but he wouldn't disregard it if others felt like they were about to come under attack.

"Ready your shields," Cassandra called. If something attacked them from above, there was little that her sword or her spear could do unless she threw them. She began to wish that she'd brought a shield as well. Her armor and the charm would keep her safe enough but Strider would not be so well protected.

The Pack looked at Langven, who nodded for them to do as they were told. There would be no time to fumble for weapons and shields when something was attacking them and if there was nothing to be worried about, they would not be overly inconvenienced to put their weapons away.

Strider was the first one to see them and he neighed profusely as a head peeked over the edge. It was followed by another and then a few more until about two dozen pairs of eyes looked down on them. They were mostly human as far as she could tell, armed and armored and ready for a fight.

"Take cover!" she shouted and drove her heels hard into Strider's flanks until the horse broke into a gallop as a volley of arrows plummeted from above. There was no time to consider who they were or why they were waiting for someone. Those questions would have to be answered later, provided they all survived the assault.

"Keep moving!" Langven shouted and gestured for his men to move to where the ravine sloped somewhat and provided a little more cover. There was an open section between them and it, however, enough area for those raining arrows to turn it into a killing field.

Two men were felled with the second volley when they lowered their shields to try to push their horses faster. Cassandra raised her hands and projected a shield above their heads, which provided some respite from the barrage. Not only arrows, but spears, bolts, and even rocks were flung at them.

If they could reach some cover, they would be able to find a way out and attack the bastards. It was a tenuous position to be in but they had to make it work.

Her shield caught a handful of projectiles before she was

forced to lower it and take control of Strider's reins again. She looked over her shoulder to where the twins lagged behind.

"Move!" she bellowed and Tandir did as she said and heeled his horse into a gallop. His brother remained, however, and looked up as he drew one of the spears from the saddlebag.

It was exactly like a barbarian to want to retaliate while in the open, but even his position on a saddle failed to slow him as he flung the spear with enough power that it chipped an edge away from the rocks above them and forced those who stood nearby to take a few steps back to avoid being struck. Still, not all were driven away and what looked like an orc stepped close to the edge. He swung what appeared to be a sling over his head a few times before he launched a stone fast enough that she could hear it whistle through the air.

"Bandir!"

Cassandra jumped off her saddle and slapped Strider's rump to send him galloping to where the rest of the mercenaries were gathered. Langven was already positioning them in formation to surround Verda and ensure that she was not a part of the fight.

It left her with the task to go to where her barbarian now slid from his saddle, his body limp. A trickle of blood had already appeared on his temple as the stone that struck him clattered onto the ground nearby. She heard the whizzing and whispering of arrows and spears following her as she rushed to catch him before he landed.

The barbarian was a weighty bastard and she grunted as she caught him and managed to twist him to ensure that he landed on something other than his head. Her first inspection told her that he was still breathing and so still alive, but he'd been knocked unconscious and had a cracked skull to show for his efforts.

"Damn fool," she whispered, pressed her hand to his head, and reached out to the damage to his skull to help him to heal. He was out and would not join them for the rest of the fight, but if his wound was not addressed quickly, permanent damage would ensue—the kind that even she couldn't cure. Only a handful of mages could accomplish the healing of a human brain or said they could anyway. It was more difficult than it looked.

The mysteries of the human mind extended beyond the madness that filled it.

She ducked as more arrows streaked down. For some reason, they were not aiming for the horses, only for those who were riding them. Maybe they were sensible raiders—the kind who knew that live horses were worth more than horse meat.

One of the spears cut a little too close and buried itself deep into the ground next to the road, close enough that she could snatch it. Cassandra wasn't sure what was going through her mind. Perhaps it was the same thing that had gone through Bandir's when he chose to fight back instead of running. She pulled the spear free and made sure the barbarian wasn't close enough to the horse that it could trample his head if it acted nervously.

With no thought and driven by pure instinct, she stepped out from behind the beast and targeted one of the archers who was reaching for more arrows from his quiver. Now would have been a good time for the massive bow that Skharr liked to carry around, but a spear was about as good as she could hope for. As it left her fingers, she knew that it was a good throw—even a perfect throw. The archer hadn't even seen her before the spear gouged into his chest and launched him back into his comrades who uttered startled shouts.

A distraction was all she needed. Cassandra pulled Bandir's arm, yanked it over her shoulder, and groaned as she heaved him up and began to drag him to where there was some cover. The enemy would recover and find an easy, slow target to fire at, which would leave her with nothing to show for her efforts except for a handful of arrows sticking from both their bodies and one of the bandits dead.

Suddenly, the weight was lifted. Not all of it, but some was lifted from her shoulders and she turned to see that Tandir had returned and now held his brother up on the other side and helped to carry him to cover. She couldn't understand how they hadn't been hit yet until she looked up to where they were going.

The mercenary leader had organized his men to form a shield wall to block all the arrows, spears, and rocks cast from above. They had also begun to retaliate. Archers had retrieved their bows and began to choose their targets as well to force the men at the top to where they were no longer in a position to threaten them. This provided the moment of respite they needed to move the barbarian into the protection of the shields.

"We attack," Cassandra shouted when Strider trotted to where she was standing.

"What?" Langven snapped and marched closer to her. "We have a defensible position here."

"It will not be defensible for long. And even if they do not attack us, we'll have these skirmishers nipping at our heels every step of the way. That is if they do not move forward and warn a larger force of our presence here."

She made a point of directing her gaze at Verda, who still looked terrified and refused to meet it. Langven noticed but both knew this was not the time to address it.

"You three—with her now. The rest will hold this position."

She smiled and caught Tandir by the shoulder.

"No, I have you—"

"Remain here if you wish. Remind me to ask you what the fuck was accomplished."

"He was injured—"

"I healed him. Now, stay at his side or take vengeance on the men who injured him. It's your choice."

By the time she had mounted, his decision was made and he took to his horse alongside hers. The three mercenaries joined them as they galloped back the way they'd come. Tandir tossed two spears at the bastards to ensure that they did not grow any courage while they waited.

She swung her horse around once they reached the top of the ravine. It was rocky, treacherous terrain, which made it difficult to ride the bastards down, but she noticed them trying to regain their position. There were fewer than she'd counted before, which meant the archers had lowered their numbers to something a little more manageable. With the boulders and thick, stubby trees around them, it was difficult to make their ranged weapons useful before the mercenaries were on them.

An archer had barely looked up before her spear tore through his throat and splashed blood onto the rocks around them and his fellow fighters. More began to drop their bows and reach for weapons that could combat their attackers.

Cassandra buried her spear into the chest of another and made sure that it went in deep. She dropped from Strider's saddle, whirled quickly, and leveraged the bandit's body off the ground to fling him into his comrades.

As a distraction, it did its work well and made them catch the man as the other mercenaries barreled into them. Tandir screamed something she couldn't make out as he jumped directly from his saddle into a pile of four or so of their adversaries and swung his mace into the face of the one closest to him. It was a smooth strike and crushed the skull even through the helm before he impaled the spike through the neck of the one behind. He continued to bellow as blood spattered his face. The mace was stuck and he left it there, drew two smaller axes from his belt, and swung into the bandits like a whirlwind of fury.

She had no time to consider whether he needed help as she drew her sword and managed to control her spear with one hand and use it to keep most of the others at bay. Her blade opened the throat of one and cut through padded armor to bury itself into the chest of another. It wasn't her finest strike as the man's fall wrenched the weapon from her. She used both hands to hold the spear and twisted it. The men in front of her backed away, suddenly terrified to attack.

A quick thrust punched through the thick padded leather armor of one, almost like it wasn't there. She assumed a weapon that could slash through a dragon's scales would find little difficulty with armor. Her teeth gritted, she yanked the spear to the right and the longer blade opened the man's guts and spilled them onto his comrade who stood next to him.

Perhaps they understood their peril now. Or maybe they didn't. Cassandra didn't care much. She had fallen into something her trainers had always called a battle trance. Others called it the blood fury. Her mind had gone silent and allowed her body to do what it had been trained to do. She whipped the weapon around and hammered the butt of the haft into the closest bandit's gut. He doubled over and she planted the spearhead into his back and forced him to the ground.

It came out again smoothly and she twisted and drove it toward the nearest moving figure but paused when she realized it was one of Langven's mercs.

He had his hands raised to show he had no intention of fighting and it seemed like he was afraid she wouldn't care.

There was blood fury and there was blood rage. She had never allowed herself to reach the point where she would kill any and all who set foot in her path. Some paladins had gone down that road and stripped their armor off and shouted as they charged into battle. She'd known of one she had trained with since she'd been a child who had watched his own arm be cut off, laughed, and directed the spray into the faces of those he was fighting.

It was sheer madness but nothing was quite as liberating or tantalizing. Which was why she knew she had to resist. Once she had gone into it, there would be no coming out again.

"Good fucking hells," Langven muttered when he caught up

with them. "You and one barbarian are capable of this. It makes a man wonder if you need us at all."

"It makes a woman wonder the same." She paused to wipe the blood that had spattered onto her face. Tandir showed no inclination to follow suit and simply sat on a nearby boulder, breathing heavily as the axes in his hands dropped to the ground.

"Bandits?" Langven asked.

"They were too heavily armed and armored for simple bandits," Cassandra pointed out and dropped to her haunches to study their weapons. Even the orcs were equipped with human-forged weapons, although they hadn't even reached for them during the fight. "They follow the common tactics but I have a feeling they were waiting for us."

"Bandits would be waiting for anyone who passes by," Tandir said and pushed to his feet to wrench his mace out from where it was buried.

"No, I mean they were waiting for us specifically." She leaned a little closer and pushed one man's hand to the side to reveal the image emblazoned on his chest. It was a little faded and difficult to make out, especially with the blood covering it.

She narrowed her eyes and her gaze traced a skull lacking the lower half of the jaw and horns jutting from the brow. It was a simple sign, the kind generally used to identify fighters in combat —signs used by armies.

"Are they all marked with the same sigil?" Langven asked and checked a few others. Cassandra didn't need to wait to hear the result.

"Yes," one of the mercs answered once he'd checked a few others. "All of them."

"Deserters?" Tandir suggested.

"It's possible but unlikely." The mercenary leader shook his head. "Most deserters will cut all signs that they were a part of any military from their garb. That way, there will be less of a chance for them to be recognized and dragged back to be hung for the crime of desertion."

"Do you know a lot about what happens to deserters, then?" Tandir asked and finally began to clean off the blood he'd spilled.

"I do."

"Is it a matter of experience?"

"Possibly." Langven was suddenly anxious to change the subject. "No, these men are still with whomever that sigil belongs to but I have not seen it before."

"Me neither." Cassandra didn't want to bring up the fact that if there was a sigil, it practically confirmed that they weren't dealing with a few rogue bandits. She knew that he was thinking the same thing and hadn't raised it for the same reason she hadn't. He wanted to address it with Verda in private, where others would not be able to interfere.

"If these are scouts for a larger party, they will wonder what happened to those they sent," he commented as the rest of the party arrived and began to search the bodies.

Bandir was awake and present and roughly shoved a mercenary away from one killed by his brother. "We hold the rights to the loot. It's all the coin we are making on this fucking venture in case you forgot."

There was no need for further convincing and the twins continued to search the bodies that had been killed by Tandir or Cassandra. She decided to leave them to it as she approached Langven.

"You have ideas, yes?"

He regarded her carefully and chuckled. "A few. We have the means and the opportunity to plan a trap for the bastards and if all goes to plan, we might even be able to turn the tables on them."

CHAPTER NINE

There was something powerful about being in her proper armor again. Cassandra wasn't sure why it felt like that, but the way the sun glinted off her exposed skin was liberating. She was the barbarian princess and she was on her own. Only her with no other mercenaries to fall back on if something went wrong.

It seemed entirely odd to feel this calm about it. She was sure that panicked thoughts were supposed to race through her mind as she nudged Strider toward the open gates of Torsburch.

It had all the signs of a thriving, industrious town, already on its way to becoming a true city. Her gaze noted the walls, towers for defense, and even a moat around them to ensure that any force attempting to attack would need to funnel in through the bridge she now crossed. The buildings were growing but still showing signs of improper techniques. They were built by those who had no real training and whose only drive was to make a home for themselves. A small market area was situated beyond the gate. Wells had been dug to ensure that there was water for the whole town and a rudimentary sewer fed into the moat. Perhaps it was meant to fill it one day, although she couldn't understand why they would want to. She preferred to think this was a temporary measure until a better waste disposal system could be constructed.

All the signs of a prosperous town were there aside from the people. They hid in their homes, peeked out of the slatted windows, and tried to understand what and who they were looking at.

Men in familiar uniforms watched as well and studied her as she continued to ride toward one of the wells.

When she reached it, she realized it wasn't a well, but a spring. The water seeped naturally from the ground and fed into a handful of other areas where the townsfolk could gather and use it at their leisure. It was likely the reason why Torsburch had been founded there in the first place. There could not be many places in this area where water simply pushed from the ground. They were close enough to the desert to make water more precious than gold.

More of the men approached and scrutinized her carefully as she dismounted and approached the spring. A handful of buckets and cups had been placed around it. She found the largest cup, filled it with water, and took a sip as her gaze was drawn to the path to the longhall at the top of the hill.

Two stakes had been driven into the earth and two people had been bound to them. They were still alive—or still breathing, at least—but their backs were covered in welts and wounds where they had been whipped and left out as a warning to the rest of the populace. A man and a woman, exposed to the sun and the elements, to demonstrate the dangers of rising against the city's new masters.

Heat filled her cheeks while something cold touched her stomach, the kind of feeling that generally came before she drew her weapons and left a pile of bodies behind her. For the moment, however, she needed to control the impetus and keep herself calm.

Cassandra distracted herself by taking a sip of the water. She let it cool both her mind and her body as she noted that men who wore the same horned skull she'd seen before were approaching. This all but established that Verda had lied to them. This was not some mish-mashed group of renegades in need of a good trouncing. The uniform was that of an army, the kind that would not be intimidated when a small group of well-armed mercenaries rode up.

With that established, she took a moment to splash water on her head and sighed as the cool, clean liquid washed over her body. There was nothing quite like washing the sweat and grime of the day away under cool water on a hot day.

It was considerably less appealing when it was cold and muddy but still necessary.

"Nothing quite like cooling off after a hot, sweaty ride, eh, love?"

One of the men spoke. She wasn't quite sure which one it was but it didn't matter. She wouldn't take the risk of addressing him directly. Men like him would see that as an invitation on her part, and any clear thought would be gone from their minds. The end result would be a pile of bodies with hers at the top.

If she was lucky.

"Some time giving the ride might help," another commented with a chuckle and the rest joined the laughter. "Although no less sweaty, I'm sure you'll feel the weight of the day far less."

Cassandra took another sip of the water, well aware of the tantalizing image she presented to them—a scantily clad woman, her skin shimmering and reflecting the blazing sunlight. There were men who would not be attracted by such things but they were something of a minority in the world.

The one who spoke first showed more courage than the others, took a few steps closer, and made no attempt to hide how his gaze wandered over her body.

"What brings you to this fucking shithole of a town?" he asked.

"A shithole, is it?" Cassandra countered and regarded him steadily. "If that is the case, what does it say of the men who inhabit it?"

That caught both the man and his followers off-guard. Unlike him, however, the others laughed at the comment, at which their overseer looked embarrassed at first and then annoyed. He glowered at them as if ready to deliver a sharp reprimand before he turned his attention to her again.

"Any number of things, I suppose," he answered and tried to play his discomfort off as nothing but a momentary lapse. "But that does not answer the question. What are you doing here?"

Cassandra moved to where Strider browsed a small patch of grass growing by the side of the road. "I've come to trade. I was told there was a market here for those who were willing to make the journey. It is unfortunate to see there are none here to trade with."

"There are those who you see before you." He gestured to his men. "All are heavy with coin and intent on spending it should the right product present itself. And it has, by the looks of things."

She raised an eyebrow and nodded as she shifted a few of her saddlebags aside. "Truly."

He approached, grasped one of the heavier sacks, and yanked it off the saddle. "Indeed."

It fell at their feet and the contents spilled out and drew a strong reaction from the men. The one who had come a little too close stepped back, his eyes wide. It had taken a fair amount of work but the idea was better than the one of dragging all the bodies back. Strider would not have stood for that kind of work in this heat.

Instead, they'd settled on bringing the heads, still wearing the helms they'd been sent out with. They had already begun to smell a little ripe from the heat.

She slid her hand under the remainder of the packs and drew her sword from where it had been hidden. Despite the tension of the moment, she could not help a smile at the shocked expressions of all the men who had leered at her mere moments before.

"How much will I get for those?" Cassandra kicked one of the heads closer to the man who appeared to be in charge and gave him her most convincing smile. "I'm sure you'll offer a lady a fair price, yes?"

"The price will be your fucking head!" he responded belligerently and retrieved what appeared to be a whip that was held on his belt by a hook. She had a feeling he was the one responsible for beating the man and woman still bound to the nearby stake.

"I fear that price is too dear for you." She couldn't help a small grin as he unfurled the whip and raised it above his head with the full intention to strike. "None could afford to take on the Barbarian Princess!"

She didn't wait for a reaction but darted forward and closed the distance between the two of them faster than he could blink. Whips were interesting as weapons—generally useless but they did work to intimidate the uninitiated. She was initiated, however, and she pushed in close before he could jerk the weapon forward.

His hand dropped to the ground alongside the whip, severed from the arm it had been attached to seconds before.

Alarms resounded around the city and more of the men began to rush toward them. They became the focus of attention as the overseer stumbled back, clutched the stump, and tried to stem the flow of blood from the wound.

"You...fucking bitch!" he roared, tripped over a rock on the road, and was helped to his feet by one of his men. "Do you know what this kind of wound means for a man like me? I'll fucking end you for it!"

"You'll die trying."

More of the men gathered as Cassandra kicked the hand away. It tumbled end over end on the road and she wondered idly if there was perhaps some way for him to attach it to his body again. A handful of healing mages said they could regrow a hand from a stump, but she wasn't sure if she believed it. She would if she saw it, though.

"Is anyone else willing to pay my price?" she shouted and raised her sword to the group that grew larger by the minute. Dozens of them looked around and tried to decide whether it would be a sound idea to attack the woman who stood calmly in their midst, wearing almost nothing and armed with only a sword.

There was the question of why the fuck they hadn't attacked yet and she wasn't above admitting that she'd taken the idea from Skharr. The mad fuck had walked in on dozens of enemies in the middle of their evening meal, killed two, and sat for a drink while his enemies decided it was time to leave.

This wasn't quite the same situation and there would be a very different result but she could not deny that the inspiration had come from the DeathEater.

She spun her sword in a smooth figure-eight before her to loosen her wrist and wondered when the right time to retrieve her spear was. It would help to keep them at bay—not that she had much of a choice. She had no idea how long it would take for Langven to bring his men through while most of the soldiers were focused on her and what she was up to.

They would make a scene of it so there would be no chance that she'd miss whatever the hell the merc leader had planned but her part was done. She had already drawn most of the soldiers away from their posts to see what was happening, and it wouldn't take long for them to decide they could deal with one woman.

And they might have even been right too, for all she knew.

Cassandra drew a deep breath, kept herself calm, and focused on the group that appeared to have gathered their courage and now began to advance.

Before they could reach her striking distance, however, a

whistling sound was quickly followed by a wet thud and a gargled scream.

They all turned as one of their men fell to his knees and tried to reach his back where a small spear protruded. It had punched slightly out the front as well and it wasn't long before all the fight left his eyes and he slumped in a motionless heap.

Every gaze turned to the walls, where the mercenaries had positioned themselves, armed and ready to fight. They were heavily outnumbered, of course, but with the walls used to their advantage and most of the enemy caught out of position, it had proven to be a rather ingenious plan.

The first part, at least.

She took advantage of their distraction, leapt forward, and slashed her blade through the throat of the man closest to her. Blood pumped immediately from the wound and the fighter released his weapons in a futile attempt to stop it.

A second had his throat opened and she buried her blade into the chest of another as more arrows and spears were launched by the mercenaries. The fighters were cut down quickly as they lacked the leadership to command them to attack either the woman or the men on the walls.

As she fell back, she realized there wasn't much more of a fight to be had. When the barbarians ran out of their spears, they jumped from the walls—their height inside less than it was outside—and charged at the group, bellowing battle cries. It was an impressive sight to see, she was willing to admit that much, and even Langven and his Ebon Pack made an impressive showing of themselves.

Their archers especially, who forced the soldiers bearing the horned skull on their chests to take cover as the barbarian twins rushed closer. Tandir crushed skulls with his mace and his brother removed the heads entirely with his ax. They had an energy about them that she could certainly appreciate.

With what remained of the battle well in hand and as the

Ebon Pack did their job and began to deal with the last of the bastards, Cassandra could turn her attention to those who likely needed her help the most.

"Hold on there," she whispered as she approached the two still roped to the stakes. "I'll get you clear. Mind your wounds and you will be all right."

She wasn't sure if they could hear her or if they had simply shut the whole world out altogether. Although she'd never been beaten to this extent, she assumed that some mental fortitude was involved to survive it—not only the beating itself but the way the body reacted to it as well.

When she began to heal them, a little life returned. The woman's eyes had been open but had stared ahead without much focus. Now, she turned to her and looked confused and almost afraid like she thought there would be more to come.

"Those who did this live no more," Cassandra assured them once the wounds were healed. More work would have to go into what it had done to their minds but she would never claim to be much of an expert in that regard.

The man jerked up like he had been sleeping and was suddenly awoken from a deep slumber. He flailed in an attempt to take hold of her.

"Verda!" He gasped. "You have to warn her! You have to warn Verda."

"Well, first things first." She pushed his hands away from her breasts. "Secondly, I do believe the warning would be better voiced when coming from you."

She pushed from her crouched position and glanced to where Langven was already riding in with the rest of their horses and Verda with them. The girl looked terrified and stared at the town she'd called home as if to make sense of it all. Perhaps she feared that everyone had been killed—as evidenced by the empty streets —but as the sounds of fighting gave way to silence, a few peeked out from their homes to delighted gasps from the girl.

Verda dropped from the saddle and tears ran down her cheeks as she rushed to the two Cassandra had healed. They cried with her and wrapped her in a warm embrace. It was easy to tell that they were either her parents or other members of her family. The older woman's hair looked similar to hers so they must at least be related somehow.

A younger man limped from the longhall, his face and body covered in a variety of bandages, and he walked forward with the help of a crutch. His injuries appeared to have been considerably more severe—burns, she surmised from the condition of his skin.

"You need healing," she stated and pointed out the obvious.

"I'll be fine."

"Of course. I'll simply stand here and wait for you to fall over before I offer healing magic to help with your wounds." She placed a hand on his shoulder. "There is a time to look like even mountains couldn't bury you, and there is a time to accept help when it is offered. This is the latter. The fight is over. You can rest."

He sat slowly close to the water spring and looked around as the bodies of the dead were gathered and searched. As she started to heal him, he stiffened.

"It should sting a li—"

"There are only eleven."

Cassandra narrowed her eyes. "What?"

"Eleven. Only eleven of the overseers."

"Overseers?"

"The ones with the whips. There are only eleven among the dead. There are twelve of them. Where is the last man?"

She glanced up and opened her mouth to call for the mercs to count the men with the whips. Her assumption was that he hadn't noticed the one whose hand she'd lopped off. Before she could say anything, she heard shouting and one of Langven's Pack fell and clutched his throat.

An overseer lunged out of the shadows, having taken the

smart and cowardly path of hiding himself when it was clear that the fight would not go in their favor. He was quick to make his escape, however, and vaulted onto one of the horses before the others could reach their weapons and was already galloping through the gate by the time they tried to stop him.

"He...he got away," the young man whispered, leaned back, and seemed despondent, almost like they had lost the battle to retake the town.

"Only one of them," Bandir scoffed as he stooped to search the pockets of one of the nearby corpses. "There's nothing to worry about. He'll find another bandit group with more sense and less coin."

"No, you don't understand." The wounded man tried to rise but Cassandra pushed him down and wished she could continue to heal him. "He already is part of a band. They...their leader... she calls herself the Herald of someone or another. I forget his name. She's a powerful mage who burned my father, the chieftain, to ashes and left me in this sorry condition. They left the overseers to ensure that the city remains theirs. If word goes back to them that it is not, the army will return."

"Army?" Langven asked.

"Aye. Army."

Things had gone poorly. Not quite the way Adrian had ever intended but in the end, they were supposed to anticipate that there would be problems. Someone had thought it was a good idea to not kill the woman when she entered simply because she wore practically nothing.

She had been a distraction, nothing more and nothing less. Without a doubt, she'd known she would have a rapt audience followed by an overreaction when she proved to be violent.

He wasn't sure how long he'd been on the saddle or how long

it would take to reach the rest of the Herald's forces but he pressed on. The sun was baking into his back by the time he reached their camp and alarms were raised as he approached the perimeter.

Adrian pushed harder to reach the place where the Herald was camped. It was easy to find as her tent was larger than the rest and all the others were careful to remain a fair distance away. This was never at her command but simply because none of the men had any desire to be anywhere near her.

The woman was in front of the tent and washing her hands in a bowl of water when she saw him approach. Her eyebrows lowered and her fingers toyed with a twirl of hair that hung over her forehead as she walked to where he had dismounted and fallen to his knees.

"I left you in command of Torsburch," she stated, her voice quiet but clearly heard through the silence that resulted from his arrival. "And yet here you are, bloodied, bruised, and looking like absolute shit. I assume you have something to report, Adrian, so get it out. I can smell you from here."

She had a sensitive nose and warned all those who came close to her to not bring offense anywhere near where she could smell it.

"Torsburch—" Adrian took a deep breath. "Mercenaries were hired by the locals. They took it back and killed all the others. I am the only one who made it out alive."

She raised an eyebrow, turned her attention to the bowl, and washed her hands again before she dried them on a nearby towel. Once she had finished, she motioned for one of her servants to take the bowl and towel away.

The silence was almost palpable. He could feel it ticking with every beat of his heart, a rhythmic warning that her calm response did not bode well for him.

"Who took it?" she asked and stepped closer to where he was still kneeling.

"There...they were mercenaries."

"You said that. Who led them?"

"A barbarian. She called herself the Barbarian Princess. I was not... I—"

"Barbarians do not have even the semblance of royalty." She finished his sentence for him, shook her head, and turned to where her seat waited for her. It looked almost like a throne and he had no idea why she made her people carry it everywhere she went, although it did add a certain regality to her appearance.

"They do not," Adrian answered. He wasn't sure if she had asked him or stated it but decided it would be safest to state the obvious.

"The only appeal of their whole miserable race," she muttered, raised her hand, and motioned for one of her men to approach. Savog was one of her orcs—and a massive one at that—who had the customary tusks his kind were known for and another pair between them that looked almost like fangs but were inverted somehow.

Like most orcs, he did not like to speak any of the human languages and instead, gestured with his hands. Adrian didn't like it but for some reason, it amused the Herald. She even made the same gestures in response when not pressed for time.

Not this time, however.

"I'll need you to lead a raiding party," she stated, her gaze fixed on Adrian. "Put Torsburch to the torch, salt the fields—you know how we handle these things. Enslave a quarter of the population and mutilate another quarter. Both hands will do but not the feet. We need them to travel far and wide and ensure that our message is spread. Going against Belladonna the Herald will end with death, pain, and misery for every man, woman, and child. Kill the rest and bring me this...barbarian princess. "

The orc nodded and again formed his words with his fingers. Adrian still could not understand what he was saying but the way the Herald's attention suddenly focused on him did not bode well.

"You're right. I do believe in killing the messenger, if only for the message it sends." She smirked when she saw his expression. "Do not run, little rabbit. I so hate a moving target and the only result will be a painful death."

There was no debating that. He pushed to his feet. While he wouldn't run, he did not intend to die on his knees. Somehow, dying on his feet was the better choice. It didn't seem like it would make a difference one way or another but in the face of certain death, he was allowed to make the small choices.

She raised her hand, smiled, and whispered something he couldn't understand. He closed his eyes as the flames engulfed him.

CHAPTER TEN

Of course he would make things difficult. Cassandra knew Langven was only in the business for the coin. The villagers had paid him enough for him and his mercenaries to return to Edge's Rest and live a life of debauchery for a few more weeks until the coin ran out and there was nothing else to do but to find more work.

This was the kind of life one tended to live when the next day could be the last one. She could understand that. What she couldn't understand was him pushing them for more coin.

"Your girl told us that there would be nothing more than a handful of bandits," he told the chieftain's son, who had been elevated to his father's position now that the older man had been killed. "When we arrive, we are ambushed by trained soldiers and then we have to retake a whole damn town. I would say that requires more coin in compensation."

"We have given you all we have left," the younger man stated calmly. "Food and other supplies have been offered, more than enough to cover your return journey. You have our gratitude."

"Fuck your gratitude!" Langven snapped. "Unless it can be used to pay a willing woman to wrap her lips around my cock."

"You mistake these people for leprechauns," Cassandra interjected before things turned less civil. "They cannot squat and shit gold at will. They had all their possessions of worth taken from them by the army that took their city. What little they had left already fills your pockets."

"A sob story I've heard more times than I can count." The mercenary leader was annoyed that she had not taken his side in the debate. "As much as we would all like to force the world to hold hands, feast, and fuck all day in peace, such are not the times we live in. What would you have me and my men feast on? The promise of better days?"

"You could always remain," she suggested. "Those who took all their coin will return and likely have not had the time nor opportunity to spend it. Fight them off and you will be richer for the effort."

"I know better than to position myself at the foul end of a fucking army." He scoffed and glowered at her. "Especially one led by a godsbedammed witch. You barbarians lack any sense if you do not see it the same way."

"And the alternative is that you fuck off and leave those lacking in sense to their impending doom." Cassandra tilted her head and raised an eyebrow. She had her clothes on again and for some reason, felt less comfortable in them.

But despite everything, she knew Langven was right, for all his other faults. If the threats they were facing were accurately described, they would stand against a real army.

Walls like theirs could be held by twenty or less, depending on how determined the defenders were, but it would only last until food and other resources began to run low.

The situation was even worse given that the food stores had already been raided once by this Herald's army and now again by the mercenaries.

Cassandra pushed from her seat and drew a deep breath. In

the end, the merc leader was a simple man and no number of appeals to his courage and honor would help.

"Like it or not, you have two options. Take what you have and leave to avoid the oncoming onslaught or stay and fight for the promises of more riches to be earned on the field of battle. There is no third option."

He had thought the same thing over the three days they had spent helping the town find its feet and he knew that she was right about that as well. For a moment, it appeared as though he would take the easier option.

Finally, he shook his head. "I cannot commit the lives of my men without speaking to them on the matter first."

"At least commit to scouting the area," she answered quickly. "I can afford that much from my pocket, at least."

Langven nodded and rubbed his fingers over his chin, which had started to show signs of not having seen a sharp blade for the duration of their stay.

"I can do that." With that said, the man stood and headed off to break the news to the rest of his men.

If the truth be told, she could probably pay for them to stay but she did not want to commit what remained of her treasure only for them to slip away in the night on the eve of battle.

It reminded her that she needed to talk to the twins to find out if they were willing to commit themselves to what might well be a doomed cause.

The townsfolk seemed determined to return their homes to the condition they had been in before the attack. She received smiles and waves from almost everyone she passed but a hint of darkness lingered there as well. Their minds were locked on the possibility that their oppressors would return and likely not treat them as well as they had the first time around.

For herself, Cassandra would prefer death to being ground into the dust by the heel of a foreign power, but she had never been one to speak for her family, children, and those too old or too weak to join the fight. They had to make such decisions on their own and she had a feeling they would see many of these common folk leaving before the battle started.

Yet there seemed to be more of them in the streets than there had been. She narrowed her eyes and tried to determine what was happening as more people poured in through the gates.

Her first thought was that these were the townsfolk who had escaped the invasion and now returned. It was quickly discarded, however, when she realized that she recognized these people.

"Fucking pilgrims," she muttered and broke into a jog to reach the town center where they now congregated in large numbers.

What the hell were they doing there? The very last thing they needed was more mouths to feed if the army decided to starve the occupants out instead of storming the walls.

Not that she wasn't happy to see a few friendly faces after the day she'd had. It wasn't long before she located Caephas, who helped to lift a few heavy bags from donkeys that she assumed they'd acquired since she had parted ways with them.

He saw her immediately when she approached.

"The barbarian princess is among us again." He laughed as she took his outstretched hand. "At this point, you cannot deny the influence of Theros in guiding us to you a second time."

"I fear that he has guided you all to your deaths," she whispered and drew him aside. "This town is likely to come under attack before the week is out. You all need to leave while there is still time. What in the seven hells are you doing here in the first place?"

"Well, I believe you'll understand the impact of it when I say this," he responded with a shrug, "but they were directed to come here by divine inspiration."

"Oh." Cassandra made a face. "Fuck. The damn pilgrims need to start taking their orders from someone else if they intend to live long enough to be of any use."

At any other time in her life, she would have considered such words to border on sacrilege, yet there she was, openly blaspheming. If Theros had a problem with it, he could present himself and even help them in the coming battle. It was about time he was of some use to the people who followed him.

"A battle coming, then?" Caephas folded his arms and scrutinized the walls that surrounded the city. "The defenses are sound enough. If they plan to attack and cause any real damage, they will need a fucking army."

"And a fucking army is what they have," she answered with a grim smile. "At least from what the folk here told us. I was brought here to take the town back from them in the first place, albeit unwittingly. One of the men they had left in control escaped and went to warn the rest of the force. If they consider this town to be of any value, they will certainly return."

"Which army? Imperial or of one of the city-states across the desert?"

"None as far as I could tell. The son of the chieftain said the woman leading this army called herself Belladonna, the Herald of Grimm the Cruel, son of…Karthelon. From the way she spoke, it was meant to inspire fear and awe but I've never heard any one of the three names. Have you?"

He shook his head. "Then again, I am not well-versed in the ways and the wills of the world. This is my first journey beyond the walls of my hometown, although it has been many months following this group. I can tell them that trouble is afoot and see if they are willing to depart, but if I know them at all, they will say they were brought to Torsburch for a reason, although what that might be is beyond my ken."

"Your what?"

"Ken? Knowledge."

"Ah. Why don't you say that?"

Caephas chuckled. "You know, they are handy craftsmen and women for the most part. Should they decide to stay, they will not merely be mouths to feed if this Herald's army does attack. I am sure they could be persuaded to fortify the walls, secure the gate, and possibly even conjure up a few engines that could be of good use to the effort."

That was the only piece of good news she'd heard all day. "Should you decide to stay, we could use a strong arm manning the walls as well."

"It would be my honor. And even better, I have some experience organizing and training a militia from the time after I was removed from training to be a paladin. I think I could probably make a fair fighting force of these villagers. It won't be enough for them to stand against an army on their own but would certainly provide a stronger presence if you were to lead them."

Her eyes narrowed when he said that but she pushed the niggling thought away.

"Why are you doing this?" she asked and tilted her head.

"Because it is owed."

"To whom?" Cassandra shook her head. "You should not trust Theros even if he is the one who guided you to this place. You cannot throw your life away."

He paused and looked at his hands for a moment before he met her gaze again.

"Is a life wasted if it is given to help those in need?" Caephas wore a small, knowing smile, almost like he'd managed to catch her in a trap of her making.

"You know the answer to that," she retorted sharply.

"Then what am I throwing away?"

His words made sense but she still wasn't sure if she agreed with the reasoning behind them. Any attempt to argue would be a waste of time and energy, however, so she chose to return to the task she'd set out on originally—to find the twins and ask if they would remain at her side.

It was not difficult to find them. All she had to do was follow the sound of squeals and laughing children, who had taken to following the two barbarians everywhere they went. They were helping to repair one of the houses and were not above showing off their strength and power to the horde of tiny followers they had acquired.

It was the kind of sight that brought a smile to her face, no matter what the circumstances.

"A child can find joy even in the most miserable of circumstances," said a voice a little to her left. "They truly are a wonder."

Cassandra spun and her hand reached for her weapon although she knew precisely who had spoken to her even before she noticed the old man seated on a nearby bench with his donkey browsing the grass not far away.

"You," she stated bluntly. "What are you doing here?"

"I am not quite here as you might say," Theros answered and beckoned for her to sit. "They cannot see me and fear not, they will not hear your words directed at me either. None will think you mad for talking to the air."

She looked at the group of children and realized that while they still jumped and laughed, all had slowed and the sounds felt like they came from miles away.

"You didn't answer my question," she said and deliberately remained standing. "Why are you here?"

"Am I not allowed to have a chat to my barbarian princess from time to time?"

"Not after the shit you've attempted. I have no idea what you planned that necessitated having me here, but all you're doing is preparing your people for a glorious death. I wouldn't mind so much for myself but for the people you sent here to die, that does raise the possibility that you might simply be that cruel."

She noticed a slight twitch of expression on Theros' face but it was gone so quickly that she wasn't sure if it had been there at all.

Then again, those kinds of questions tended to arise when she was in his presence now—not the how or the when or anything like that but the why.

"You have a way of inspiring people," Theros answered and pushed from his seat once it was apparent that she would not sit next to him. "Can you truly be angry when they follow your example? How would they find a way to continue fighting? All this would happen whether you were here or not but in the end, all you can hope to do is make what little difference you can in the world. None can see the ripples of those actions, not even me."

"But you can predict where they will be, yes?"

"Patterns emerge and if you live as long as I have, they do help to predict what is happening in the world. That said, surprises appear from time to time—the kind that catch even me off-guard. Encountering one in a lifetime is interesting. Encountering two...well, that is simply unprecedented."

"That doesn't change this. It doesn't change what will happen here."

"It doesn't but you can. All I can do is provide you with the tools you'll need to succeed."

"They are not tools. They are people—living, breathing folk you can't play around with like they are pieces on a game board."

"That is a poor choice of words, of course, but they want my direction. I direct them to where they can do the most good, even if it does mean putting them in harm's way. Would they not want to be where they can make a difference?"

"Did you tell them of the dangers they would face if they did come here?"

"Do you truly think that would stop them?"

He made another good point and once again, it was the kind she didn't like the reasoning of. Merely because folk didn't mind being used by the gods didn't mean that it was acceptable for the gods to use them—not to her mind, at least.

"You—"

She raised a hand to stop him. "Not another word. Otherwise, I'll commit my last days among the living to doing something truly blasphemous. I'll continue with this little plot of yours but for the lives of the folk living here. Not for you."

"Reasons can be considered. All that matters is the actions."

In the next moment, she was twisted to where she had stood before and sucked in a long breath like she had surfaced from a deep dive in the water.

"Are you all right?"

She shook her head and realized that the twins stood in front of her and looked a little concerned.

"I...yes, I believe..." Cassandra turned to look at the bench, only to realize that man, donkey, and bench were all gone. Truly, it was all madness.

"You approached the building," Tandir said, narrowed his eyes, and inspected the area she had looked at before he focused on her again. "Then you stopped and stood there for a moment. Your eyes were open and you were awake, but your mind appeared to have been seized by something else."

That was one way to put it.

"I was looking for the two of you," she said firmly to change the subject. "We need to discuss the future. With the dangers coming to this town...well, I cannot leave it. I will remain to help defend it but I don't presume to speak for the two of you. Your help would be appreciated, of course, but in the end, there is every chance that ours will be a last stand and that we would not be the last ones standing. If I know anything about the kinds of people who were described as taking Torsburch in the first place, they will want to ensure that the citizens here never rise in defiance again—painful deaths, mutilation, all of it."

"You're saying that as though you think we have not encountered the like before," Bandir stated with a small grin. "I can and will speak for my brother when I say we are well aware of the dangers facing us here, and if we had any intention of leaving, it would have been the moment after we took what we were owed."

"Which isn't much, as it turned out," Tandir commented. "I

guess those who remained behind were not left with much in the way of spoils to enjoy."

She narrowed her eyes. "You will stay, then?"

"We'll die here or in some other hole, fighting another rich man's fight over where lines should be drawn on a map," Tandir answered with a grin. "Better here, I think."

"Folk are nicer," Bandir agreed. "They are less likely to fuck us over on pay."

"They will not be paying you," Cassandra interjected quickly to avoid another situation like Langven's. "You will have to take what is owed from the loot on the battlefield."

"Which means even less of a chance for them to fuck us over on pay." The two grinned like maniacs at her. "You'll not be rid of us so easily, Princess."

CHAPTER ELEVEN

Bandir and Tandir would help to train the folks who needed it for the fight. Caephas had already lined up those who weren't busy repairing their city and showed them how to use the weapons and armor the dead had worn before Cassandra and her mercenaries had killed them.

In the little time available to them, they were preparing. There was little worse in the world than sitting and waiting for death to knock on the gates. She made a point to push that feeling aside by checking and rechecking her weapons and armor. If there was nothing else for her to do, she might as well take the time to ensure that everything humanly possible was done to ensure that her weapons and armor would serve her the best they could.

In the end, however, she couldn't resist the feeling that they were doing little more than setting up walls of sand to try to stop the incoming tide. Time would tell if she was right but in the meantime, she had her business to attend to.

The sun had not yet appeared on the horizon but the sky had begun to turn a breathtaking shade of pink by the time she approached the makeshift stables that had been set up for the horses owned by the men they had killed. It was now used to house her horse and those of the other mercenaries as well. Although not the most comfortable accommodations for Strider, she had made do on a pile of hay in a nearby barn.

Everyone had to make do in this day and age.

She was surprised to see that Langven had woken around the same time and was also on his way to the stables, although he looked like he could use a few more hours of sleep. Dark circles ringed his eyes but he was up and ready to start the day at a decent time.

"You didn't think you would leave without me, did you?" he asked as their paths came closer together.

"You sound like you thought I would simply head out," she answered with a gentle shake of the head. "My intention is to make sure you stay, not give you more reasons to leave. Besides, you've already taken my coin for the scouting journey. I would have gone in and woken you if I had to, although I am glad to find it is not necessary."

"And you sound like you thought it would be necessary."

"I did fear that I would find you drunk and with your head buried in a bucket of your vomit."

He laughed. "That was the night before last. I never drink the day before I travel. I have done so in the past and the headache afterward is not something I want when I need to travel in the future, not if it can be avoided. Especially not when the midday heat starts beating down on us."

He was not wrong about that. It was still relatively cool this early in the morning, but an hour after sunrise would see the temperatures rise to the point where it would be difficult to tolerate.

Riding in that kind of heat the day after a night of heavy drinking would be pure misery.

"Well, I am glad you made a wise choice," Cassandra

commented as they neared the stables. "I know I would have to be the one to listen to your endless complaints otherwise."

"Oh, have no fear, you will bear witness to my whining," he answered with a chuckle as they reached the door. "The heat and almost all the other things to find fault with will be complained about, have no fear."

"I assumed that would be the case," she muttered and rolled her eyes. "There is always the option of not complaining. Instead, enjoy the ride, the warmth of the day, and the sunlight. Many of those up north would kill for a day like the one we are facing."

"Only because it would be a rarity for them. Out here, where the days are always unpleasantly warm, I would say I am entitled to voice complaints."

"Who to?"

"To whoever might be listening. In this case, you and the gods if they happen to give a shit."

There was no need to point out that she tended to have regular conversations with the gods. It would only be taken the wrong way—or perhaps the right one. There was a history of good and bad things happening to folk who could prove they had a direct connection with the gods, and one of the most common effects of it was that the gods stopped talking to them.

In the end, that was probably a good thing. For her, at least. If it meant Theros stopped intruding in her life, she was willing to do almost anything.

She yanked the bolt open, pulled the door, and suddenly realized that they were not the first ones there. Verda had entered the stables somehow and had managed to lock the door from the outside while she was at it. Or, more likely, she'd simply climbed in the windows. She was still small enough to fit.

"What the hell are you doing here?" Langven asked and narrowed his eyes as she jumped up from her seat on a nearby bucket.

The damn girl looked bright and chirpy this early in the morning, which simply wasn't fucking natural.

"I came to volunteer my services," she stated and looked like she'd practiced that line all night. "I heard the two of you would head out to scout for the approaching enemies and I know I can be of great use to you."

"You must believe us mad if you think we will trust you again, girl," Langven snapped and shook his head.

Verda looked a little confused and Cassandra smiled.

"He is still upset that he was paid less than he would have liked for the amount of work he had to do," she explained.

"She said a small group of bandits and that's all we were paid for," he protested and pointed a finger at the girl. "And if you think I'll trust her again, you're as mad as she is."

"I thought this was already established, given that I was the one who rode in practically naked to distract them and still took a lower amount," she answered with a laugh. "His annoyance with you aside, I think you had better stay here. There is no telling what dangers we will face on the road."

"But see, that is where I can help." The girl took a step forward and her gaze shifted from one to the other like she wasn't sure which one to direct her argument to. "My father was a trapper and a hunter before he was killed in the original attack and I hunted with him regularly. I know the ways in and out of the whole region better than most. If you take me with you, I'll show you the best places to see most of the land while not being noticed yourselves."

The girl made a good point—assuming she was telling the truth—and Cassandra scowled. She didn't like the idea of taking someone only a few years older than a teenager on a dangerous scouting mission like this, and she turned to Langven to hear more of his doubts.

Surprisingly, he had none to give. "I'm fucked if she doesn't make some good points—if you believe a word she has to say.

You're paying for this so you make the decision any way you see fit."

"A lot of help you are," she retorted. "We have no time to waste. Gather your things and meet us at the gate."

"There is no need for that. We are both ready to depart as soon as you are." Verda grinned as she patted her mare on the neck. The beast was already saddled and ready to leave.

"Fine." Cassandra shook her head, strode to the stall where Strider still appeared to be sleeping, and began with his saddle, reins, and the rest of the saddlebags. "Does that horse have a name?"

"What?" The girl turned and her unruly hair whipped all the way over to catch her in the eye.

"The mare you ride. Have you named her yet?"

"I...I'm not sure."

"How can you not be sure about whether or not you've named a horse?" Langven asked. "My stallion is Busef, named after the famed stallion that was ridden by Argead the Third during his conquests. A proper name for such a beast, wouldn't you say?"

Cassandra noted a distinct lack of a reaction from the powerful chestnut stallion in response even as the man swung into the saddle.

"What do you call yours?" Verda asked, already astride her mount as if to drive home the point that the barbarian princess was the last one ready to leave.

"Strider," she answered, attached the last of the saddlebags, ensured that her weapons were attached, and mounted smoothly. "A kingly name if I ever heard one."

"One dimwit bastard I used to fight alongside merely called his horse, Horse," Langven noted as they rode out of the stables. "He was a little slow of words, so perhaps he called the beast what everyone else called it, thinking it was a name. He was a damn beast of a fighter, though, and used an ax and a bow better than anyone I've ever seen."

Cassandra smiled, shook her head, and chose not to comment on who she assumed he was speaking about.

"I have some skill with the bow myself," Verda commented as they approached the gates and she patted the bow she had attached to her saddle. "I've hunted with them ever since I could walk."

"But that does not answer the question," Cassandra told her once they were beyond the walls and turned to follow the direction they'd seen the overseer escape in. "How can you not be sure whether the mare has a name?"

"I...might have stolen her from one of the overseers when I escaped," Verda answered, patting the beast on the neck. "She was left unattended and all other horses, mules, donkeys, and beasts of burden had been confiscated. Most were sent away with the rest of the army, likely to prevent any of us from escaping or getting far if we made the attempt. So I am sure she has a name but I do not know it."

"You can always give her a new one," Cassandra pointed out. "For all you know, she might not even like the name she was given and will readily take to the new one."

"How do you know if a horse likes her new name better than the other?"

Langven looked curious to hear the answer as well and she shrugged and nudged her horse into a faster walk to catch up with the other two as she had lagged a little behind them.

"You'll know. She'll tell you."

The man continued to study her while Verda appeared to consider what was said. While it did not appear that she would give the beast a name soon, it was something she would no doubt think about as their travels took her farther from home.

There would be precious little else to do.

The day passed much like Langven had assumed it would. The heat bore down on them, not mitigated by greenery as most of the underbrush was the kind generally found this close to the desert. The trees were short and gnarly, necessary to survive in a land where water was scarce, and what grew thickly was the grass and bramble. It was dense enough that even pushing through it without thought of where they were going would lead to numerous encounters with thorns and dangerous animals.

Not only snakes, spiders, and scorpions of all sizes, but lions were also known to inhabit the area and preyed on the antelope and zebras that grazed on the grasslands. They were the kind that had none of the manes so many lords and ladies liked to have adorn their coats of arms. These were considerably less royal-looking, that was true enough, but it also allowed the lions to move almost unhindered and practically unseen through the underbrush.

At least, that was what Verda told them as they began to move through the hidden paths that led them away from the main road. From the position of the sun, it was easy to confirm that they were moving in the right direction and making good time.

"Listen to the horses," the girl continued as they passed through a green patch next to a small convergence of three or four streams. "They'll see the lions much sooner than we will, even high on the saddle as you are. If they start to run, give them their heads and let them break. If they get a good start, the lion cannot keep up."

Cassandra had never faced one of these beasts but according to the girl, they were not interested in humans. She said that they avoided humans as much as they could, although the horses offered a meal that might catch their attention.

Still, as they continued to move, there was no sign in the tall grass of any creature that matched the image she had in her head. A small, childish part of her wanted to finally see a lion, given how often she had heard of the beasts over the years, but the rest of her knew the dangers. Besides, where lions lived, the likes of wemices and griffins tended to as well. There were even writings of a griffin presiding as the leader of a pride of lions, although she'd learned to doubt stories like that.

They found little to scout until, over the thick grassland ahead of them, they noticed a cloud of dust rising in the distance. They were still in the thick of the brambles and followed a small trail she assumed had been created by the hunters from Torsburch. In parts, it looked like the brush was trying to reclaim it, which forced them to slow their pace from time to time.

"If I were the wagering kind," Langven commented, his gaze fixed on the dust cloud, "I would put coin on that not being a natural occurrence."

She could only agree. "Is there a branching path for us to head out there to have a look?"

Verda nodded. "Follow me."

Cassandra assumed there was no real reason to point out that it was what they had done all day, but when they reached the end of the thicker sections of brush, it was clear that a larger force traveled in the distance.

"Should we leave the horses here?" Langven suggested as they came to a halt.

"Yes." She nodded and slid from the saddle. "Verda, you should remain with the horses. Langven, you and I will take a closer look."

It was obvious that the girl didn't like the idea—although whether it was because she didn't want to be left behind or if the idea of contending with a lion on her own did not appeal was unclear—but she complied and the others advanced on foot the rest of the way. They were both careful to keep themselves low as they reached a small crest that allowed them to look over a wider plain that spread out before them.

For once, Cassandra was happy for the tall grass as it allowed them to remain upright while they tried to determine what was happening in the plain ahead of them. She wasn't sure she wanted to crawl around on the ground where all kinds of insects waited for them.

It was very clearly a larger force than they had engaged before. They were setting up for the night, which made it easy to watch them while they milled about and built campfires and defenses around their camp. It appeared that they were also wary of the lions in the region, given that they set fires around their camp and also used a few of the brambles to create a barrier.

Perhaps the lions had killed a few the night before and would do so again. It was a strange thing to hope for but it would help to even the odds.

Then again, the lions would have to do considerable killing to make things look better for the group.

"Fifty, maybe sixty men given the size of the camp," Langven said, his voice low. "Maybe more."

"Definitely more." Cassandra gestured to a far corner that had been isolated from the rest where the orcs and goblins milled about. "If my experience counts for anything, goblins and orcs require less space, especially in a human military camp. I would say there are two or three dozen of them in that little space at the very least."

He dropped to his haunches, his eyes narrowed, and rubbed the bristle on his chin thoughtfully. "What in the seven hells would convince orcs, goblins, and humans to fight together?"

"Barbarians too," she added and pointed to another side of the camp. Even from a distance, they were easy to identify from the way they gathered around their campfire. "Even dwarves by the looks of them."

She had no real answer to his question, however. There were a few reasons why folk who were so different would choose to fight together, but she had never seen any reason good enough for orcs, goblins, and humans to do so until she saw the flag raised above the camp. This was less of a sign of unity in conflict but unity through something else entirely.

Fear.

The red flag with the black skull with silver horns sent a chill down her spine and she drew a deep breath as she tried to understand the significance of it.

"This Herald," Langven muttered and mirrored her scowl at the flag. "She must be a terrifying creature for so many of these fighters to follow her without so much as a reference to their homeland."

"Terrifying," Cassandra agreed and ran her fingers over the knuckles of her other hand. "That is one word for it. I'm not sure I know of anything terrifying enough to make orcs fight alongside humans. Perhaps this Herald is an orc leader, which would mean she is one of the matriarchs."

"Wouldn't it be amazing to meet that bitch and cut her head off?" He grinned when she looked at him. "In another time, in another life, with a whole fucking army behind me as well. Before you have any ideas that I might want to fight alongside you in this lost cause of yours."

The barbarian princess raised a finger to her lips.

"No, you will not silence my di—"

She reached over, clamped her hand over his mouth, and pointed toward the area ahead of them. It was not the kind of situation that required them to do much talking and they should have considered the fact that they were looking at a small army that was establishing itself in the region.

It did beg the question of why until she realized that a few of the structures were more than merely tents. They were rundown, derelict buildings. She could even make out the remains of what looked like walls, although whatever the structures were, the people who had occupied them had left many years before.

A small river ran through the center, which made it the ideal camping place although it was clear that the positioning of the goblins and the orcs in the camp was significant. It meant they wanted whatever came out of the region to go downstream from the campsite without compromising the water they would be drinking.

Armies that were well-organized tended to send men around their campsite to ensure that no enemies were present who could attempt to spy on their movements. It was something she should have considered before she heard the men move roughly through the thick underbrush, cursing and hacking at it with falchions and the like.

Both she and Langven settled themselves low in the grass. All fears of insects vanished as the boots drew closer. Cassandra knew no spells that would mask their presence—it had never been relevant to her kind of work—and while the enemy pushed through, she grasped her sword, ready to end their lives quickly and painlessly, as well as noiselessly.

It would mean their enemies knew they were spied on, but it would give them time to escape and maybe get word to the town. Given that night was falling, they wouldn't hunt anyone until the early morning.

Cassandra held her breath and tried to not make a single sound as the group approached.

"This is a fucking disgrace," the human muttered and shook his head. "Because we were a little late to the march, they make us trudge through this gods-forsaken underbrush while fighting off thousands of blood-hungry leeches that fly through the damned air."

She couldn't see what the orc gestured in reply but it didn't seem to help.

"Do you think I care that they aren't leeches? They drink my fucking blood. That is all I know about leeches and that is all I fucking care to know about leeches. As far as I'm concerned, that is what these little flying bastards are."

The orc said something again and added a few grunts in his own language. She couldn't understand it but the sentiment was clear.

"We've come far enough. We'll tell them we did the full sweep. Come along."

Cassandra waited until they were out of earshot before she motioned for Langven to follow. They remained low for a few moments but soon regained their feet and rushed to where Verda was still waiting for them with the horses.

"What ha—"

She raised another hand quickly to silence her and they turned to ride back down the path. It was important that no word be spoken until they were well beyond the need to worry about anyone overhearing them. Once they were far enough out of earshot, she reined her horse in and looked over her shoulder to make sure that they were not being followed.

"What happened?" the girl asked and eased her mare in close. "Was it an army?"

"As good as," Langven answered. "Between seventy-five and a hundred men, possibly more, although something tells me they are only a part of the whole. Orcs, goblins, dwarves, humans, and all ready to attack."

"They were setting up camp in a place that used to be a fortress of some kind," she explained. "Do you know anything about the history of this area?"

"My father told me there was once a fortress built by barbarians who claimed this land," Verda answered and turned to face the path ahead where they could not see dozens of campfires being lit. "As it turned out, they were rather easy to drive out given that they were never much more than nomadic peoples. They abandoned their fortress and it crumbled into dust for almost a hundred years."

There was something a little off-putting about that story, although Cassandra couldn't quite put a finger on what.

"Why have they camped there?"

"It is likely that they have based themselves in a defensible location," Langven answered as they continued. "Any army moving through this region would have to always find a place where there is water. Otherwise, horses and men will die of thirst alike."

"My father always talked about how to keep an eye out for watering holes and for the animals that visit them," Verda answered as she and the merc leader started to ride on a little ahead. "Would they need someone who knows that territory with them?"

"Possibly. But the more likely explanation is that they have riders who go out in the morning and know how to scout for water. They would usually ride back before the midday sun with a report of where they might be able to camp that night. Otherwise, the army will have to return and camp in the place they had left earlier."

"Doubling back? Doesn't that lose them time?"

"It does, but given the option is death by thirst, it is a necessary evil."

"Have you campaigned in an area like this before?"

"Many years ago. Back when I followed a banner of my own accord instead of merely fighting for money."

Cassandra narrowed her eyes as the two continued to talk. They almost completely ignored her and left her the responsibility of keeping an eye on the path behind them to ensure that they were not being followed. It was not the fact that she was relegated to rearguard that annoyed her the most. Although annoyed wasn't the word. Suspicion was more accurate. Earlier in the day, Langven had complained about how he couldn't believe a word the girl said but now, they shared stories about her father and his military past.

It was an extremely odd turnaround but not what she ought to consider. She knew what she would do but there was no telling what it would mean for herself, not to mention for others.

"We should find somewhere to spend the night," she commented as they continued to retrace their earlier path. "I don't think we'll be able to light a fire out here, not without risking being seen."

"Better seen by them than by maneaters," Verda answered. "Fire keeps most of the beasts around here at bay."

That was a decision to be made as well, she conceded. They could probably ride a few more hours away from where the camp was and where scouts might notice them and risk a small fire to avoid anything untoward walking into their camp.

CHAPTER TWELVE

The ride to Torsburch was terse, at least for Cassandra. While Langven and Verda appeared to be more comfortable in conversation with each other, she could tell that the man avoided speaking to her. And she had a feeling she knew why, too. It was the kind of situation a man found himself in that he did not want to deal with. He needed time to consider what he would do and she suspected that she knew what his decision would be.

There would be no need to address it with him. Pressing him would not help her cause but he would have to answer soon or he would find the decision made for him instead.

As the walls of Torsburch rose in the distance, he grew more silent and sullen.

It was a few hours after midday by the time they entered the gates and the change that had come over the town was clearly visible. The defenses were being shored up and fortified, with additional crenellations added to the top of the walls to protect the defenders. The lack of machicolations was something of a worry, but it was about as good as they could expect on such short notice.

Meanwhile, those who weren't working were being drilled in

the use of spears and shields as well as the various ways they could make themselves useful on the walls when the fighting started. Bringing water, arrows, rocks, and other such items for the defenders would be a vital, if overlooked, part of the defenses.

The lack of weapons was a worry and most of them would have to work with sticks that had been sharpened to a point.

Even so, it was difficult to put much in the way of faith, given the numbers that they had seen approaching.

Caephas was the first to see them ride in. He still helped to drill the village folk but left it to the barbarian twins and jogged to where the trio was dismounting.

"You have long faces," he said but kept his voice down. "I suppose that means you come with ill news."

"We'll speak to the chieftain's son on the matter," Langven responded. "Although I should remember that he is the chieftain now with his father dead."

Caephas nodded and joined them as they started up the path to the longhall. Word of their return had spread and the young barbarian stepped out to greet them. He gestured wordlessly for them to step inside so they could speak with some assurance of privacy.

"What did the scouting tell you?" he asked once they'd been provided with water to wash the dust from their hands and faces. "I assume that your early return does not bode well."

"You assume correctly," Langven answered and sat with a soft groan. He was tall and like most tall men, so many hours on the saddle made his back hurt. "A raiding party approaches, less than two days' ride from here if they move with purpose. I believe them to be an offshoot of a much larger force but they still boast at a bare minimum seventy-five fighters, probably far more—possibly a hundred or more."

"Easily outnumbering the whole of the village," Cassandra added. "Each one is armed, armored, and ready for battle. If we all stand as one, we might have a chance at victory, but it is a slim one. Defeat is likely and the survivors...well, I have to say there won't be many and it will not be a pretty sight. Monsters like this will likely make you bleed twice for every drop of blood we take from them."

"This is grim news."

She nodded. "If I were you, I would abandon the city, take what can be carried quickly and easily, and leave them nothing but empty buildings. Some might be lost and there is no promise regarding where you might find yourself, but staying will likely see a much higher death toll."

The young chieftain shook his head vigorously. "This land is hard and to live in it costs a great deal. The fact is that we've all paid that price ten times over with our blood, sweat, and more blood. I'll offer them the choice but I already know what their answer will be."

"It is better to die fighting for your home than fleeing from it." Cassandra frowned and folded her arms. "I suppose I can understand that."

They agreed to gather the village to speak to them as to what they would do once the work for the day was done. When the time came and all were present, she scanned the faces and noticed that Langven was not among them.

"The other mercenary," the young chieftain said in a soft voice. "Has he gone?"

"I would not put it past him," she answered. "You cannot expect the man to stand his ground against such odds for coin alone."

"And not much of it." His smile was a grim one as he stood. His wounds were healing well but he was still far from his full strength. Magical fire had a way of sapping the life of those subjected to it. "Every man counts. Every departure robs us of what little strength we have left, even if I cannot blame them for it."

Of those present, she already knew many who would remain.

Among them were Caephas and the twins, as well as the people who had been training. The pilgrims would also and she didn't need to ask to know what they would choose. She couldn't force them to leave but she couldn't help the feeling that none of them were truly aware of the danger they were in. It was the kind of bravado that was instilled into folk when they listened to stories and songs about battles and glories and all that shit.

There was no telling if their courage would hold once the arrows were launched and the screams of the wounded filled the air.

"Every hand capable of helping in the defense will make a difference," the chieftain continued, his hands clasped together. It was obvious that he was not used to speaking to large numbers of people but he assumed the responsibility with an encouraging amount of poise. "But no lies will be spun. It is likely that we are peering into our deaths. None who choose to leave will be stopped. If all wish to leave, I will join them, but as long as one man, woman, or child remains within these walls, I will fight to my last breath to defend them. Contrary to whatever this Herald believes, the true riches of Torsburch are not the items that can be found inside but the people—all of you."

He'd gone off on something of a tangent but there was no questioning the fact that every man, woman, and child in the longhall hung on to his every word.

"I offer the same promise," Caephas interjected and his voice carried through the room. "I am here to do as Theros guides, and my every breath will be spent defending those he has called to me."

"And I," Cassandra answered, although she didn't like the look of hope in their eyes. It appeared as though the decision was made and not the one that she'd hoped for.

She stood and moved away from the room when she noted that Verda was not in it with the others. The huntress had taken to Langven during their time together and while she wasn't quite sure she understood it, she could at least sympathize with the poor girl.

As she suspected, he and his men were already preparing to make their departure. That was a decision she could understand although she neither approved nor sympathized. Then again, she'd never been one to turn away from lost causes. It was more or less a requirement of a paladin and there wasn't much that would change that.

Still, she was surprised to see that Verda was there with him. She showed no signs that she planned to join them in their departure but she was in conversation with the mercenary leader. While she couldn't hear what they were saying, the way he took her hand and the way she didn't snatch it away like Cassandra would have showed that there was something more there than met the eye.

She kept her distance and let the two exchange their words. It was clearly not a conversation that would be better for her inter-ruption, and it wasn't long until the torches around the stables glittered in the tears running down the girl's cheeks as she lifted his hand to her lips.

The oddest part was that she could see a few slide from beneath his control as well, although they were brushed roughly away by his forearm.

The conversation had not gone the way either of them had hoped, and Verda pulled away almost violently to run down the streets toward her home.

It was a strange thing to see. Langven was not the man she ever expected would be so taken by the young woman, but his gaze followed her and a haunted expression settled on his face until he realized that she was watching. Perhaps a little too closely, she realized, and snapped her head around to look at something else.

It was too late, however, and she heard his footsteps approach before he sat on a nearby cart.

"How much of that did you hear?" he asked with a raspy edge to his voice.

"None of it," she answered. "It did not seem the kind of conversation I would be welcomed to."

He nodded slowly and looked at his hands for a moment.

"The raiding party won't move quickly, not in this region," he muttered and cracked his knuckles. "It will take them three, maybe four days if they are the kind to spare their horses. There won't be dust on the horizon for a while yet but it will come soon."

"They don't need to move quickly," she pointed out as she sat next to him. "Torsburch is not moving at all."

That did draw a laugh out of him but it was a curt, unsettling sound quickly followed by a silence that felt a little too heavy for both of them to tolerate for long.

"You could always come with us," he said at last. "It's not your fight. These villagers should pack their things and run as far and as fast as they can manage. I'm not sure what possessed them to stay and fight, but the madness need not claim our lives. That is one of the appeals of being a mercenary. Nothing is ever truly invested."

She turned to him with a grin. "I've never been a mercenary, only a paladin and a barbarian princess. Investment has always been what has driven me. I've never entered into a fight without the full knowledge that I would carry it through to the end, for better or worse. It has generally ended for the better, but a bleak outlook is usually expected."

"How so?"

The fact that he had no questions about a barbarian princess having once been a paladin was interesting and it provided some insight into his state of mind.

"Well, there was a time when myself and a few of my fellows were attacked by a dragon. It killed both of them and left me almost dead. I managed to survive and with the help of a friend, killed the dragon."

"What?" He laughed and shook his head. "Impossible."

"You tried to steal my share of the dragon hoard, moron. And my spear was the weapon that finished the creature. I could bring you a few scales as well if you like."

His laughter sounded a little more genuine this time, and Cassandra smiled.

"Well, for what little it might be worth, I do hope you survive this. And if you do, we will have to speak in Edge's Rest again over a few bottles of wine about how your investment paid off."

She looked over her shoulder at the two stakes where Verda's family had been bound and whipped to within an inch of their lives. The sun had mostly set but there were still streaks of orange matching the fires to illuminate them and made it seem like they were still bathed in blood.

None of the other townsfolk had taken them down or so much as approached either of them. She had a feeling it would be years before any of them had the courage to remove the monument to the oppression that had shadowed their lives.

"Fuck surviving," she said after a pause. "Any halfwit with legs to run with can survive. It takes a great deal more to win and when we share a drink, it will be about how I won."

CHAPTER THIRTEEN

She had been involved in a handful of siege defenses in the past, although generally more as a symbol to show the men that the gods were on their side. As ridiculous as it was to think that Theros, Janus, or the others would involve themselves in the petty squabbles of humanity, it did have a beneficial effect on morale.

It did the same in this situation as well, she realized, although she was not the cause of it. Too many already believed that the gods had decided what would happen among them and the presence of a barbarian princess only served to reinforce that. She had no intention of telling them that she had been a paladin herself once lest that serve to further cement their belief.

There was little she could do to change it. All she could do was ensure that their faith was not in vain and move on. It meant there was still considerable work to be done and she could almost hear the sounds of the raiding party approaching their walls, telling her they would not be ready in time.

At least she wasn't alone. Bandir, Tandir, and Caephas did good work in preparing the locals for a fight. They had a fair number of hunters among them and their bows would be put to good use, and arrows were being made by the dozen to ensure that they were well-provided for. Long sticks with sharpened points were better than nothing, and some weapons had been taken from those they'd killed.

But it was not enough.

A voice in her head said the same thing repeatedly, even as she worked to prepare them. Langven and his mercenaries had gone and left her as the most experienced member of their group to organize and ensure that no precious resource was wasted.

If there was ever a marker for how bad things were, that was it. She was giving her all but her place had always been at the front line, never in the back to manage logistics and make sure they had enough water.

"Something's on your mind."

She looked up as Tandir approached the fountain she was drinking from.

"I'm trying to judge whether or not we'll have any issues with water if their attack turns into a siege," she answered. "One of the benefits of being in this region is that we could probably outlast them if they cannot breach the wall."

The barbarian chuckled and she knew why. Preventing them from breaching the wall was the sole deciding factor as to whether they would survive.

"They'll want to take it quickly and with overwhelming force," he asserted and crouched next to the fountain. "They cannot afford to have this last too long. Then again, they will likely not have to."

"We'll make them pay for every inch of this town they try to take," she answered with a small grin. "If nothing else, I can promise you that."

"It's been a while since I fought for an impossible cause. I suppose it was about time that I did again. I might have wanted a few real archers among our numbers, though. They could have turned the tide."

"No barbarian worthy of the name goes far without his bow."

"Maybe for some clans. Ours were determined to be good throwers of the spear although for the life of me, I can't think why. Tradition fucks everyone in the ass from time to time, does it not?"

"Maybe. Or it could simply be that those who came before in your clan knew about the dangers of troops advancing with shields. A well-thrown spear or javelin like those you carry can rend a shield and leave it unusable until it is removed. I would assume that gave them a great advantage when attacking shield walls."

He nodded. "I suppose. Then again, you would know the power of the bows the DeathEaters carry. They are fucking disastrous to almost anyone, shield or no shield."

"True enough. However, it takes a great deal more strength to draw a bow that heavy than it does to toss a spear, but the result would be more or less the same."

Tandir chuckled and noticed that his brother was approaching as well.

"I'm out there drilling with the rest of the recruits and you're here drinking water and chatting?" Bandir did not appear to be fatigued in any way by his efforts but was still annoyed that all the work had been his.

The other barbarian didn't answer and merely filled one of the tin cups with water and offered it to him. It was the hottest time of day and the locals recommended rest or at least working in the shade until the heat had passed. She wasn't sure if she would follow their suggestions but there was no denying the appeal of wanting to escape the heat.

"How does our new army fare?" she asked once Bandir had drained the cup.

"They do not lack enthusiasm. Natural skill, experience, and technical abilities, yes, but not enthusiasm. Then again, if we can manage to keep any rams they might bring to bear away, enthusiasm is all they need. Not much else required to be at the top of the wall and push over ladders and cut grappling hooks."

"They didn't have any engines with them when we saw their advance," Cassandra recalled and took another sip of water. "It might be that they are building some on the way but I would assume a simple ram at the most and otherwise, ladders and grappling hooks."

Then again, assumptions tended to leave people dead by the end of a battle, which meant they needed to prepare for the worst.

One of the younger lads—those who had been judged to be too young to be on the front lines—ran across the road at full tilt and Cassandra narrowed her eyes when she saw that he was rushing toward them. He was barely ten, judging by his size, but he certainly had considerable energy to sprint the way he was.

"Princess!" the boy shouted as he skidded to a halt and his sandals kicked up a small cloud of dust in the process. "Karva... Karva..."

She laughed, drew more water up, and handed it to him. "Take a moment, catch your breath, and tell me what you need. I won't waste my time interpreting everything you're trying to say between pants."

He sucked the water up greedily and spilled some on his shirt in his eagerness before he dragged in a deep breath and finally spoke.

"Karvahal wishes to speak to you at your earliest convenience."

Her eyes narrowed. "Who does now?"

"The...the chieftain."

"Right." There was no need to consider the fact that she hadn't thought to ask the young man his name before, given that this was the first time that she had heard it.

"As soon as you are able, he said."

Cassandra looked around. Her time from when the sun rose

had been spent overseeing the work on the walls and schooling the archers on where they needed to be when the attack came. From there, she'd helped to drill those who remained in what they needed to do when it came to carrying supplies and everything else. The whole time, she'd watched the east and waited for any sign of dust clouds in the distance.

It had already been a long day. Perhaps she had become a little more used to spending her time resting and recovering instead of having to focus on the constant strain of knowing that something was coming for them.

A conversation with the chieftain's son might help. Karvahal was his name, she reminded herself. She needed to remember it.

She stood and gestured at the brothers. "Spending time on your asses instead of working won't save anyone's life. Get back to work or I'll have to find one of those whips the overseers used."

The barbarians laughed but Cassandra immediately regretted the joke when she noticed the pained expression on the boy's face. The memories of people he'd known since he was a child and perhaps even friends and family being subjected to those whips were perhaps still a little too fresh in his mind to find any humor in the situation.

She could think of no gracious way out of the situation and all she could do was slink away and hope that the joke would pass without negative effects. Her sudden guilt was an unsettling feeling and she hoped that all those present would forget about it. Perhaps it wasn't her best choice but it was the one she chose to make anyway.

It was a long, silent walk to the longhall, where the young man already waited for her. She'd healed him as much as he would allow but there were still signs that he struggled to recover from what was done to him. He had difficulty walking and even standing unaided.

Of course, she could have continued to heal him but he had

refused all her requests to help. Barbarians still did not like magic in any way, shape, or form, and he was no different from the rest. It was annoying but not a problem she was ready to take on at the moment.

"It's good of you to join me," he said and gritted his teeth with the effort of standing.

"You called and I came. I am easy to work with that way. Is there something you need?"

"Of a kind. Follow me."

He nodded and began to move toward the door. She knew better than to help him, even though he looked like he was about to topple at any moment. To his credit, he made it to the door.

Only once it was shut and none of the town could see them did she take his arm to help him remain on his feet.

"A...appreciated," he whispered.

His flesh was cold and clammy but from the way the sweat coated his skin, he had issues with the heat as well. This meant that healing was not his only problem. Sickness remained, which would slow his recovery even further.

"You have to let me help you," she said.

"It's not...not why I brought you here. I need you to do something for me should all go wrong and end in your hands to resolve. There will be nothing for it but to get all the people out as quickly as you can. You would have to be alive for this to happen, but I assume you would be the most likely to survive anyway."

They reached the back of the longhall—the section where he lived, she assumed—and continued to what was a bedroom.

"I would question your intentions if you weren't struggling to stand," Cassandra commented as he dropped into a nearby chair with a soft sigh.

"I have no covert intentions," he whispered. "I assure you. This longhall was built by my great, great grandfather, a power-hungry barbarian who thought he could take control of the whole of this region if he managed to build enough fortifications in enough key locations. In the end, the barbarians under him did not like having to stay in one place forever. There were insurrections and challenges to his control. He lost all the other forts but this one and in the end, he proved to be as paranoid as he was power-hungry. Because of that, he devised a way to escape if his men decided to attack."

"Another way out?" Cassandra asked. "In this room?"

He motioned to the far side of the room where a heavy copper bath was positioned. "It moves easily enough and leads to a cellar, which in turn leads to the springs under the ground. You will find a path to safety from there. Try it."

She did as he instructed and sure enough, the bath moved almost effortlessly to reveal a trapdoor. The opening led into a cellar, where she could hear rushing water in the distance.

"I am not entirely sure how you can use it," he said and clenched his jaw. "But I thought that it would be best if you understood all your options—everything this town offered to those who lived in it."

She smiled, moved the bath into its place, and crossed the room to a chair. Instead of simply sitting where it was, she picked it up and carried it to where she could sit in front of him.

"Thank the gods for the madness of our relatives, eh?" She chuckled and he followed suit, only to grit his teeth again and fight off a convulsion.

Suspicions had nagged at her but they were confirmed now that she was seated not a full pace away from him.

"Your wounds are healed but your condition is worsening," Cassandra stated calmly and looked him firmly in the eye. "I understand the traditional barbarian aversion to magic and I might even support it depending on the circumstances, but in this case, you do need my help."

"I'll be fine," he whispered.

"You'll be dead," she corrected him and placed a hand on his shoulder. "As you said, we need every man out there who can stand to be on the field of battle, and your refusal of help undermines your words about doing everything and anything you can to keep the people here safe. Wouldn't you agree?"

It was perhaps a little manipulative on her part but in the end, a little manipulation was what was needed in cases like these.

"Do...do you know what is wrong with me?" he asked through clenched teeth.

"I'll need to perform a closer inspection but I have my suspicions. I survived a dragon attack not long ago and I suffered something remarkably similar to what you are experiencing. Convulsions, sweats, chills, and clenching of your jaw tightly enough to make your teeth hurt, yes?"

He nodded slowly.

"It's a disease called lockjaw, common in those who suffer burns. Your condition will continue to deteriorate, the convulsions will worsen to the point of breaking your bones, and you will have a fever and difficulty swallowing. You will likely die during one of the convulsions, which will seize your breathing. I remember those and they were...they were not pleasant."

"Can...can you help me?"

"I can. It will take a great deal of energy. Given that your wounds were caused by magic, I can only assume there is still a little of that mixed in to make your life that much more difficult. I will need to be thorough in cleansing your body of it or it will return, although in a milder form. The way the healing mage explained it is that the body learns to fight the disease if it is somehow resisted the first time."

"Will it hurt?"

"Me? Certainly. You...probably."

After a moment of thought, he nodded and grasped the arms of his seat. "Get on with it, then."

She chose not to point out that he was taking it almost as though he expected her to torture him or something, but there was little else for it. It wouldn't be pleasant for her either but she would recover from the effort far quicker than he would if he were left to recover on his own.

If he did at all.

Cassandra closed her eyes, put her hands on his wrists, and focused on everything she had been taught. It was not an exact science. All bodies were unique and there was no telling if he had non-human blood in him that changed everything.

All appeared to be more or less normal, however, and she could feel the sickness battling for control of his body. Magic lingered where the wound had been inflicted, but the disease had grown past it. The magic was easily pushed to the side but the lockjaw was not. It fought back as though it had a life of its own, and she realized that she now held his arms with a vice-like grip, almost as though she was scared of being physically pushed off him.

The initial surge was formidable but the disease felt almost cunning in its strategy. Once it realized that it could not fight against her, it began to spread quickly through the body and hid to make itself difficult to eradicate.

A thorough cleansing was required, and it was what she was determined to put herself into even though the effort was starting to drain her. She could feel a headache readying to plague her as she worked, her eyes closed and her whole body tense, and focused as she fought to cleanse the man of his illness.

Karvahal grunted softly but his fever began to abate as her work progressed. It was always encouraging to know that her efforts were successful. The physical signs were generally the last ones to come, given that it was at the point where the body was done fighting for its life and tried to calm and recover.

A few strong sweeps did not reveal what she was looking for. She would have to keep a watchful eye on the man over the next few days to ensure that the disease was gone, but her work was done.

She exhaled a soft sigh as she finally relaxed her hold on him and leaned back into her seat. Her whole body ached and her head's throbbing would not cease or go away. She knew better than to think a healing potion would help in this situation since all it did was take the resources of the body to heal whatever needed it.

Unfortunately, her body's resources were spread thin. She'd found that some koffe had the pleasant effect of at least soothing the symptoms but she had none with her.

Karvahal, on the other hand, appeared to be invigorated. His eyes opened wide and he looked at his arms and hands, drew a deep breath, and massaged his jaw gently.

"That is truly amazing," he whispered, stood quickly, and walked around the room. "How... I feel healed, but also...as though my body has energy where it has been sluggish since...since..."

His voice trailed off and she knew his mind had gone to the day when he had been injured and his father burned to nothing but ash. It was the kind of thing that stuck with a man, no matter how strong he was.

"Your body used a great deal of energy to combat the illness and keep you alive. As it has no more illness to fight, it is recovering appropriately. You will feel more energy for a few hours but I would suggest you eat soon or that might end and you will find yourself sluggish again. The body requires fuel as much as any fire does."

He grinned and rolled his shoulders and she knew he was thinking about how well he could fight at this point. Barbarians were a predictable breed.

"Are you all right?" he asked when he suddenly realized that she had sagged into her seat about as far as she could.

"I will be," Cassandra answered, closed her eyes, and rubbed her temples gently. "A headache that will feel like a thousand tiny dwarves using my skull as an anvil will come along shortly, and the only cure for that is rest and sleep. But…I need to discuss my plan with you."

"Plan?"

"Yes, plan. Do not interrupt me. I have less than five minutes before the contents of my stomach come up and I will curl into a ball. I need to tell you all before that time comes."

CHAPTER FOURTEEN

She'd dreaded it from the beginning although it was practically inevitable at this point. Every day had been spent scanning the horizon, watching for any sign of movement or attempt to approach them. It had been three days since they'd returned with news of the troop advancing on their position.

And there it was. As the sun began to crest the horizon, a cloud of dust rose to herald their arrival. Cassandra watched as it grew and its size indicated that their original numbers had been a little underestimated. There were at least a hundred of them, by her count.

Perhaps the early morning sun was playing tricks on her mind. She wasn't sure one way or the other and it was an unsettling thought. They were all about as ready as they could be and the waiting had been the worst of it. She had sensed it burrowing into the minds of those they were fighting with, which made it impossible to ignore.

Now, at least, would be the culmination of their efforts.

They had made camp out of sight, likely intentionally to ensure that they had a full day to assault Torsburch if they had a mind to. She didn't doubt that they would attack when night fell either, but they would want daylight to have a look at the defenses and plan their attack.

If they had a sharp mind in charge, which wasn't always a given. A raiding party was generally sent out with the finest fighters but not necessarily the keenest minds.

Karvahal's position had been made official the day before. Not that there had been any doubt but having him as their chieftain certainly made sense. How long he would remain that would have to wait for the day's events but from what she knew of him, it was a sound choice. No others had stepped forward to claim the position either.

She could tell that the responsibility weighed heavily on his shoulders by the way he stared at the dust cloud as well. He had strapped an ax at his side, carried a shield and a spear, and wore the kind of armor she had come to expect from barbarians. They were not particularly fussy about aesthetics and appearances and as long as something worked, there was no real need to replace it.

A thick gambeson and a hardy helm were about all that was needed. His gauntlets had studs on the knuckles that allowed him to fight with those as well, and his boots were capped with steel. A solid round shield of wood with a bronze boss and cap around the edges meant it could also be used as a weapon if it was needed.

If it was not broken, there was no need to fix it. This was why she stood there in naught but her specialized armor that lacked all modesty and grasped her spear as she watched the invaders begin to advance on the walls.

As much as she would have wanted to, the walls needed at least fifty more men to properly defend it. Holding on would only see them spread too thinly. An initial attack could be repelled but it wouldn't take long for their enemies to find ways to exploit the areas that were poorly manned.

The decision was made. They would not hold the walls. A few

arrows would be cast and a small fight offered, but they would immediately retreat to the secondary defensive position.

All Cassandra could hope was that the courage they all displayed would hold. The foolish tended to die first in these situations, but the worst of the group had a way of escaping it so that others died in their stead. It was on her to ensure that they stuck to what little training they'd had and the tactics they'd drilled to the point of annoyance in the days prior.

"Come along, now. We don't have all day," she muttered, held her spear a little tighter, and focused on the advancing force. They were still on horseback. No ram was in evidence and no ladders, but ropes and hooks were easy to carry on their horses.

What the wall was able to do was prevent them from attacking on horseback, but it wouldn't last.

Karvahal laughed softly and shook his head at her words but said nothing as their archers stepped forward, a handful of arrows at the ready while they waited for the enemy to come into range.

Surprisingly, they did. With no pause in their advance, they pressed forward toward the gate and attempted to make their way through quickly and press an advantage.

"At the ready!" Cassandra called and mentally measured the distance they were covering. The previous day had seen how far their archers could fire and they had left markers about ten paces closer than that to allow them effective range.

The barbarian twins were waiting as well, although their range was considerably shorter. They would hold the line and make their enemies think that the walls were still manned while the rest retreated to their proper positions.

She motioned for the archers to fire whenever they were ready when the horses crossed the fifty-pace mark. That had been about as far as they could send their arrows, which meant that seconds remained before the time came.

Her heart raced and fingers tingled with the need to join the fight as the air was suddenly filled with the song of bowstrings and the arrows streaked to where the riders suddenly reined their horses in.

There had been no high expectations and as expected, shields were raised to catch most of the projectiles. She counted two dead and a few more wounded, as well as a dead horse when the second volley struck, but the intention was met. The charge was stopped and the invaders milled about in confusion.

Surprisingly, not all of them were on horseback. Cassandra couldn't believe her eyes and for a moment, she thought a familiar barbarian stood among their enemies, the image made easier to believe by the fact that he ran along on foot. But the way he roared at the other raiders told another story. His armor was about as modest as hers but he wore a thick steel helm that obscured his features.

There was no mistaking the muddy-gray skin tone, however. It was an orc, not a barbarian.

That was a relief, at least. She would not wish to be on the opposite side if Skharr assaulted a wall.

"Get your horses moving, you miserable whoresons!" The orc bellowed his insults and the man who had lost his horse was forcibly picked up and thrown forward into another arrow that took him through the throat.

"Nice shot," Tandir muttered, hefted his weapon, and remained utterly focused on the group.

The orc leading them did speak the common tongue—although with the kind of slur that reminded all those present of the tusks in his mouth—and he used it to ensure that his men continued to attack regardless of the arrows that streaked toward them from the walls.

Cassandra had thought this would be a possibility and beckoned the two barbarians forward, their spears at the ready. The group was approaching the fifteen-pace mark and a few of them had already drawn their bows and began to return fire, but most hid behind their shields and watched for any of the arrows coming in their direction.

Both barbarians were ready and needed no direction before they flung their spears. They did not even appear to throw the javelins particularly hard but with a flick of the wrist, two were suddenly airborne and hammered hard into their targets that waited for them below.

There was a deceptive force behind the throw and it was interesting to watch as the two men were knocked from their horses. They had stopped the javelins with their shields but there was enough force behind the strikes to throw them clear, cut through the shields, and strike their arms instead.

It was better than being killed but it was enough to give the others pause, especially as one of the archers came in too close. He carried no shield and so had no possibility of defending himself as the javelin buried itself in his chest.

The brothers were more than eager to continue to rain death on the raiders, but Cassandra knew the time was coming when they would no longer be able to.

As if he'd read her thought, the orc leader realized that they would not be able to assault the walls directly, at least not without putting a little thought into it. Their horses wouldn't get over the moat, and there would be no attempt to attack the gate, no matter how hard they pushed for it.

Instead, they formed into a small shield wall and their archers continued their steady volleys to make the walls suddenly not as safe as they might have been a few moments before. If they had simply charged, she could have adjusted the fight for the wall and rendered all their work irrelevant in a very short battle, but the orc proved to be no fool, which meant they would be able to reach the walls.

The crenellations did allow the defenders to move without being seen by those below, and she motioned for them to do so. Making as little noise as possible, all those on the walls immediately retreated deeper into the town. It had been built with inside defenses in mind—probably thanks to Karvahal's ancestor and his paranoid mind—and it had taken comparatively little effort to set everything up the way they needed it.

She watched as the twins headed off to man one side of the defenses. There were three more, of which one was entrusted to Caephas and the other to Karvahal. Each would lead a small troop of fifteen or so of the locals into a fight for their lives.

Cassandra would face the side that was closest to the gate. It was a simple decision given that she was the one most likely to give the rest of their small force the time and space to retreat to the longhall, their last line of defense. She spun her spear in her hand and looked around to ensure that all was well and prepared. There was nothing else they could do.

Their attention was drawn to the section of the wall closest to the gate, where they could hear hooks thrown up and gaining purchase on the wall they had abandoned. There were enough of them to say that a significant portion of the invaders would attempt to scale the walls but not all.

They climbed quickly and arrows arced over the barrier as they appeared to consider the possibility that the defenders were still waiting for them. Those who reached the top had their shields up, ready for some kind of attack. They could have put effort into hacking the hooks from their ropes but all it would do would be to spread their attackers out to find a section that was not properly defended. It wouldn't take them long and it was better to control when and where the shits got through to ensure that all the surprises happened in front of them.

A few arrows were shot at the men on the wall, mostly to keep them attentive and moving slowly behind their shields as they dropped to ground level. One of them took an arrow to the calf and while he uttered a cry, more than a few of them were ready to cover for him as they continued to move toward the gate.

They lifted the barrier that held the simple gate closed and looked around like they had expected more from the defenders. In only a moment, they noticed that the group had gathered deeper in the narrow streets of the small town leading directly to the longhall.

She would not cede these defenses without a fight.

Cassandra spun her spear in her hand and studied the group that approached steadily on foot. She identified the orc at the front, his sharp eyes gleaming inside his helm as he studied what the defenders were doing. Intelligence was not something most people associated with orcs and many even thought that they were outright stupid, given their dislike of the human languages.

They were similar to a few barbarians, although not much was being done to change that about their situation.

This particular orc, however, was a sharp one. He had been put in charge of the raiding party not only for his brutal commanding style but also because he knew how to take a fortress without killing every last one of his men. She had a feeling that the falchion he carried was not merely for show either.

He uttered a few grunted commands and the men organized in front. They wouldn't divide their troops but rather take advantage of how the defenders had to split their forces and attack head-on from the front.

It was more or less what they had feared would happen if they were defending the walls but to a lesser degree. Their forces were spread a little thicker this way.

Archers fired at them, courtesy of the hunters who had likely never aimed their bows at humans before. While the troop moved forward quickly, they did not abandon their shield wall and thus prevented any of the arrows from finding their targets.

Their advantage was finished and it had claimed a handful of their men and wounded a few more. The rest would have to be done the old-fashioned way.

Well, not all the advantage, she reminded herself.

Cassandra stood her ground. She couldn't look back, not for a moment, to make sure that the rest of the defenders were still there behind her. At least she could hear them in the clattering of their improvised spears. She knew that their courage would be faltering and their minds would consider all the options that might allow them to leave this place before they were killed.

By now, their mouths would be dry and their bladders would suddenly feel full. It was the body's response to being put in danger that they were unfamiliar with. Hearts would race and a numb, tingling feeling would likely touch their fingers as well.

It wasn't that a person like her who had been in so many battles and fights before didn't feel the same way. At this point, she'd learned to bear it and had picked up all the tricks necessary to keep her mind on the matter at hand.

A smile touched her lips as she heard the tell-tale sound of boots on wood. They had disguised the traps well enough but the sound was not something that could be hidden as they advanced. The orc heard it too, turned, and pulled back a step as the weakened planks, supported by twigs, immediately snapped when weight was put on them.

Five of the men at the front fell through and screamed as they faced a short drop that ended with all five firmly impaled on the spikes that had been positioned below. It was the kind of trap that generally didn't work, given how much effort went into hiding it and how easy it was to notice. But needs must and the defenders had little to work with so they had put the effort in. It brought a sense of satisfaction when the rest of the troop skidded to a halt and tried to stop themselves from falling in after their comrades.

It didn't help as three more were pushed in by those coming from behind. All but one was killed and she could hear the sole survivor screaming in pain below. She assumed he'd missed the spikes for the most part but had broken a leg or something when he reached the bottom.

The archers had been drilled over what to do, and she smirked when four more were caught with arrows to the chest, legs, and throat before those coming behind could lower their shields in their defense. It was a good start but it wouldn't take them long to push through the rest of the fight. She wanted to make sure they wouldn't simply jump over the damn spikes. They had to work for it.

One of them did try, to his credit, but was pushed in almost effortlessly. She couldn't help a soft laugh, which was echoed by those behind her. Nothing quite cured the nerves they were experiencing than the sight of their enemies dealing with similar difficulties. She raised her hand and waved to their enemies across the line as another two tried to leap across the gap. There were walls on both sides, and they assumed that more dangers were waiting for them in the other avenues of attack.

And they were right as they would soon discover.

Cassandra moved forward, caught the one closest with her spear, and shoved him back as he blocked her strike with a shield. The second managed to reach the other side but she twisted and caught the back of his knee with the butt of her spear as her comrades rushed to aid her. In a matter of seconds, the man was skewered on the end of a handful of spears that looked suspiciously like the spikes at the bottom of the trench in front of them.

A few of the raiders learned their lesson and attempted to send a couple of arrows to the other side. Those villagers who were with her had already raised their shields made from wooden boards to protect themselves, but she raised her hand, narrowed her eyes, and pushed the projectiles back.

The sight of magic used by the immodestly dressed woman gave the group pause. It was one thing to pit themselves against a few villagers and what hired blades they could gather to their side. Facing a mage was another thing entirely and she could see the hesitation in their eyes.

The orc, on the other hand, was not impressed and she assumed that had to do with how he likely worked with the Herald himself. She reminded herself that the woman had summoned fire to burn Karvahal and his father.

"Get your miserable corpses over that fucking trench or I'll toss you over myself!"

His accent was still heavy and there was no question that the men feared him, but they clearly needed a little more encouragement. The orc was more than willing to deliver on his threat. He grasped one of his men and heaved him over the trench using both hands but barely showed any pause in the effort.

It was a good throw, although Cassandra's spear intercepted the man, cleaved cleanly through his shield, and punched through his armor and chest to come out the other side.

As he slipped into the trench to join the rest of his dead and dying comrades, she laughed.

"You might want to throw a few others over to be sure," she said, flicked her spear, and watched the blood slip away, almost like the weapon was happy to be clean of it.

If they did find another way over, she would have to discard it for the moment and take up her sword and shield. As much as she liked the weapon, it was not fit for an engagement in close quarters.

And it did not appear as though the invaders would be stopped for long. Spurred by the threat of being tossed over by their orc commander, the men were driven to action and looked around the area to find something that would allow them to cross without too many problems.

Unfortunately, a few beams were found. Combined with planks, they could make a bridge. Cassandra moved forward and resisted their efforts, but it didn't last very long and she pulled back, strapped the spear to her back, and drew her sword. She retrieved her shield from one of the locals who had held it for her.

A proper battle would soon commence. Well, a skirmish by the looks of it, but she wouldn't be fussy about it. Of all the places she could be, defending a town on the border of the desert from an army driven by a madwoman who could summon fire certainly seemed like the kind of situation that would ensure tales were spoken of her as well.

Provided she survived.

The shield walls closed and there was a definitive difference in the weight behind both sides. The villagers heaved the way they had been taught to and they held the line for a moment, but it was immediately apparent that even though their enemies were on perilous ground with their improvised bridge, they still pushed forward.

They would at least make a small part of a day of it, and she growled and shoved as hard as she could before she suddenly gave way and let the raider who had pushed against her stumble forward. She left him to be killed by the others and stepped into the hole he left behind.

Her sword cut into one enemy and her shield hammered into the other, and both lost their footing and dropped into the trench. It had been a risky move on her part but in the end, standing and holding the line until they were forced back into where their numbers could be brought to bear was equally as risky.

At least this way, they were finding a few kills. As she pulled back, however, it was apparent that killing the one who had fallen had not been as easy as they thought and two of her people had died before they'd managed to kill the bastard.

The raiders now pushed in again. The locals had been taught how to hold a shield wall when they were all in it, but as all the muck started to fly and they could hear their friends scream in pain, all the drilling and training they had received went out the window. Panic set in, and she knew it was only a matter of time until she stood in the line on her own.

Cassandra knew she needed to take control before that happened.

"Retreat!" she called, took a step back, and watched the enemy step off the little bridge. She saw an opening and slashed her blade across the first man's throat. A gaping wound opened and the warm spray caught his comrades and gave them a moment of pause.

With all her experience, she knew better than to turn her back on the troop, but there was no telling if she would be alone. She could only hope that the rest of their force knew what was happening and would come to their aid—not only for her sake but for theirs as well. The raiders were in and if the defenders didn't rally immediately, they would be torn to pieces. It would be a massacre.

Her responsibility was to hold them off long enough for their people to realize what was happening and retreat. If she was lucky, they would have the presence of mind to help her do so while the others escaped.

But it couldn't be counted on. Of all the reasons to get herself killed, having it be because she fought alongside farmers, tanners, and trappers was a little insulting.

Suddenly, a whoop filled the air and two of the men fell back as their shields splintered under the weight of two javelins flung straight into them.

Barbarians certainly knew how to make an entrance. Cassandra didn't bother to look back but darted forward and slashed the throat of one as he tried to yank the spear out of his shield. She buried her blade in the chest of the second, whose arm had been cut through by the javelin.

It was about as close to an opening as she would get and she spun and rushed back to where the twins charged toward her, their weapons swinging as they barreled into a handful of the invaders who had tried to catch her as she ran. She couldn't help but laugh when they killed three of the men before they were forced to rejoin their fellows.

"You didn't think you could have all the fun without us, did you?" Tandir asked.

Or maybe it was Bandir. Since the former's nose had healed, she could no longer tell them apart. She then recalled that Bandir was the one with the ax and Tandir carried the mace with the spike at the end. That was how she could tell them apart now.

After another war cry, two throwing axes careened into the troop, followed quickly by Karvahal throwing the last one into the bandits as Caephas rushed in.

The man who would have been a paladin carried no shield, but she didn't think for a moment that he was in any kind of trouble. He roared something—or maybe it was simply a roar with no other meaning to it—and he hammered the maul he carried into the closest of the shields. All the power he had in him drove the blow and the shield shattered and fell apart as he twisted the weapon to crush the raider's skull.

The fact that he wore a helm didn't help at all and the man dropped to his knees, then toppled without so much as a sound.

In that moment, she knew he was in trouble.

Also without a shield, the orc stepped forward with only the wickedly curved falchion she'd seen him holding earlier. It was unsettling to see Caephas stand his ground in front of him and twist his maul as the massive orc walked across.

The enemy leader wore a gauntlet on his other hand. Spikes on the knuckles made it look almost like it was meant to be used as a mace, and its wielder showed no fear despite the steel-like resolve of the man he faced.

A second later, the orc blurred into motion. It seemed like he hadn't even put his feet down before he attacked and the falchion flashed in an arc that cut across Caephas' cheek and pushed him back. The man did not back down but powered his maul into a short swing that was blocked by the falchion and followed it immediately with a heavy sweep that caught the orc in the ribs.

The impact cracked a few bones but his adversary trapped the maul quickly with his arm and jerked his head forward.

Cassandra winced when their ally fell back and blood flowed from a cut on his brow. She rushed in to help him as the huge spiked fist hammered into the side of his head. Her feeling was that the orc enjoyed beating people to death with his hands and she would not allow that to happen.

The barbarian princess sheathed her sword, drew her spear to intercept the strike, and put her shield in the way of the next punch. The power behind it almost staggered her, but she slashed with her spear in hand and opened a small gash in the orc's exposed side. The intention had been to stab him through the chest but the miss came as she reeled, and the orc's speed did her no favors.

Frustration surged when she realized she had missed. She'd had him and fucking missed. Before she could strike again, the enemy leader backed away and returned to where the raiders continued to push forward. The defenders' bows loosed a determined barrage into their ranks to slow them enough for the rest of the people to retreat into the longhall.

Those who hadn't been fighting had been holed up there, waiting with spears to bring the others in and ready to close the doors and bar them. It wasn't the kind of situation they might choose for themselves if they had any say in the matter, but the only consideration was survival.

She grasped her spear and watched the doors close to make sure there was no attempt to break in immediately. The door was made from heavy wood, which meant that a forced entry would be no easy feat.

Small slits in the walls allowed them to see out without necessarily opening themselves to arrows from the enemy. This was yet another item they had the paranoid great, great grandfather to thank for.

The raiders began their approach but the orc put his hands on shoulders to force them back and stop his men from attacking the longhall outright.

He certainly was clever, this orc—intuitive and he also had all the right instincts. It would be difficult to make him commit to an attack that would give her the advantage.

"You will need to come out eventually!" he roared, took a step forward, and flicked his sword up to catch it smoothly. "You will die! The manner of your deaths is in your hands! You can die like cowards or you can fight!"

Shouting around his tusks sounded like it was a chore, but she knew that no one would survive. Perhaps a few would be punished, left maimed and mutilated, and sent to spread the word. That was how people like this Herald liked to work.

"Dying like cowards! Like cowards it is!"

It was a ham-fisted attempt to draw them out and it wouldn't succeed. He probably didn't think it would work but his people no doubt expected that he make the attempt anyway.

He could smell a trap and he made a show for his men while he tried to determine what it was.

"It's not only about rebellion against the civilized world," Cassandra stated from where she peered out of a murder hole. "It's about making decisions. Deciding where you will take your stand and that nothing—and I mean nothing, not men, monsters, or gods—will make you back down. That is what it means to be a barbarian. You made your decision when you stayed with me. Now it's time to be a barbarian."

The twins nodded beside her, their expression grim and determined. The orc shouted about setting fire to the building and burning them out, although it was difficult to tell what he said exactly from this distance. His men cheered and shouted agreement like they didn't realize that the longhall had been built from stone.

There wasn't much to burn, thankfully for the defenders.

"Time to be a barbarian," she whispered and glanced at her two companions before she faced the murder hole again.

"What will you do?" Bandir asked.

She didn't answer him and instead, leaned closer to the aperture.

"Oy! You—the big one so ugly he has to cover his face!"

The roars and yells from outside stopped as the orc looked at the longhall.

"You must be a powerful mage if you think you can set fire to stone," she continued once she confirmed that they could hear her. "We have a powerful mage among us as well as you saw. You would be amazed at what can be done with a little magical power. You could walk into this longhall and find all of its inhabitants disappeared!"

A mixture of laughter and uncomfortable silence rippled among the raiders and all tried to decide how likely it was that someone could do what she had said they could.

They'd seen her magic and the lack of understanding of how magic worked certainly played in her favor.

"Do you doubt me?" she called. "Do you doubt my power?"

The twins nodded. It had been planned almost to perfection as they pulled a handful of the windows open to reveal what was inside. Where a little over sixty men, women, and children had been before, all had now vanished.

There would be no need to tell them there were tunnels involved rather than magic. All she needed was for them to believe.

From the orc's enraged roar, she could tell it had gone about as well as they needed it to. She grimaced as he led the rush to the longhall and the open windows.

"I hate it when my plans work so well," she muttered, drew her sword again, and kicked the first jar of oil over.

CHAPTER FIFTEEN

Cassandra had no idea how she'd managed to convince three of them to stay, but there they were. Bandir and Tandir were practically inseparable and might as well have been joined at the hip. Neither showed any sign of fear but their usual boisterous nature was long since gone.

Caephas was one she had hoped would take her invitation to leave with the others. His pilgrims needed him, after all, and she wanted him to have a long, healthy life of rolling his eyes as he followed them around.

With his face swelling, she had hoped he would change his mind but he remained where he was and held fast to his maul, his jaw clenched.

Four of them were now left there. She counted about twenty of the raiders dead, perhaps thirty if she'd missed a few during their retreat. They'd paid for those, however. About fifteen of their villagers had fallen in the fighting from what she could determine.

That left four against maybe fifty but probably more.

Skharr might have made a joke about how he liked the odds. Then again he was probably not the kind stupid enough to stay.

He would have told them to leave as soon as they saw what was coming and folk would have listened to him too. She had no idea how but he would make them see things his way.

But no, she had to stay and fight with the oil burning all around them as the first of the raiders entered.

Cassandra targeted the first one, jumped from a nearby table, and uttered a cry as she stabbed the goblin through the chest with her spear. More of them surged in and the twins rushed at those who pushed through directly behind their now dead comrade. They took five of the goblins with them, engaged them, and pushed them out of the main fight. A handful more of the oil jars were upended in the scuffle.

By the time she had dragged her spear out of the first one's chest, Caephas had joined the fray. His maul split the head of one of the orcs and he turned his weapon and cracked him on the skull with the haft before he finished the job with a heavy swing.

As another one of the raiders moved in to attack him, Cassandra lunged forward and slashed the blade of her spear across his face to give her ally the time to turn and sweep the man's legs out from under him.

He began a swing to crush that man as well but one of the raiders screamed in battle lust and hurled him off his feet.

This time, it was up to the twins to keep him alive as three more of the bastards managed to surge through the windows and swing their swords at her. They forced her back but she blocked their strikes with her shield and buried the spear in the chest of the one closest to her.

One of the raiders—an orc small enough to be mistaken for a goblin until it was up close—stepped through the opening and grasped the spear where it was still buried in the body of one of his comrades. It left her with no other options but to release it and she took a few steps back again when she had to ward off a heavy strike from a mace with her shield.

She jerked the shield forward and hammered the boss into the man's face. That forced him to take a step back and allowed her to draw her sword and immediately slice his chest open, even through his padded armor.

It wasn't quite a killing blow but enough to force him away and she dragged in a breath as more of the men poured in. The twins kept more than a few of them occupied while they shouted, yelled, and killed as many as they could.

Caephas had regained his feet. His face was covered in blood although from the dagger in his hand, she could surmise that most of it was not his.

"You simply had to stay, didn't you?" Cassandra shouted over the din of the fight and ducked under a heavy swing at her head. She parried a stab and twisted her wrist to slide her blade around one of the raiders and cut his throat before she shifted to push her shoulder into one of the goblins to drive it into a nearby wall and cut its head off.

The smoke began to fill the longhall and made it difficult to see, and she knew it would be difficult to breathe before too long.

Still, their little ruse appeared to be doing precisely as they had intended and she wouldn't complain about a plan that had been mostly of her devising.

"I couldn't leave you all the glory," Caephas shouted in response and swung his maul in low to crush one of the raider's knees. He reversed his strike quickly to snap his neck. "A former paladin and a man who never finished his training to be one, paired with two mad barbarians. I can't think of a more fitting place to be."

She laughed. "Nor I!"

Calling the twins mad did feel a tad hypocritical given that they were standing there with them.

"A courageous death, after all!"

The orc leader had rushed into the fray again with that single challenging statement. There was no telling where he'd come from or how he'd managed to move so silently through the fighting and remain unnoticed—not that the explanations mattered. She leaned away from his falchion and avoided it hacking her arm off at the shoulder. The attempted strike was followed quickly by a blow from his gauntleted hand that hammered her hard in the jaw with enough power to catapult her into a nearby pillar.

The armor—or rather the amulet that acted as her armor—did its work well. The blow should have crushed her jaw and shattered her skull but she only felt stunned as the orc approached and his hold on his falchion shifted slightly.

"The Herald would want you alive to see the fate of those you fought so hard to protect," he told her coldly. "But you are too dangerous. Best dead and imagine the suffering."

She reached for something to try to pull herself from the floor but the blow she'd received made her see white spots all around the room.

As the falchion raised, she heard a cry and before she could blink, Caephas appeared beside her, swung his hammer low to catch the orc off-guard, and pushed the attack out of the way. She wasn't able to do much but roll away from the danger and curse her limitations as her faculties returned all too slowly to her.

It was disorienting and watching her ally engaged in a fight he'd lost the first time made her feel even worse.

The orc recovered from the surprise of the man's sudden intrusion and pounded his fist into his opponent's helm again. He twisted to block a swing from the maul, slashed his blade over the man's chest, and forced him to take a step back. Unfortunately, a step was all he could manage as his back met a wall and the falchion followed without pause.

"Caephas!" she shouted and scrambled to her feet, still gripping her sword.

She wasn't sure if he could hear her as he stumbled back and looked at where the weapon had gutted his stomach through his padded armor. A look of shock touched his eyes and he frowned at the wound, dropped his maul, and tried to contain his innards as they began to spill out.

The orc placed the tip of his blade on the man's neck. "Where has your courage brought you?"

"Right here," he replied through gritted teeth and stretched to one of the torches in a sconce on the wall. "Standing between you and what you would have done to the people of this town."

The orc tilted his head for a moment as if to understand what the man was talking about before he looked at the floor and realized what covered the stones he stood on.

"*Burhaka mon.*"

Cassandra couldn't understand the words precisely but she assumed it was some kind of insult regarding his adversary's parents. The man ignored him, dropped to his knees, and touched the torch to the floor. The flames were hungrily received by the thin coating of oil and immediately blazed into a spreading fire.

She couldn't hear Caephas. He was still alive as the flames engulfed him but they traveled quickly carried throughout the room and caught at least a dozen of the raiders while holding the others out of the longhall.

The orc was unfortunately not among those who caught fire although his eyes widened when he realized how quickly the tables had been turned on his men. Still, she knew better than to think of him as beaten yet.

"Come on then," Cassandra snapped and flicked her sword, her body now almost fully recovered from the blow. "You intended to have me imagine the suffering of the people I fought to protect."

Slowly and deliberately, the orc turned to face her. The flames made his eyes gleam red and for a moment, the madness in them told her that he would die trying, no matter how everything turned out. It wasn't determination but something way beyond it —fear. She didn't want to think about what the Herald was capable of to inspire this kind of borderline terror in the people who followed her, but she was happy to leave the questions for later as she circled him and watched for his assault.

She knew he would attack first. That was what the desperation meant, after all. A cornered animal was a dangerous one. He moved with surprising speed and she almost didn't realize that he had begun his assault before he swung his falchion and barely missed her head. She raised her shield immediately to block what came next and grimaced when the punch from his armored gauntlet was almost enough to knock her off her feet.

Her adversary was fast and strong and for the most part, he seemed to rely on those two elements to win his fights. Now that he was under pressure, he grew predictable with his strikes and easy to anticipate as long as one survived the first few attacks.

Therein lay the rub, of course. Surviving against the kind of onslaught he was capable of laying down was a profoundly difficult task. Still, she knew what to look for and ducked under his spike-armored fist and shoved her shoulder into his chest to drive him back.

A glance confirmed that the twins had happily engaged the rest of the troops despite the fires that gained impetus, but time was running out for them to leave the longhall. Soon, the whole building would be filled with smoke and they would all die from the fumes.

That couldn't happen until she had finished the enemy leader.

He attempted another swing and a punch and Cassandra swayed back barely enough for the fist to scrape past less than an inch away from her nose. She darted forward and blocked another strike from his blade before she buried hers in his stomach.

The orc's gaze fixed on where she pushed the weapon in deeply enough that she could feel his spine against her sword.

A twist brought him to his knees and he stared at her through his thick helm.

"Who is the Herald?" she demanded. "How does she inspire such fear in those who follow her?"

His shoulders moved and an odd, grunting sound issued from him, and she realized with no small amount of shock that he was laughing.

"You...will...find out!"

His final words were annoyingly vague but before she could ask him to clarify, he pushed against the sword to drive it deeper. The blade killed him quickly when it found the artery buried deep within.

Orcs and humans were similar in so many ways and she'd lost count of how many men and women she'd seen make the same choice. She drew the sword out and gestured to the brothers.

"We need to leave!" she shouted. The flames blazed fiercely and their heat, together with the acrid smoke, made it increasingly difficult to hear or even see. Her eyes watered as she pulled her spear out of the chest of the raider where she'd had to leave it.

"We had only begun to enjoy ourselves!"

"They'll pursue us!" Cassandra moved hastily toward the opening in the back. "You'll have more than enough time to continue fighting once we're away from the fire."

They appeared to agree and made no protest but followed her into the tunnels. As it turned out, she was not wrong about the raiders following closely. There was little else for them to do but continue to press forward.

"Get down!"

Both complied with alacrity as she spun immediately and thrust the spear toward the men on their heels. She killed one and forced the others back a pace to enable the three defenders to continue moving.

The smell of smoke persisted through the tunnels but the sound of rushing water beckoned them and in moments, the narrow area opened into a cave carved out of the rock by the river they could hear ahead of them.

There was the small matter that they were now in an area that was more open and thus would allow those with the greater numbers to have the advantage.

Conscious of this, they moved as quickly as they could through the cavern but had to negotiate a safe path which slowed them a little. They could hear the raiders coming in behind them.

Cassandra saw an opening that she assumed was the exit to the caves. If they could reach the other defenders, they might have a chance to push the raiders back into Torsburch and allow the locals to escape too. They would have lost the city but most would still be alive to tell the tale.

"Get down!"

A massive body collided with hers and she fell heavily with a muttered oath. It took her a moment to realize that Tandir had tackled her the moment they exited the cavern.

His timing brought her safely clear a split second before the air suddenly came alive with the sound of bowstrings and whistle of arrows on a sure trajectory into the raiders behind them.

"Attack!" roared a familiar voice and Langven pushed forward, followed by his Ebon Pack as they rushed in to deal with the last of the raiders.

More arrows streaked in and enough had already fallen to make driving them back a simple task, especially since they were aided by the Torsburch locals as well as Karvahal.

It was over quickly. The invaders showed no intention to retreat and any fear they might have had of the defenders was overwhelmed by what they knew was likely waiting for them if they failed.

Cassandra managed to push up from where she had sprawled and rubbed her shoulder gently.

"My apologies," Tandir muttered from beside her. "I didn't think there would be time for you to move clear of the arrows before they were loosed. If the archers had waited, it would have destroyed their element of surprise."

She groaned softly and scowled at a few sharper rocks that had dug hard into her ribs. "I know you were right to do it but it doesn't mean it was a pleasant experience."

"What happened to Caephas?" Bandir asked as he helped them both to their feet.

"He fell," Cassandra answered and lowered her gaze. "And he set the flames that turned the tide of battle for us."

Both brothers bowed their heads as well, a moment of respect for their fallen. She looked to where Langven was checking to ensure that those raiders they had killed were truly dead.

When he saw her looking at him, he raised his sword wordlessly in acknowledgment. She smiled and returned the salute.

———

Their inexorable drive west was what pushed them through. They were to make the name known and spread the fear of it throughout the countryside. Any and all who were found would be educated in what was coming.

Belladonna looked out toward the walls they were approaching. Most of the towns they had encountered thus far had been walled off by logs and wood and other such primitive forms of protection if they even had them. More than a few had not had any defenses at all and had been pitifully easy to take.

Others had put up more of a fight but all had been subjugated. Her men were well-educated in the methods necessary to ensure that the fight was thoroughly stamped out of those who were placed under their control.

Despite this, one offered far more resistance than expected. She drew a deep breath and pushed aside her intention to press onward to a more civilized town with stone walls that appeared to be something of a challenge for her troops.

Not as much for her, of course, but it was time for them to pull their weight in these matters. She would give them the time and the opportunity to prove themselves as a real army against a real challenge before she stepped in to do the work for them.

For now, however, all her plans had come to a grinding halt. She had received no report from Savog regarding the success of his raiding party in retaking Torsburch from the idiotic sell-swords who had made themselves a problem. With no news, all she could do was wonder why.

Finally, she had been told that their scouts had seen riders coming from that direction. From the reports, they appeared haggard and wounded and showed all the signs of defeat that she wished they wouldn't.

Like any army, they would inevitably encounter problems, of course, but Belladonna had assumed those would rear their heads when they began to invade the empire in earnest, not the outer edges. It seemed both ludicrous and entirely unacceptable that they should manifest while her forces dealt with the small towns that dreamt of independence.

She closed her eyes, ran her fingers through her hair for a moment, and calmed herself when she heard hoofbeats approaching her tent.

They were, she knew, bringing bad news to her doorstep. Savog had been entrusted with a simple task and he had failed. She knew this since those approaching did so on horseback, while the orc preferred to use his two feet.

The aversion to riding was understandable, of course. The orc was head and shoulders taller than she was and horses were unnerved by his very presence. That would only be exacerbated if he tried to ride one. In the circumstances, then, she could now only assume that he was dead.

It unsettled her that they were so close to driving themselves to the edge of prominence. They were preparing to move against a real city this time with a significant population to subjugate and instead, she was being reminded left and right of her failures.

Well, not hers to be precise, but given that she was the leader of the force, nothing would be said or thought that might absolve her of the ultimate responsibility. The coin stopped in front of her seat, as they liked to say.

She turned slowly to the small group that had gathered and now faced her, narrowed her eyes, and tried to remember why Savog had chosen them from among her men to take with him on his quest. Perhaps their time riding had been harrowing enough to leave them looking particularly unimpressive, but she could see nothing in them to explain his choice.

They knelt in front of her, their gazes lowered, and everything about them suggested that they were seriously considering trying to run. While she couldn't blame them for it, they would remain in place no matter what they faced. They were well aware of how she felt about hunting her prey.

Belladonna stood in front of one of the men, her eyes still narrowed. She held her hands clasped together in a traditional meditative gesture that allowed her forefingers to tap idly on the opposite wrist to indicate her annoyance. The staccato rhythm was enough to tell each and every one of her soldiers that they were on the thinnest ice possible.

"Speak."

Her voice carried, although it was soft and the word almost whispered. The silence in the camp was palpable and even the barbarians made the effort to silence themselves for the matter at hand.

The man she had focused on didn't so much as dare to look her in the eyes. He kept his gaze firmly on the earth beneath his knees and likely wished very desperately that he was anywhere else in the world.

"Have they said anything?" she asked and turned to one of her lieutenants.

"Nothing of import, Herald," he answered and bowed his head slightly. "All they did was ask for mercy and to not be brought before you. Even so, I thought you would like to have words with them yourself."

"How thoughtful," she murmured and placed her hand on the head of the man she had asked the question of. "I suppose they will need to be reminded of what I am capable of when displeased."

The heat in her hand began to grow. Her fingers clamped on the man's skull and her nails dug into his skin as he uttered a soft cry of pain. It would only get worse as she tightened her grip and warm blood flowed from the small wounds she inflicted. Pitiful cries of pain turned to screams as the pressure increased over the bone and made it impossible to avoid the fact that this was how he would die.

His shrieks increased in pitch and intensity. The pressure caused by her hand was like a vice and in a few agonizing moments, one of his eyes popped clear of his head. Suddenly, in a soft, wet crunch, the whole skull shattered and succumbed to the pressure.

She looked at her reddened hands and wondered if perhaps she had allowed his death to occur a little too quickly. The dead man slumped and a handful of his former comrades rushed in to remove the body as she turned her attention to the next one.

"What about you?" she asked and pointed a finger at the orc. "Have you anything of note to tell of what happened in Torsburch?"

"Please...you must understand—"

Even if he intended to tell them, there was no need to press for it. Fifteen men had returned from Savog's raiding party of a little over a hundred. It was pathetic that they chose to run instead of fight and even more alarming was the fact that they had chosen to fear whoever commanded the troop—the barbarian princess came to mind—more than they did her.

Examples had to be made—reminders of exactly who these men were dealing with and who they should fear. Belladonna took a step forward and pressed her fingers into the man's eyes to hold him forcibly in place as he screamed pitifully.

His death should last at least as long as it had been since her orc was supposed to have replied about the status of Torsburch. There was no need to put too much effort into it and all she had to do was be creative. Gouging eyes out was always a favorite of hers but if she infused her touch with a hint of fire and lightning, the man would be crawling on his hands and knees, whimpering and begging for it to stop before the end.

His body convulsed and he fell, in too much pain to shout a plea or even scream his agony for the rest of his troop to hear. Perhaps she would need to learn how to apply the torture in a way that would not leave the recipient completely and utterly catatonic in his pain.

There was always a place for screams, although others were generally required to watch their comrades being punished. It served as a gentle but effective reminder of what would happen to them if they chose to make her life even more difficult than it was.

"You," Belladonna snapped and pointed at a third raider, this one a woman. "I assume your tongue is still intact. If you wish for it to remain so, you will tell me what happened in Torsburch. And where is Savog?"

"You sent him...us back to Torsburch to reclaim the village that was taken," she answered quickly and showed no interest in remaining silent like those who had been interrogated before her. "Savog pushed us day and night to reach the walls, and when we did, they were held by a witch with at least two dozen mercenaries fighting at her side."

Something about the explanation struck the Herald as odd from the offset. Savog was sharp, even for an orc, which meant he would have pushed his men, yes, but not to the point of exhaustion. He would have made sure they had defensible camps and sufficient water and resources.

She raised her hand and closed her eyes for a moment and a gust of wind swept through. The woman fell, her hair suddenly aflame, and as much as she tried, there was no way to extinguish it.

"You." She pointed at the next one, a dwarf whose gaze was fixed on his comrade's burning hair that had begun to cook her skull. The sight made it difficult for him to focus. "Your friend was a liar and I will not stand for exaggeration. Tell me the truth."

"There was a witch," he stated and tried to focus on answering the questions instead of the screaming woman. "She could raise shields and heal, I think, and she had an enchanted spear. There were a few trained soldiers, but the rest were merely villagers."

"And they managed to drive your attack off?"

The dwarf gulped. "More came toward the end and they had a trap waiting for us. We followed them into the longhall—that was where Savog was killed—and they set fire to it and escaped through some tunnels. By the time we reached the end of it, men were waiting for us in an ambush. Those of us who managed to escape returned to our horses and returned here as quickly as possible."

Belladonna smiled and patted the dwarf's head for a moment before she turned to her lieutenant. "As a reward for this one's honesty, they will die swift, merciful deaths."

"But—"

"You failed me despite your honesty." She nodded, and her men moved in behind their fellow fighters, their swords drawn, and immediately ran them through.

A quick death was a reward but there were other reasons for it.

"Pack the camp," she snapped and the soldiers scurried to their duties. "We have a new target to focus our wrath on."

CHAPTER SIXTEEN

A celebration was in order as was always the case when there was a deserving victory to mark the occasion.

Cassandra didn't know why she wasn't in the mood. They had won and it was a positive thing that they were in good spirits over it. A few drinks had been spilled in honor of Caephas and the signs of his sacrifice were all over the longhall. The whole building was carved from stone, which meant that the fire had burned out before the day ended, although clearing the bodies out had taken a fair amount of work.

Unfortunately, it was not finished. The bodies and the horses had not accounted for all those who had initiated the attack, which meant a handful of survivors had escaped. In light of this, they would inevitably have to face another force and would have to start the fight all over again.

At least this time, they had a better force to fight with—assuming Langven decided to stay.

"We are celebrating and yet you do not look like you are joining in."

She turned to where Karvahal stood near her, a cup in each hand.

"I'm sorry. Something about so much death—even if it is those who would kill us—has a way of making me feel...maudlin. Pensive too, given that what we will likely face again also weighs on my mind, if I'm being honest."

"Is it too much to ask that you live in the moment?" He handed her one of the cups and she could smell the wine. It wasn't particularly good quality but they wouldn't be choosers, being beggars and all.

She took the cup and tapped it lightly to his.

"To our continued health," she said before she drained it in one gulp. It was a heady vintage and it hit her immediately and made her stomach warm.

He laughed at the toast but also drained his in a single gulp before they both tossed their cups over their shoulders. It was an old tradition and one of the finest since it was supposed to be performed by those seated at a round table and it almost never was.

They turned when two yelps came from behind them.

"Oy, watch it you two!" Bandir growled and rubbed the back of his head. Tandir did the same and she still couldn't tell one from the other. It was time to break one of their noses again.

"Aye, having too much to drink is no excuse to hurt people."

"It might be the best excuse but never you mind that."

She grinned at them. "I'll have to hurt both of you if you don't stop your whining. Now head off and find us a jug to share."

They looked like children and both pouted but did as they were told. She and Karvahal continued their laughter as the two shambled across the room.

It wasn't long before her gaze shifted to the east again and a little to the north. That was the direction the orc's raiding party had traveled from, which meant it was more or less where the Herald's army was.

"I would say the drink worked," the chieftain commented and shook his head. "Although not quite as well as intended."

"It did the trick," Cassandra answered with a shrug. "But we don't have time for another. We have to start preparing and we need to gather the craftsmen together to travel. Tonight."

"Tonight?"

"What's happening tonight?" Bandir asked as the twins sat again.

"You heard her fine, you moron," Tandir answered and took a swing from the jug instead of pouring it into a cup. "But why? All the wine is here. Not that there is much of it but more than enough to drink ourselves silly for a couple of nights. Then we start hunting for something a little stronger to raise our spirits."

"Tonight," she insisted.

"You are the mother of all killjoys."

"I suppose that is what comes from being of a royal barbarian bloodline. I might be the last but there will be time for that later. Fuck off."

The twins complied but took the wine. It was probably for the best, all things considered. She needed her head on straight if she wanted to set all the wheels in motion that needed to be.

"Come along then," she snapped to the young chieftain. "I have to spend the night sober but I'll be damned if I will spend it alone."

"If I didn't know any better, I would think that was a proposition."

"You do know better. Come on. If they won't listen to me, they will listen to you."

It was not something she had expected, but the people of Torsburch had taken to the young man's style of leadership. As much as they respected her, she was still an outsider, the kind who would not have their interests at heart. That was the assumption, at least, and it was proving problematic. Folk second-guessed everything she had to say.

That was why it was best to have the chieftain beside her.

Once it was clear that he trusted her, the rest of them fell into line.

"Join us!" one of the pilgrims shouted. "We have recounted the tales of your heroics during the battle of Torsburch. Would you care to check the facts?"

"I have business. In fact, I have business with you."

Many folk thought Theros' followers were the pious ones and entirely different than the assholes who followed Janus. The latter were loud, annoying, drank too much, and got into trouble where they were not wanted, all because that was what they believed Janus wanted from them.

From what she could make out, the god himself was equally as annoying, which made sense. But the Theros followers were only quiet and pious by comparison. They were still as willing to indulge, enjoy, and annoy all who encountered them as much as all the other humans.

"Business?" one of them asked and appeared to be deeper in his cups than most. "Business tonight?"

"For fuck's sake, yes. Tonight."

Her curse caught their attention and it was interesting to see that they took her a little more seriously now. They weren't quite as sober as she would like but were sober enough.

"I know of fortifications that need to be shored up. Are you up to the task?"

"Our walls?"

"No. A small fortress not far from these walls and in a sorry state of disrepair, but they can be restored. And made better than they were before given that we might need to defend them this time. We have large quantities of stone inside the walls. Can you use those to fortify them?"

"Yes…yes, I suppose we could."

"What carpenters you have will also need to be prepared to work alongside you. There is a reason why these people surrendered their city the first time around when the Herald was present, and I think it means they would be able to raise a proper force against us. Not only soldiers but engineers, ready to take the wall down if they cannot come over it. I would see them thoroughly disappointed."

"As would we."

"If you are willing, I have a few plots and plans that might allow us a few advantages those bastards won't see coming."

"We shall make them pay, Princess."

That was a first. And it didn't even sound like they were joking with the title like the others tended to. Perhaps these folks had begun to think of her as a princess. It could be the garb she'd worn during the battle. They hadn't ever seen anything like that, not as practical armor that would aid her in a battle aside from being a distraction.

Them using the title was not a problem, although she didn't particularly like it. She could stand it as long as it let them help her help them survive, which was the kind of concession she usually hated to make. Still, it was necessary and in this case, especially so.

"We'll get to work as soon as the sun rises," the pilgrim promised with a broad smile and raised his cup to her and the young chieftain as they moved away.

"Is there a reason why you want to do this tonight?" Karvahal asked as they continued between the small groups gathered around fires in the longhall. "It could all be done in the morning."

"It is an unfortunate necessity," Cassandra stated and fixed him with a firm look. "We will face an interesting and dangerous foe. While we celebrate tonight, I want all those we need at work to be there as quickly as possible come the morning. No loitering, complaining about aching heads, or standing about, unsure of what they have to do."

He laughed and shook his head. "Even if it means it casts a shadow over the celebrations?"

"The shadow is already cast. We know our enemies

approach and pretending they aren't will result in deaths in the future. As we prepare to stand our ground, I would rather have everyone ready and waiting for the attack as quickly as possible. That way, less of a shadow will be cast over the coming days. They will have something to occupy their time and keep their imaginations from running wild. Your people remember well what happened the last time Torsburch was taken. This way, their hands and minds will be focused on the task at hand."

They paused as they reached the doorway, and Cassandra looked out into the distance again. There would be more than a cloud of dust to announce their arrival. Assuming their numbers matched her assumptions, they would know the force was approaching days before they arrived. Of course, there was a tactical element to that as well. The Herald would want people to know she was arriving.

She wanted fear and terror to do her work for her and perhaps convince them all to give up again.

"We need to find Langven," Cassandra said and shook her head. "As long as he plans to remain this time, we'll need to coordinate our efforts."

"Has anyone ever told you that you are the largest and most unsettling of killjoys?"

Both turned to the man with a mug in hand and a broad smile on his face as he approached.

"Regularly and with great fervor," she replied. "And they were alive when they did so too, so I'll take that as what needed to happen. A necessary sacrifice."

"That is fair, I suppose. You do seem like the type who is willing to do what is necessary to ensure that lives are saved. Although you probably realize that many more will die if we are successful than if we fail, right?"

"I doubt that." She shook her head. "That army was assembled for a purpose, and it wasn't merely to take a handful of small towns on the border of the empire. It's preparation for an invasion. A herald for one, perhaps."

The mercenary nodded and ran his fingers over his jaw.

"If that was your thinking, why did you return at all?" she asked. "I wouldn't have thought that you would be willing to fight for anything less than your weight in gold."

"Jewels make better payment, between you and I," he answered. "And...well, I have something that might prove to be a little more valuable to fight for. Did I hear correctly? You intend to shore up the defenses of the fortress we saw the orc's party camping in?"

"The fortress my ancestor built? That one?"

She raised an eyebrow. "Are you willing to throw your life away again?"

He studied her as he tried to discover what she was speaking about for a moment before he chuckled softly. "If you happen to have a plan to make my sacrifice worthwhile, I think I might."

"I do and I'll explain. For the moment, I need you to gather as much firewood and materials for tents and the like that you can find."

"And you'll explain what all that is for after I've done all this work?"

"I don't trust you not to leave again. Therefore, I would have you put some investment in before I tell you the news that will influence your decision."

"Devious. I like it. Consider this mysterious task of yours done."

She winked and he returned to where his men and young Verda were waiting for him. Despite what she'd told him, she didn't doubt that he wouldn't leave, not with the way he and the girl exchanged glances that would likely lead to something more as the night wore on.

Still, she had to make sure and finding a way to push her jabs in when they presented themselves was part of that.

The craftsmen would come in and ask her about specifications soon and Cassandra wondered how the hell she had been landed with the work of resolving the logistics. Generals had specialists when they had to put in this kind of work but she was no general, which oddly meant she currently shouldered all the responsibility with far less authority and almost no pay.

"You would think a princess would be able to raise a real army," she muttered. "And folk to do the shit required for it."

"Most princesses are holed up in palaces and waited on by servants, while every aspect of their lives is controlled and contained. Husbands, lovers, and even children are chosen for them," Karvahal pointed out and drained his cup again. "You would not want to be a real princess. Your place is out in the wild, protecting folk and killing monsters of all shapes and sizes. It's the barbarian in you."

"I am not an actual barbarian. You realize this, yes?"

He shrugged. "You encapsulate the spirit of freedom that comes from being a barbarian. All I can think is…what the fuck is the difference?"

That teased a smile out of her. She never felt that she was pretending to be something she was not. In the end, it was not a real title so no one would care if she claimed it. But being a barbarian was more than simply being born into one of the many clans. They were known to take folk in. Criminals and exiles who faced death or worse in civilized society were said to find a home out in the wilds with the barbarian clans.

Perhaps she would as well, someway or somehow.

"You know," Karvahal said as he refilled the empty cup she still held in her hand. "That place might have been a fortress once but it will not be again, not without considerably more work than we are capable of putting into it. It's a noble idea, of course, and I don't deny that as a camp, it might be the ideal situation, but there is no way to have that ruined fortification repaired enough to repel an attack. While it's an interesting idea, it's also one I fear will not work."

Cassandra grinned and winked at the man. "The fortress cannot be held then, you think?"

His narrowed eyes and his curious expression told her that he was trying to work out what she had in mind.

"You don't intend to hold it?"

"I intend to make it look like we will hold it," she answered and continued to grin like she was twelve and was waiting for someone to bite into a pastry she'd spiked with blazing hot peppers. "I intend to set a trap."

CHAPTER SEVENTEEN

She had been right about one thing—they had no difficulty seeing the advance of the Herald's forces.

The enemy had made good time too by the looks of it. They had only been at work on the crumbling husk of what had once been a fortress for two days before the dust clouds began to rise in the distance. There was the intention to deny their enemy the water that they were going to need while marching through the arid landscape, but they could only expect it to be partially effective.

The sound of horses immediately drew her attention and she looked to where Langven approached with a group of five men. He'd left with five too, which was a good sign. Not all the other scouting and raiding parties the Ebon Pack had sent out had been so lucky.

"How went your hunting?" she asked as he stopped at the small gate their carpenters were still working on to make it functional.

He gestured to the blood on his armor. "Productive, as hunting goes. Have the other teams reported in yet?"

"Yes, but they all took casualties. I would say you were lucky enough to run into the least competent of their scouts."

"You could give me a little credit."

"When you've earned it." Cassandra looked at the fortress they had invested so much time, effort, and work into. It had been a considerable challenge. At first glance, it would appear that they were attempting to make it defensible again, but a closer, more careful look would reveal the other work they had put in.

While certain positions had been fortified, others had been sabotaged and traps rigged to turn the structure into a complex maze of death. It had not been as difficult to accomplish as she had feared it would be given that Karvahal's ancestor had designed it to be something of a death trap for any who might have tried to invade it.

Madness and paranoia aside, however, he was also something of a genius. All she could do was attempt to recreate some of his work.

Any good scout would see what they were doing. They had come to that realization about a day into their work, which was when Langven volunteered his men to harass the scouts and ensure that they would never have a decent look at what was being done inside the dilapidated fortress. With luck, all the Herald would hear was that they intended to defend it with a real force.

She'd received no word about the dust ploy they had been working on. In the meantime, Karvahal had kept his people busy. Those who were not hiding about the town put tents up and built fires to make it appear as though people were camping outside the fortress.

It was one thing to plot and plan their deception but another to think about the consequences if she was wrong. Looking at the cloud of dust that obscured the sun rising in the east failed to settle the uneasy feeling that had plagued the pit of her stomach over the past few days.

Things would be better when the enemy arrived and everything began to go wrong. Faced with reality, she could react and work to fix it. There would be no time for conjuring and internal debate. Her imagination would not need to run wild every time she had a moment to herself.

Langven rode into their little camp and left the work of harassing the enemy scouts to the rest of his men while he took a moment to rest. Cassandra hadn't had much sleep at all. She'd stayed up working until deep into the night and had woken with the sun, only to find that she was not the most productive one in camp.

The weariness did little to ease her unsettled feeling. As it stood, she was in desperate need of koffe.

"Do you think it will be enough?"

She turned as Verda approached and looked like she had just woken up herself. There was a hungry, worn appearance to almost everyone in the camp, but she did not want to overwork any of those who would end up fighting. It would not end well to fight alongside folk who were dropping from exhaustion.

All she could spare was a wry smile before she returned her attention to the horizon.

"I suppose that makes sense." The girl sat next to her and sounded oddly like Skharr did when he was talking to Horse and acting as though the beast had answered. "If it isn't enough, we'll all be too dead to consider the alternatives."

"Not all of us," she muttered and scratched her chin. "The chances are that they will enslave a few and mutilate others, all to instill a sense of fear and dread on those who might choose to fight against them."

"Wonderful."

"That about sums it up, yes." She patted the woman's shoulder before she slid her arm around her. "But we've done all that we can and that is all anyone can do. Now, we wait, which is the hardest part."

"I would have thought the battle was the hardest part."

"That has not been my experience. Battles are bloody, confusing, and terrifying but simple overall. The outcome is already determined ahead of time, whether you want to talk about preparation and weather or the will of the gods. We'll have the skill and strength to kill that bitch or we won't. When the time comes, that is the full sum of it all. Whether we will or will not. It's simple enough."

"So, what makes the time before so difficult?"

Cassandra sighed and lowered her gaze to the ground for a moment. "Before the battle, your mind wanders, considers, and feasts on your imagination. There is always something to think about that provides a tactical advantage to those attacking, to be used or discarded at the peril of the commanders in question. It's the time when all you can do is wonder about whether you did enough to shift the predetermination of the battle. Did we bring enough men, set enough traps, and provide our people with enough food and water? How tired will we be? All that rages through your mind."

Verda chuckled nervously. "I thought I was the only one who felt that. All of you seem so calm and collected."

"It is the illusion of the duck."

"What?"

"The duck." She nudged her. "Have you ever seen a duck in the water?"

"Yes."

"It's calm on the surface but paddling like all the demons from all the hells are after it under the surface. I like to call it the illusion of the duck."

The girl laughed softly at the comparison and shook her head. "I'll have to remember that."

"Please do. In the end, you'll find that the battle you fight against yourself is the more challenging one. Compared to it, fighting the enemies who present themselves will be considered a sweet release."

They were complaining. Part of her felt like they did nothing else.

It wasn't like they weren't paid enough for their efforts. She would have been content to spend a great deal less on the bastards but the decision had been taken over her head.

And as usual, she had to live with the consequences. They wanted to slow down, to rest, or to take in the fucking scenery like it wasn't one of their overpaid maggot comrades who had lost them Torsburch in the first place. None of them seemed to consider the fact that she was the one who had to retake what they had lost through their incompetence.

Of course, none of them were brave enough to bring their complaints to her face. It was all bow and scrape and avoid her gaze when she was present—the kind of cowardice she probably should have taken into account before she brought them in to fight for her. Still, she had what she had and for the moment, their fear of her drove them to do whatever she told them to and the complaints only came after her back was turned.

Reports that the rebels had begun to establish their camp up in the old fortress had not helped morale, of course. There was little enough water in the region, which meant that she needed to push from one larger source to another to keep her troops watered and properly fed. The fortress was built on what was easily the most substantial water spring in the area, so if they could not take it quickly, they would die of thirst before the week was out.

Those same reports were starting to come in less frequently and the reports were that this barbarian princess who led their defenses sent troops out to harass her scouts and keep them away from their camp.

It was an interesting detail. If they were working to rebuild the fortress, there would be no need to harass the scouts. A more effective strategy would be to delay the approach of the main force to give her people more time to fortify the building.

Killing scouts was an interesting tactic. Some might even consider it to be foolish but she was well aware that the woman they called the Barbarian Princess was no fool. Which led to the question of what she didn't want the scouts to see.

This would be answered soon, she assured herself as she pulled her horse to a halt within sight of the fortress. The dilapidated walls showed signs that they had been shored up and improved, but she doubted that it would be too difficult to overthrow, even if they brought the ladders up to it. They would lose a few men but that was what they were there for.

She would consider it just payment for complaining about her behind her back.

Still, something burned inside her, hot and hungry and angry, and it filled her with a consuming white light. This need for the sight of the bodies and hundreds killing each other was something she'd never been able to explain, only revel and bask in.

Belladonna licked her lips at the thought but reined in the impulse to attack the damn fortress herself as she nudged her horse to ride ahead of the rest of the army. She raised a hand to stop her troops from continuing.

There was no need to look back. The sounds of their marching ceased as she rode in front and isolated herself from them to study the ruined fortress. Her keen gaze immediately noticed a handful of defenders on the wall.

Of course, Grimm the Cruel was as intolerant of failure as she was. One might have even said that she learned that particular trait from him. If she did not emerge from her mission with anything but complete and utter victory, she would be dead—and it would not be a pleasant death.

He'd taken to having an orc chieftain at his side—the kind who liked to crush skulls with her bare hands or simply gore them with her tusks. That was, of course, when he wanted a very public death. Grimm the Cruel had not earned the moniker through exaggerated stories. Making deaths last years was something he relished. The story was that he'd made his own father's death last a decade, although it had all come before her time.

Still, those were the stories she believed. There weren't many beings in the world whom she feared and even fewer humans. Grimm unsettled her and she wasn't sure why.

Her tenuous relationship with him somehow added to the flames that raged within her as she brought her horse to a halt a full thirty paces ahead of the rest of the army. She estimated that she was probably a little out of the range of the bows the defenders carried. Although if their leader truly was a barbarian, the chances were that they would have a few of the stronger bows her kind were famous for.

None had joined her army who could shoot with purpose, of course, but by now, Belladonna was getting used to the fact that she'd been saddled with the rejects. They were still good soldiers —strong, experienced, skilled, and almost as sadistic as she was herself. It was an intriguing situation, the kind she was most interested in examining to its deepest and more appealing levels.

She could always run away, of course. With her abilities, she could keep herself ahead of any force sent to retrieve her. But the idea of returning to her life as a vagabond and a thief, on the run from the empire and any other army large enough to pose a threat to her, was not an appealing one.

It had its moments but they were few and far between.

"This is your final warning!" she called and amplified her voice so it carried across the whole damn valley to ensure that even her softest whisper was heard by all those inside. "I am

Belladonna, the Herald to Grimm the Cruel, son of Karthelon, and your rebellion against him has made your lives forfeit. But even in this, they can yet hold meaning in service to your betters. Surrender your fortress, hand over the one who calls herself the Barbarian Princess, and avoid this pointless loss of life."

Her voice echoed and faded but silence was all that remained. The wind whipping her cloak was a slight nuisance but her helm prevented her hair from being affected. She took a deep breath when a handful of the men raised their bows and let the arrows fly.

They were good shots, especially from that distance. She noted that the arrows were not as affected by the wind as she had hoped they would be. Or perhaps the archers used the wind in her banners as an indication of where to place their arrows. Five of them arced upward and dropped again in her direction.

Without a moment's panic, she raised her hand and focused her mind on the air directly ahead. It was almost effortless by this point, but she could remember a time in her life when it would have taken everything she had and even then, there was no guarantee that it would work.

The armor did help, of course. The original assurance was that it would infuse the wearer with mystical powers of an uncertain nature but after wearing it, she found that all it did was improve her abilities and make it easier to access them and plumb them for more. It was a dangerous artifact given that an untrained mage could possibly kill themselves if they took the power too far or used too much and failed to account for the limits of their body, even with the armor. There were no defenses that would help the user remain alive if they pushed too hard or too far.

But stopping a handful of arrows was nowhere near what she was capable of. As she focused on them, time felt like it slowed and her grasp caught the projectiles. Her fingers closed in a fist again, and the army watched in silence as they turned to ash and dropped harmlessly to the earth.

"I'll take that as your answer, then," she whispered, lowered her fist, and pointed it at the wall, specifically the palisades that had been shored up directly in front of her. The heat built within her until it was a raging inferno and illuminated her eyes so they gleamed through the eyeholes of her helm. "Just die!"

CHAPTER EIGHTEEN

In the end, most of the work that had gone into shoring up the walls and palisades had been for naught. There wasn't much in the world that could withstand that kind of attack.

The woman who rode ahead of the invading force—wearing a black cloak and full plate armor, complete with a helm that matched her sigil with the horns rising from the temples—called for them to surrender. When the Pack gave their answer, none of them truly expected the arrows to kill her, but to watch how easily she turned the arrows to ash was merely a taste of what was to come.

As Cassandra saw the woman's eyes starting to glow through the eyeholes in her helm, something else far more powerful surged violently to the point where she could feel it across the battlefield.

"Get down!" she shouted. "Away from the wall!"

The men needed no further encouragement and immediately scrambled away from the palisades as a bright flash—almost like a second sun—illuminated the whole area. Something stung her cheek as she ducked away from the blast. It was powerful but focused, struck the poles to shatter the wood across them, and made it difficult to see for a moment.

They had known that the bitch was powerful but this was something else entirely. It was practically unfair.

She hauled herself to her feet and brushed off a few pieces that had collected on her. Thankfully, she wore her traditional armor—the amulet and little else. Even though she had been closer to the blast than most, all she had to show for it were a few bruises and a handful of splinters in her cheek.

The amulet certainly did its work and aided her where it was needed, although it did raise the question of exactly how much punishment it could take before she was suddenly caught without it.

She knew it didn't withstand dragon fire, but little did. The question of where the line ended would have to be considered.

For the moment, they needed to jump into action. Her ears were still ringing and there was a tiny blind spot in her eyes from when she was not quite able to close them in time for the blast. Her people were still in motion and they jogged and scrambled to their second point of defense. She had hoped they could force their opponents back from the walls in their first push but that was no longer an option.

They had no choice but to move into the deep end of the fight.

She grasped her spear a little tighter as the cloud of dust began to dissipate to reveal their enemies starting to rush forward.

"Langven, are you ready?" she shouted.

"All prepared!"

"Are you sure that you won't rush off at the first sign of trouble?"

"You will never allow me to live that down, will you?"

"Only if we survive this."

It seemed like an odd time to trivialize their situation but in the end, there wasn't much she could do to change what was happening to them. All she could do was try to lighten it and hope there was nothing to be worried about.

Their enemies surged toward the hole that had been made. Those on horseback reached it first and she adjusted her hold on the haft of her spear. She was alone, with most of the others already having retreated deeper into the fortress to prepare the rest of their traps.

Langven and a handful of his men remained in the positions they had prepared overlooking the hole. They had assumed it would be the focus of the assault and this was why it was made to look weak and inviting.

And it had worked. A little too well, but it had worked.

As the first horses reached the opening in their wall, the twang of bowstrings told her that she wasn't alone in this, at least. Two of the raiders were felled instantly by arrows in their throats but the rest failed to pierce armor.

A few more dropped from their saddles with wounds and three of the horses neighed loudly, reared, and tossed their riders as the projectiles hit them as well.

Horses in pain wasn't a pleasant sight or sound but the goal was successful. The charge was slowed and it gave her the opportunity to thin the herd.

"Come and find what awaits you when you battle the Barbarian Princess!" Cassandra roared, leapt lightly off one of the logs that had been knocked over when the palisades were destroyed, and jumped high enough to lance her spear through the chest of one of those still on horseback.

It was certainly satisfying to watch the blade of the spear—somehow magical, although she couldn't quite understand what enchantment had been used on it—cut cleanly through armor, hook the man off his horse, and bring him to the ground as she landed.

She dropped to her knees as a lance brushed past her shoulder, rolled over it, and regained her feet as she twisted the haft to drive it into the side of another's head. As the attackers raised their shields to defend themselves from the arrows raining on them from above, she found all the targets she could ever need who were distracted.

Another fell when her spear sliced between his ribs, and the next strike eliminated another. Their advance was choked both by the resistance and the narrow hole, which made it difficult for any of them to pass through even without the panicked horses that could so easily trample anyone in their path. The arrows and the chaos were all she needed to ensure that their focus was never on her, but she knew it wouldn't last.

Eventually, those who could command the men would organize them, pull them back, and attack with something a little more subtle than an all-out charge into the trap set for them.

"Look out!" Langven warned.

He had a view over the wall, even though he and his archers were hidden in the murder holes directly above the entrance. And if he told her to look out, Cassandra intended to pay attention. She sprinted away from the wall as the raiders continued to push through. Now that they were no longer harassed by the woman on the ground, they renewed their assault in earnest but she could see the light building on the other side of the barrier.

It was difficult to ignore but at least this time, she was able to close her eyes before the blast struck. The difference this made was minimal. She could see the bright flash even through closed eyes as well as feel its powerful impact. While only enough to knock her off her feet, it still felt like someone had punched her in the chest and forced the breath from her lungs.

"I…do not…like that," Cassandra muttered and eased slowly to her feet to inspect the damage.

Another cloud of dust hung over the battlefield and made it difficult to see what was happening beyond the wall. The structure itself was in pieces. A much larger hole had been created that tore down the stones and logs that had been positioned to shore it up.

It had been made to stand against catapults, ballistae, and even the odd ram, as long as they didn't put too much work into it.

There wasn't much in the world that could withstand a blast like that unless it had been reinforced with a little magic behind it. It also didn't look like the Herald cared much about her men given that at least a dozen of them and their horses had been caught in the blast. It had killed them all and turned the area into a charnel house.

The bottleneck was broken, however, and more troops moved through it. This made it difficult for her to decide whether it was time to leave or if she should remain for a little while longer to thin their numbers further.

She looked up as Langven lowered the rope with a small loop at the end of it, a clear message that his better view of what was happening told him that now was the time to leave.

One last look behind her said the same. The rest of the army pressed through and she would no longer have any kind of advantage in the area, even with her magical spear. She put her boot through the loop and clutched the rope with one hand but took the opportunity to slash the throat of one man before the rope jerked her up. The weight of the boulder attached was enough to drag her higher at an impressive speed.

It hurt her leg a little but she was soon at the top of the secondary wall with those in their murder holes that they would have to abandon shortly.

This wasn't quite the way she had expected the first few minutes of the battle to play out. Then again, she had expected it all to go to shit with their plans immediately meaning nothing as soon as the battle lines came together. That was always how it went.

"It looks like you came out of that no worse for wear,"

Langven noted, nocked an arrow, and loosed it at the group that had begun to gather below them. "Next time, I'll have to join you."

"We didn't have the time for two ropes to pull us up. We discussed this." Cassandra looked down and scowled when one of the men threw a grappling hook up to try to climb to their location. She waited for him to move a few feet above the ground before she slashed at him with her spear as a couple more grappling hooks were tossed up. The man fell with a gaping wound in his chest. She caught another across the throat before he realized that he was expected.

The Ebon Pack archers were quick to cut the rest of the ropes but the time was coming for them to abandon their little perch. More men poured in, using shields to keep the arrows from doing too much damage. The ladders were dragged up as well.

She and the mercenary leader both realized at the same time that the time to leave was upon them.

"Come on then!" she shouted to the army gathering below. "We don't have time to waste."

A few arrows shot from below were all the answer they needed as the group of six archers, together with Langven and Cassandra, hurried carefully across a handful of narrow bridges that would allow them to continue moving without having to touch the ground. The fortress was already something of a maze, created to be the kind of place that would allow defenders to continually fall back to defensive positions until they reached the very center.

There would be no escape from it, of course, but they would make their enemies pay for every inch they managed to take. And the best part was that there would be no escape for their enemies either given that they needed the water flowing from the very center of the fortress as well.

Assuming this Herald didn't have a way to conjure some water from the ground with her powers. It was unlikely, but Cassandra wouldn't start to doubt the woman's abilities now.

"Keep moving. Keep moving!" Langven yelled as another handful of arrows streaked toward them. They were in an exposed position above one of the avenues leading to where most of the other fighters were. A few skirmishers on horseback had reached them and fired a handful of arrows in time to catch one of Langven's men.

An arrow hit him in the back and drilled through the chain mail. Another punched through his boot and continued into his leg and he stumbled forward with a cry. Immediately, the others raised their shields to protect one another as they slipped back into cover.

"Shit, Neeru," Langven muttered and dragged the man in to check him, but he'd already begun to cough up blood.

"The arrow's pierced a lung," Cassandra told him and placed a hand over the wound. It had injured more than that judging by the way his eyes started to drift. In seconds, he was unconscious and would be dead a few minutes later.

They needed to continue moving but she could see the impulse in Langven's eyes to try to help or at least drag his man to safety. While she could understand it, she knew he had to push on or they would be overrun. The decision was made in the blink of an eye and he patted Neeru's cheek once before he let him fall.

If they survived, they would return to ensure that he had a proper burial.

For the moment, they needed to focus on the priority—continue to run to where most of their traps were waiting. Cassandra had not known Neeru very well. She had seen him about, of course, but this was the first time she'd heard his name.

Oddly, it saddened her, but there would come a time for mourning later. For the moment, she would fight and stand her ground to save the lives of the others, even if she never learned their names. It wouldn't be the first time, of course, but sadness lingered nevertheless.

Cassandra checked her weapon and shifted it to a ready position as she looked to confirm that Langven had led the others on before she followed. Once they were all in position, they dropped carefully to ground level again. She could hear their enemies still negotiating through the traps that had been left for them. The purpose of these had been an attempt to continue thinning their numbers and see to it that none of them were in any other state than furious.

There had once been a time when she thought any army would simply go on a rampage in any town they had attacked, but she remembered speaking to one of the soldiers who had told her about how the folk in a city had been poorly led. If they had been well-led, they would have been the poorer for it.

She hadn't understood his point until he explained that armies tended to be worked up when they committed those atrocities. Watching their friends and comrades killed before the walls would make even the most stoic of knights feel the impulse to wreak vengeance on those responsible. Only one was required to snap and the rest would follow.

And in this case, she needed their control to be gone. It would turn them into a mob instead of an army. No strong hand would enable them to surge into battle without a care that they would be rushing into the jaws of the defenders.

Waiting for them was an unnerving feeling, especially when they could hear and feel the heavy hooves of their horses charging forward. The streets were narrow and made more perilous with the traps and holes that had been dug. Screams issued from those who fell to their deaths.

It had been her decision to stand her ground. She knew Langven wanted to be there as well but the fact remained that she needed him to command the defense with the rest of the men. She trusted his instincts better than hers and there was the fact that she was the least likely to injure herself. It was the right choice given that she had magic on her side with her weapons, amulet, and her abilities that would be able to hold their enemies at bay longer than anyone else could.

These were a simple series of facts that he had to agree with, even if he didn't like it.

She held her spear with the blade forward as the skirmishers rushed forward and checked the ground ahead to ensure that no more traps were waiting for the troops. There were five of them, and she now waited for the rest of the force to push forward for them to progress to the next step of their defenses.

There was no telling what the mindset of the men was. They wore helms which obscured her sight of them, but the reckless charge into an area that they could not know was not bristling with traps was likely a sign that their keen minds had long since abandoned all thought of caution at this point.

They rushed past the initial trap. All those ready and waiting behind her would know that the skirmishers were not the true targets for it and it would be her work to ensure they were kept busy while the rest of the army approached.

The first of the horses charged toward her and Cassandra dove to the right, rolled over her shoulder, and came up smoothly as the second approached.

Her spear was already raised and her arms were jarred as she buried the head into the raider's stomach and lifted him off the saddle. She groaned, planted her feet firmly as well as she could manage, and twisted to pound the man into the ground to ensure the kill.

The other three rode past her but one fell from his horse as the arrows peppered him and finally found a narrow angle to penetrate his throat.

She grinned as the other two were caught when a wall was pushed on top of them. The horses were knocked down and neighed and whinnied pitifully, but they scrambled up again and darted away while their riders were still stunned and tried to drag themselves upright.

Those who had pushed the wall over were already waiting with daggers and weapons in hand. They were not among the warriors, but they still had sufficient numbers to overwhelm the last two men who were still dazed and struggled to recover.

These were not those she could pay attention to, however. The main force was still moving forward. Any powerful charge they might have had planned was slowed when the Pack's arrows picked their men off one by one. A handful fell but the rest had enough presence of mind to raise their shields to create a wall.

She could hear the twins yell and shout insults, especially to the goblins that were a little too small to join the shield wall and tried to rush forward instead.

They were killed easily despite the heavy armor they wore. Tandir and Bandir now tossed their javelins into the formation. They hadn't been pleased that they were forced to stay in the back to organize the rest of the defenders and they were experienced enough to take it out on their enemies instead of making a scene that would help no one.

The javelins didn't cut through the shields like they had hoped but the enemy began to lower their shields and let the archers take a few more lives as Cassandra hefted her spear. It was useful but not as useful in the close quarters in which they now fought.

All the invaders felt the itch of delayed combat and wanted to rush forward and kill the one woman who stood in their way. She was not only waiting for them to do it but wanted them to do it.

"Come on then. I don't have all day!" she called, twirled her spear, and narrowed her eyes in focus as the first line passed the edge of their trap. The instinct to tell them to snap it shut was strong but they wanted more. This was one of their best plans thus far, and it had taken considerable work to ensure that they had it available to them.

She wanted as many of them to be caught in it as possible to maximize the damage.

The invaders continued their march—three then four lines past the marker. At five, she looked at where Langven was watching. His bow was lowered, his hand was raised, and his fingers closed as he frowned in concentration at the lines marching forward. He was well aware that she was moments away from having to engage hundreds of them on her own and he wanted to ensure that she was not alone.

His arm snapped down. The sound of neighing horses was suddenly heard as five of them were suddenly put into motion. Ropes were engaged and even pulleys. Some of the most complicated work she'd ever seen was put into action and the mechanisms brought out a pair of spiked walls that had been cleverly concealed to match their surroundings. It hadn't been that difficult, as it turned out. The unfinished look of the fortress allowed them to conceal a great many things and in this case, the weighted trap was suddenly in motion and the walls closed in around the first few lines of the raiders.

Screams and the hard squelch of wood on flesh made it difficult to watch as a large number of them were crushed by the trap. While she had a stomach for the violence, it was not something she enjoyed. The twins did, however, and from the cheers coming from the top of the wall, it sounded like all the others did as well when dozens of their enemies were crushed to death.

All she could do was heft her spear and focus on the twenty or so men who were in there with her. It wouldn't take them long to hack their way through. The trap was weighted but not reinforced. She doubted that it would require a ram to get through.

They would need to finish them quickly. Archers were already choosing their targets and she needed to do the same. She hefted her weapon again before she flung it directly into the chest of one of them. He had his shield raised but it made no difference. The spear cut straight through it and his chest and pinned him to the wall behind them.

"Princess!"

She looked up as Tandir tossed her a shield to use, caught it smoothly, and drew her sword to block an attack and slash a throat. Her wrist rolled to parry a strike at her head and she retaliated immediately and opened the side of the young woman's neck in the sliver of a gap where her helm stopped and her armor started.

Another wave of the enemy surged in and Cassandra was forced to pull back. She raised her shield to deflect and upended another opponent who fell with his guts spilling out and his fingers working to contain them.

Before she could reach the position where they could help her to the tops of the buildings, she could hear the battle cries. The twins bounded down to join her despite the shouts from Langven to stop them. They had assumed she was in danger and rushed to help her. Their last two javelins were thrown and she could have told them that she was in less danger than they were about to be as she could see the army behind the wall already hacking through.

"You're a pair of fucking morons!" she yelled over the din of the battle as the villagers and pilgrims began to throw rocks from the top to hit whatever they could.

She was a little worried that someone would hit her in the head by mistake but so far, they were able to keep the attackers on the defensive, which allowed her and the barbarians to decimate their ranks as quickly as they could.

"We take after your example," Bandir answered and cut two of them down with his battle-ax. With smooth clean strokes, he hooked the ax into another man's shield and yanked him away before he beheaded him with a single attack.

Both barbarians were powerful fighters and very little could stop them aside from the swarm starting to attack through the wall. It was already starting to splinter and come apart.

"Get your fucking asses up here!" Langven bellowed and

jumped down to join them. "We will be in the thick of it if we don't pull away."

He had left his bow and as the first man pushed through the ruined trap, he hacked his blade to remove the raider's head from his shoulders. A spear was thrust at him but caught on his shoulder pauldron. He shrugged the strike aside and grasped the spear, dragged its wielder through, and cut into the back of his neck before he moved away.

Three more men pressed through. Cassandra caught one of them with a slash to the throat and Tandir crushed another's skull as she sheathed her sword, recovered her spear, and gestured for the others to fall back as another group poured in. It was, however, all but impossible to attack and still maintain a solid defense. There wasn't enough room in the hole for them to hold their shields up, and the archers made good work of clearing as many as they could.

"I suppose the three of you have some bright ideas about how we'll get out of this one alive?" she asked. "I was supposed to retreat on my own, draw them out, and force them through that fucking trap. Now, it's the four of us."

"We go," Langven answered and twisted his sword. She wasn't sure why he didn't carry a shield but his plate armor was more than able to block attacks and the way he grasped his sword with both hands certainly worked well for him. As a few more enemy troops rushed at them, she tripped the first one and Tandir was able to leap in front and kill him easily. His body hindered those behind so there was no easy way for them to continue their push.

So far, tactical prowess, ingenuity, and more than a little luck had allowed them to hold the line, but they would run out of tricks soon. She knew that once that moment came, it would be time to stand and fight, even if it meant doing so with their backs against the wall. That would be the point where they had no other choice but to survive.

The barbarian princess hefted her spear and focused on

where the remainder of the Herald's forces began to surge forward now that they'd managed to destroy most of the trap. Her narrowed gaze noticed that there was something wild about the way they attacked. A handful of pits with more spikes claimed the lives of three or four more of them and it only made them angrier.

Their rage drove them into a relentless assault but Cassandra realized that the four of them were not alone. Those villagers who had pushed the wall over to kill the skirmishers had stepped in to form an additional defensive line. This would not be the last stand, but if they could push against the tide and drive them back, there was the possibility that they might break their spirit.

It was very unlikely to happen but there was always hope. She advanced with slow steps and shoved the raiders back with her shield as she ducked under a strike and speared the man who lowered his shield and retreated. Langven covered for her as they forced the enemy back with each deep cut and strike that kept them on the defensive.

Suddenly, one of the raiders jumped forward. The orc—judging by his size and the tusks that protruded from his helm—arced a massive, two-handed saber to sever the head of one of the villagers who lowered his shield to attack unwisely. The line was broken and the second man fell.

The fighting devolved quickly from that point. Cassandra noticed a handful of arrows aimed in their direction. She raised her shield hand and pushed them away in an attempt to stop them from killing more, but the defenders were already being driven away. Their courageous formation fell apart and turned what had been a push and pull between the two lines into a melee.

She planted her spear in the earth and drew her sword instead as she was pushed in with Langven, a few of his Pack, and Tandir. The other brother was separated from them and had no choice but to join the remainder of the Pack and the handful of villagers where the wall had been pushed down.

Tandir glanced at his brother and swung his mace to try to clear a path for them to get through and reconnect with the rest of their party.

The barbarian princess sucked in a deep breath, took a step back, and thrust her consciousness forward and out of her body. Powered by the full weight of her will, it battered the men and women who separated the group and forced them back. It felt like each shield, each sword, and each spear ravaged her body but she gritted her teeth and maintained the pressure to sweep them aside and clear a path. A handful of the raiders were pushed into the pits and others were knocked off their feet by the force of her assault.

It wouldn't last but it would be enough.

"Go!" she shouted.

Tandir merely nodded his thanks, vaulted over one of the fallen raiders, and rushed along the path she'd created. There was something to be said about the twins fighting together. They had an uncanny ability to know where the other was, fight alongside each other, and even coordinate their attacks without needing to plan, plot, or practice. She assumed it had something to do with them being twins and the fact that they had fought together for so long. As such, keeping them together was the finest chance those villagers and pilgrims would have to survive.

There was also the concern that each one would be distracted every moment that he was not at his brother's side. She needed all those in combat with her to have their minds in the moment and the battle. If that didn't happen, they would all die.

Langven grinned, parried a strike, blocked another with his steel bracer, and impaled one of the raiders with his sword. A smooth retraction and a sweeping strike beheaded one of those who were still recovering from her wave of force.

"You like to keep the brothers together, eh?"

She shrugged and caught a vicious swing on her shield. "That is how they fight best."

"You and me together. Do we fight best that way as well?"

Before she could answer, they heard a bellowed war cry and the grinding of stone on stone. Karvahal had waited impatiently for his turn to join the battle and made an entrance of it when he knocked a wall over with three of the Pack archers who had run out of arrows.

Six or so were caught under it and the barbarian chieftain roared again, his eyes wide as he grasped his claymore. The weapon cleaved one of the raiders almost in half at the shoulder and he ducked as he yanked his blade out into a powerful sweep to behead another with a single strike.

"I think the three of us make a good team, yes," Cassandra answered and smiled when she sensed the energy of the defenders renewed with the arrival of reinforcements.

Still, huge numbers of the invaders had to be vanquished. The fight was far from over, and she knew that even if they forced the raiders back, they had the Herald to deal with.

It wasn't something to look forward to but they would meet that challenge when it presented itself.

CHAPTER NINETEEN

They were prepared, of course, which was a source of annoyance given how the battle had gone thus far. She had hoped that her men would be enough to crush what amounted to a small insurrection by peasants and mercenaries.

This barbarian princess, however, displayed a level of cunning she hadn't expected. Belladonna would never understand why she chose to wander about the battlefield in nothing but armored undergarments. Perhaps it had something to do with raising the morale of her men.

It didn't matter even though it felt like some kind of challenge. She had assumed that the princess would be killed immediately when her armor proved to be woefully ineffective but she continued to fight. More than that, they had designed the whole fucking fortress to be a series of traps and defensive positions, which allowed them to harass and kill her men to the point of extreme vexation.

Belladonna ascended the walls overlooking the battle, knowing she had a squad of warriors beside her. Not that she needed them. Their help was entirely superfluous but it was always a good thing for people to know that she did not fight alone.

Unfortunately, it now seemed like it would end in a situation where she would have to intervene. She had hoped that her first step out—the first true display of her powers—would be in front of a grander audience. It seemed only fitting that all the many peoples in a larger town should be the first to be made aware of the extent of her abilities.

They would unfortunately have to see it the second time she used it, although they would have heard about it already and the impact would be less.

Or perhaps it would be greater. They would have heard the stories and not believed them until the moment their walls were turned to dust. That would be the most forceful impact.

"Hold your positions," she whispered, raised her hands, and closed her eyes. Her previous blasts had been of light and channeled the power of the sun. It was easy enough once one had learned the tricks involved, but channeling darkness—something that was always there and yet not—was something else entirely. It fought back like it had a mind of its own and she had to wrestle it. She had spent years learning how to do it and stop it from ripping her or her men to pieces.

They were years well-spent but in the shortest moment of weakness or distraction, it would turn on her. Unlike the light, it felt almost sentient like there was a being in it that did not want her to channel its power.

Her hands closed slowly and all the tension left her body. Belladonna relaxed more than she had in days. She let it wash over her, summoned the power, and allowed it to soak through her body. The blackness would turn her whole body dark. She'd heard it described as a hole in reality in the place where she stood —uncanny, powerful, and unnerving.

It had an added advantage in its effect on her men. She could hear those who stood beside her backing away slowly. The sight of the blackness was said to turn those who peered into it quite mad and there was no telling what would happen to those who used it.

She was already well beyond mad. Gone was the terrified urchin, and madness had its own power. Her whole body rippled with it, sucked the light out of the air to feel more of it, and filled her almost to bursting. Her teeth gritted and fingers clenched as she lowered her hands slowly to point at the fortress around them.

The words of power came naturally. The darkness knew what it wanted to do and it guided her. Each syllable burst from her mouth like a wave and the power rushed out to savage the world ahead of them. She would never understand how it worked and given that her entire body was wrapped in the darkness as well, there would be no way for her to discern what was happening.

She could only imagine it. That was another trick to using the darkness—to project her consciousness so she could see what was being done and it was glorious. Resolute and unshakeable, it attacked the structures that until now had seemed to mock them, those that these people had put so much work into creating.

It was almost a shame to watch. They had shown all the kinds of ingenuity she admired to create the death trap of a fortress. If she had an army comprised of these kinds of people, she would be unstoppable. She would not even need the help of Grimm the Cruel.

But she had to make do with a group of sadistic but uncreative minds that would simply rush into a fight without considering the possibility that greater minds had expected and prepared for them.

Unfortunately, it meant that the better folk would die because she had to come away with the victory. This meant tearing the whole damn stronghold apart. Perhaps the time would come when she was allowed to make her home in one of these locations. She could rebuild it to its former glory and take a few ideas from those she had fought against.

The part where the wall closed in and crushed her people while on their horses was particularly inspired. Despite this, it had to come down. She took no real pleasure in it aside from the power that accomplished her desire.

She had to enjoy it to retain control of the madness that roared through her body. It was an unsettling feeling for the uninitiated but for her, those days were in her distant past.

Finally, the darkness was spent and left her body feeling drained and a little jittery. Belladonna drew a deep breath, closed her eyes, and steadied herself before she looked out at the destruction she had wrought.

The fortress looked like it had been put into the path of a twister. What makeshift buildings had been erected were now scattered and mixed with the stonework of the original stronghold, which made it difficult to tell one from the other at this point. Most of the traps were exposed and the walls were all but demolished to level the area.

In moments, the darkness had laid waste to everything except for a few sections here and there, including the place where she stood. Some of her people had been caught in it and she was sure it would cause even more complaints but it was the price they paid for allowing things to reach this point in the first place.

She turned to look at the men who stood with her. Their wide eyes watched her in utter shock and horror at what they had witnessed. Awe was present as well but tempered by the knowledge that they might have been at the front of the battle with the others and thus caught in the blast.

What they thought or felt was irrelevant.

"Come along, then," she snapped and approached the steps that were still more or less intact. "It's time to kill the bastards once and for all."

The devastation wreaked on the fortress was something utterly new to her. Cassandra was not the most knowledgeable mage by any means but she had thought she'd heard of all the different assaults that could be used against them. It was part of a paladin's job, after all—perhaps not to use all those abilities but certainly to know of them, if only to be able to defend against them.

What she had seen was something altogether new and chillingly terrifying. The blackness had appeared to suck the light out of the brilliant, sunny day before it suddenly ravaged the whole fortress. It attacked and destroyed everything in its path, uncaring whether raiders were killed or others.

They didn't even have time to evade or find cover—not that there was much to be found against this kind of onslaught. All she could do was brace herself as the impact catapulted her back into Langven and for a moment, everything was unmitigated blackness.

Although she could imagine that immeasurable damage had been done in that time. There was no telling if the blackness was because this magical attack did, in fact, suck all the light out of the world and everything it touched. Then again, they might have simply been unconscious when it struck.

All she knew was that by the time she could see, the sight that greeted her was one she needed a moment to consider. They all knew how much work had gone into creating their little death trap and to see it all leveled like a twister had touched down on it jolted her heart into her throat.

Exactly what in the hell could this Herald do?

Cassandra managed to pull herself to her feet and grimaced when she registered a few cuts on her back and shoulders and more bruises than she could count across her body. Overall, however, she was alive and nothing was broken, and a quick check revealed that nothing untoward was bleeding or would pose a danger later on.

With that done, she turned her attention to Langven. The entire stronghold was still covered in a thick cloud of dust, which made it difficult to see much of anything beyond three or four paces. Still, given that the blast had hurled her into him, it was only good manners that she check to ensure that all was well with the mercenary.

He was alive, at least, judging by the soft groan that issued from him. It appeared that his armor had protected him from the brunt of the damage, although he was stunned and dazed.

"What in the fuck was that?" he asked as he took her outstretched arm and she helped him to his feet.

"I hate to say it, but it might have been me who hurled you off your feet," she answered and brushed the dust and splintered wood from his armor. "But that was the result of some kind of magical attack that destroyed the whole fortress, more or less."

"How does a magical attack destroy a fortress more or less?"

She didn't reply and merely gestured at the area around them as though that was a sufficient answer.

"Ah." Langven nodded and retrieved his sword from where it had fallen when she knocked it out of his hands. "Why... How—"

"I think the pertinent question here is who else survived the attack." Cassandra peered into the wreckage and gestured to the bodies buried under the rubble of a wall that had collapsed on the invaders. "She attacked them as much as us, honestly. I would hate to be under her command."

It was likely that the feeling was very much mutual for the rest of them—both raiders and defenders alike. There were more survivors, however. A few cries of pain and the sound of rubble being moved told her that while the assault had been powerful, its intention had been to level the battlefield as much as possible rather than kill anyone fighting on it.

Those who died on the Herald's side were likely simply collateral damage.

"Come on." She patted Langven on the shoulder. "We need to find the rest of our people and make sure they're all still alive and ready for a fight. More of the bastards might be coming, even if all those already here were killed or left unable to fight."

He nodded and joined her in the attempt to pick a safe path through the tumbled masonry, stone, and fallen logs that had once been their improvised fortress. She knew more or less where the others had been and a few had already picked themselves up and dusted themselves off and gathered around them.

There were casualties, though. The bodies scattered across the ground were not only raiders. A few of the Pack and some villagers and pilgrims had fallen and very clearly would not rise again.

Their losses were fewer than the Herald's forces had suffered but only because they had fewer people to lose. She assumed that even if they lost one fighter for every ten their enemies did, it would still come away in the invaders' favor.

Finally, they reached the place where Karvahal and the twins had fought and thankfully, they had been mostly spared. Still, given the condition of the fortress close to where they were, it had been frighteningly close.

More than a few of them were up and about again and Cassandra realized that they had begun to dig the others out from under the debris. Karvahal was on his feet and Tandir as well, but Bandir was nowhere to be seen and his brother worked the fastest to clear the wreckage.

"How many are in there?" she shouted as she helped to drag a few of the logs away.

"This one's brother," the chieftain answered and made her wonder if he also had difficulty telling the two apart. "A few of the Pack and some of the pilgrims. If we can get them out quickly, we can regroup and see about driving the shits out of this place for all time."

"Well, you say that, but…"

She turned to look at him and tried to understand what he was talking about until she realized that his efforts weren't on freeing their fellows. His attention was turned the opposite way to stare at the cloud of dust.

There was movement in it but there was movement all around them and she couldn't quite make out what he had seen. Wind whipped through the destroyed fortress and made it difficult to tell which was simply wind and dust and which were survivors trying to get themselves clear.

It took only a moment for the reality to become clear.

Something was blasting the dust clear. The Herald did not want to breathe it in the way the rest of them did and it was immediately obvious that she wasn't alone.

"Langven, you're with me," Cassandra snapped and pushed clear of the rubble. Fatigue dragged at her heavy limbs. The fire within had vanished with use and the days of working until she was exhausted, followed by a long fight.

All she could think about was a soft bed and no one needing her services for a week, but there she was, standing on the battlefield and waiting for the hardest part of the fight.

The Herald approached them with a slow, measured tread. Her armor was distinctive and hard to miss, especially given the horned helm on display.

What was more obvious, however, was that she was not alone. A dozen of the raiders marched in step with her, their demeanor resolute and ready to continue the fight regardless of the fact that they likely faced their own deaths as well.

She always knew the soldiers who followed the Herald were more afraid of her than any threat the Barbarian Princess could pose and now, she finally understood why.

"Which one do you want?" she asked quietly, hefted her spear, and adjusted her hold on the haft. "The witch-bitch or her lapdogs?"

Langven shrugged as he shouldered his bow. "I've always loved dogs. Besides, I would say the ladies need time to learn about each other, all things considered."

"You're afraid of facing her."

"I should be mortified at that statement but I'm not. I would face her if it were necessary but since you have some magical powers, it might prove to be the fairer fight."

He made a good point. The chances were that the Herald could light him up like a damn torch as she had Karvahal and his father, even with his armor. She could certainly understand why he was more than willing to face a dozen or so trained and armed killers.

"I'll deal with her," she answered with a sigh and climbed over the crumbled remains of their defenses to step out into the open. The other woman saw her and likely had the same thought as she motioned for her men to head off and find survivors while she confronted the barbarian princess.

They stood almost fifteen paces apart for what felt like the longest moment. Cassandra could already hear the clash of swords from where Langven had engaged the men while she stood her ground and dared her adversary to blink first.

"I've heard a great deal about you," the Herald stated finally and her voice carried unnaturally. "The Barbarian Princess. Well, to be honest, that is all I know about you, aside from the fact that you have a knack for killing my men, have an interesting taste in armor, and have some magical powers. You have done impressive work here. I'll be the first to admit it."

Her accent was odd. It hadn't been present when she had shouted her demands while out of bow range, but here and now, it had a soft, rolling lilt to it.

"I'll always be glad to stand between the innocent and those who would see them dead."

"Innocence is a point of view, but I suppose that kind of debate is better had over a cool pint and food. You want to stop me in my tracks and I cannot allow you to do that. Fate intervened to see this occur."

"Not...quite fate."

"What do you mean."

"There might have been influence involved but that too is the topic for a time when we don't intend to kill each other."

The woman's smile was visible even through her helm. She had an odd beauty to her when she hadn't wrapped herself in enough power to level a fortress, but it was cold and removed like looking into a diamond and appreciating what it was but with no sense of depth to it—fragile, indestructible, transparent, and impassive all at the same time.

"Whatever you're fighting for or are afraid of, we can help you fight it."

"No, you can't. You have no idea of the forces you stand against. I am merely his herald and in a sense, it is a mercy that you die at my hand instead of his. You should thank me."

"It'll be difficult to do so while prying my sword out of your throat, but I suppose I could give it my best effort."

The woman laughed. "And there is the barbarian side of the princess. You know, do you not, that you can't win this?"

"Well, damned if I won't make my best attempt regardless." Cassandra twirled her spear.

"Can I ask you one thing before we begin?"

She narrowed her eyes. It almost sounded like she didn't want to kill her but had to. Once again, she feared the consequences of not doing it far more than the alternative.

"Ask."

"Your name. I've heard the Barbarian Princess all this time and assumed it was a title."

"Cassandra. And yours? Assuming it's not simply the Herald."

"Belladonna."

It was an interesting name and likely not one that was given to her by her parents. Perhaps it was chosen by her since it was the more pleasant nickname given to the plant known as deadly nightshade.

Cassandra tightened her hand around her spear to help her to avoid the distractions that small talk could engender. She knew Langven was at least still alive from the shouted curses and insults at the men who attacked him.

Her focus could not waver, not even for an instant. She was reminded of that when the Herald plucked a few hairs from under her helm, muttered a few words of power as she looked down at them, and held them like they were weapons in their own right. The strands in her hand ignited immediately and became pure flame in seconds. They burned hot enough that the air shuddered away when she whipped the tongues of fire from side to side like she struggled to control them.

That was an opening if she ever saw one. She bounded forward, her shield in position as she feinted to the right. The fiery whips followed and she lunged to the left and thrust her spear out to catch the woman's neck.

Her opponent swayed to the right and the spearhead passed inches away from its intended target. Cassandra followed it up and kept her body moving as she swung her shield in and hammered it hard into her adversary's chest before she circled away and bounded clear of another sweep of the flames.

The Herald was taller than she thought—taller than her by at least half a head—but she wasn't a fighter at her core. A pure mage, she relied on it to finish the work the rest of her soldiers couldn't.

Then again, that was more or less how most mages fought.

Cassandra studied the movement of the whips and noted how they jumped forward before she vaulted off a nearby fallen log and drove her spear down in a hard thrust. It clashed loudly against the mage's shoulder pauldron and sparks flurried although it didn't cut through the way it would have had the armor been of a regular kind.

Instead, it was magical and easily repulsed the attack, and the barbarian princess could do little more than land, dive, and roll when she felt the heat of the flames bite at her back.

There was no real damage but her amulet had begun to heat as well, which told her that it would have been a killing stroke had she not worn it. In fact, she would have been killed a few dozen times over had she not worn it this day. But this attack was something entirely different. It pushed the abilities of the amulet to the very extreme and with another close encounter like that, she would be killed.

She shook her head and found her feet again, unable to stop a smile from touching her lips as she watched the flames moving again. The Herald followed her every step as Cassandra moved in, watching and waiting.

When the whip swung in a little too close, she lowered her shield onto it and immediately felt the heat radiate from the magical weapon and into her hand. It scorched the wood and she pushed it away quickly, took a step forward, and thrust her spear hard to catch the woman's head. Her adversary was immediately on the defensive and swept her whip around to push the spear-head away.

She succeeded but Cassandra twirled the spear in her hand, spun the butt, and hammered it hard between her adversary's eyes and forced her back a step, while the barbarian princess twirled the spear for another thrust with the head. It drove powerfully into the woman's helm again and more sparks issued but without enough power to do any real damage, which left her open to attack.

Instinctively, she swayed and leaned back under a sweeping strike from both whips and again felt the blistering heat on what should have been her exposed midriff. She turned, dropped to one knee, and spun in to kick the mage's legs out from under her.

Her mistake was made apparent a second too late and she yelped, jerked back, and felt the strike-back from where she had kicked the plated greaves the woman wore. It forced her back but had done her more damage than her intended target.

"Fuck." She hissed through the pain and stood. The two women separated and took a moment to study each other again.

She was the more active aggressor in the fight and the more skilled of the two as well, but there was a problem with her tactical approach. She could hammer the woman's armor for as long as she liked and it wouldn't do much damage if any. All the Herald needed was one mistake to deliver a single attack that would surely kill her.

And she still needed the fight to end quickly. She was rather proud of her stamina but there were limits to her body's ability to keep up with what she needed it to do.

Belladonna knew this.

Cassandra drew a deep breath, twirled her spear in her hand again, and watched the way the flames moved in clean, clear circles around the witch. They acted like a shield as she stood her ground.

The barbarian princess moved in, avoided a strike at her head, and thrust her spear forward. She felt it pushed aside and spun it to hammer the butt into the Herald's chest repeatedly, aiming for the gap between her helm and chest plate.

Unfortunately, she wasn't fast enough.

One strand of flame deflected it and the other wound around the head to hold and push it to the ground as Belladonna moved forward, stepped on the haft, and knocked it firmly out of Cassandra's hand.

Desperation took over. She lifted her shield and took a blow on it, raised her free hand, and extended another shield to block the strike that would have wrapped her leg in flames. She tripped as she tried to move away, caught her foot on a small rock, and stumbled.

On one knee, while the heat of the strikes rained relentlessly on her, she uttered a roar, drew her sword from her hip, and slashed at the Herald. The woman took a step back as the blade's tip made contact with the bottom of her helm.

A few blisters had developed on her arms from the heat but the pain was somehow pushed to the back of her mind when another lash of the whips brushed her shield. This time, the wood caught fire and she flung it as quickly as she could into her adversary's face to force the other woman back again.

A soft shout caught her attention for a moment. She turned to where Langven fought on. With five of the raiders dead, more of them had pushed in and he had slipped and dropped to one knee as he tried to defend himself. She snapped her head away barely in time and knew how lucky she was that the moment of distraction hadn't ended in her death as she felt something burning into her arm.

The pain had an odd effect on her. In that moment, she could feel it and somehow, it rushed through her body like a thing alive and surged into something angry within her that wanted to retaliate. The power lashed out, crackled in her hand, and wound it in a protective shield that prevented the heat from injuring it any further. She grasped the flames and felt them fight against her shield and lose.

Slowly and reluctantly, the fire began to lose its intensity and burn itself out.

It was only the one and the mage still had control of another, but a look of shock touched the Herald's face as she tried to pull herself free and find a way to explain what had happened.

For the first time, Cassandra realized that the flames were burning into her hands as well. Holding them so tightly so she could control them was taking a toll on the witch in a way that hadn't been apparent at first. She frowned as she healed the injuries, and Cassandra grew suddenly bolder. Perhaps it was because of the power rushing through her body or something else entirely. Or this power she felt would dissipate and she needed to use it immediately.

Forming flames was still a little too advanced for her but she lashed out and the potent energy within surged through her body, into her hand, and out to pound into the mage.

Her armor protected her but the force was still enough to launch her from her feet and she landed heavily with a clatter of armor and a soft groan.

The barbarian princess wasn't sure if she would be able to press her advantage and she probably should have but instead, she turned to where Langven was still on his knees. He tried to regain his feet and used his fist to knock one of the men back as he drove his sword through the chest of another.

She was about to break away to help when the mercenary leader was pushed to the ground as a third man barreled forward to grapple him. Before the man could take advantage, however, a battle cry erupted and the raider's head was suddenly crushed, helm and all, and Tandir rushed into the fight.

A second was felled when Bandir severed his head, and a third barbarian charged as well. His massive sword cut into one and as they were pushed back, buried itself into the chest of another.

It looked like they had all recovered from having the fortress ravaged around them, although they sported a handful of injuries.

She would care for them later. Now, she turned to where Belladonna began to push slowly to her feet.

Perhaps blasting two holes in a wall, leveling a fortress, and summoning flames to fight in a duel had drained her more than Cassandra expected as she struggled to find her feet.

"You do know," she stated as the barbarians and Langven dealt with the last of her men, "do you not, that you cannot win this?"

The Herald watched as the last of her squad were killed. Once it was done, the four began to close in on her. There was nowhere to run and even if she did, she would not go far.

The princess picked her spear up from the ground and held it at her opponent's neck.

"I don't suppose I can talk you into surrendering?" she asked and tilted her head.

In that moment, she wondered if Belladonna would agree but something pained and angry twisted the woman's face behind her mask.

"I would rather die," she snapped, her tone almost a snarl, and flashed the whip. Karvahal blanched at the sight of the flames but stood his ground.

"That can be arranged," she answered and simply waited and studied the woman in front of her.

As the first foot slid forward to ready herself for an attack, Cassandra was already in motion. She took one step forward and made a powerful thrust, extending her spear almost to its full length in as perfect an attack as she had performed all day. The spearhead cut through the gap between the mage's helm and the breastplate. The armor was spelled but even it couldn't stop a strike with that much force and precision and from a weapon that likely carried spellwork of its own.

The Herald gasped and choked in quick succession. Blood poured from the wound and her lips as she sank onto her knees and the last flame died in her hands.

She drew her spear back out and the woman dropped for the last time.

The silence that carried over the battlefield was its own kind of deafening as she wiped the blood carefully from the spearhead and looked around for any sign that they would still be attacked.

"Well…she was a tough one," Bandir muttered and wiped the blood and dust from his face. "Who do you suppose we should kill next?"

"We?" she asked. "I had that one all to myself."

"Only because she knew that if she killed you, she would have to face all of us," Tandir pointed out. "I assume she was scared and chose a quick death instead of dragging it out."

She smiled and turned to Karvahal, who had made no effort to join the banter. There was a haunted look on his face as she placed a hand on his shoulder while he planted his sword in the ground and rested his hands on the guard.

"I suppose I should have saved the final blow for you," she said. "You might have had your vengeance on her for what she did to your father."

"My father is avenged." The chieftain grinned at her. "Who did it doesn't matter. It's probably best that it was you. I might have let my emotions reign and allowed her an opening that you avoided."

"I'm glad your father was avenged, at least. And your people are safe for the moment."

"Your people can be glad that none of this destruction happened in Torsburch," Langven added and shook his head. "Can you imagine having to rebuild after such devastation?"

CHAPTER TWENTY

There was still an unfortunate amount of work to be done. Langven was right. It was good that they could leave the fortress where it was and the way it was, but there was still effort required to get all the villagers and their people to their homes.

Which meant they would likely not find a way to leave before the morning.

Langven and his Pack took on the work of clearing the rest of the Herald's forces, although Cassandra doubted there was much to do there. They were mercenaries, which meant they would not fight if the person paying them was dead. It was likely that they were ruled by fear as well and once the source of that fear was gone, the chances were that they would be in the wind at the soonest opportunity.

Provided they survived having the fortress dropped on them by said source of payment.

She shook her head and continued to brush Strider's coat. It felt like forever since she had the time to simply relax and spend time with the beast. She was looking forward to sleep as well, but that would have to wait. Regrettably, she couldn't simply rest while all the others were out and about, getting the work done.

Although it could be argued that her work in the area was accomplished. It was time for her to continue on her journey. The twins could follow if they had a mind to, but she couldn't make any promises about how she would pay them if they did.

"I think they might owe me still, though," she muttered. "They will be well-off from the loot on this battlefield and I bought their drinks. And kept them from getting killed in a pointless fight, let's be honest."

Strider had no answer for her but she didn't need one. Having someone to talk at was somehow easier than someone to talk to.

"You talk to your horses, then?"

She turned to the opening of their little stable—although she supposed a paddock was a better name, given that there was no roof over the heads of the horses—and saw that Karvahal now joined her and approached the section where his horse was stabled.

"Barbarians do that from time to time," she answered with a small smile. "Although not all of them by the sounds of it."

"No, but I suppose you are entitled to do so if you feel the need."

"How go the preparations to leave?" she asked and continued to brush Strider once he reached his horse. "Your people must be thrilled to return home after this time away and without fear of being attacked."

"They would be." Karvahal lowered his head. "And yet, as we discussed, it seemed that returning to Torsburch might be a little more distant in our future than we might have thought. What troops remain might decide to take their vengeance on us if given the chance, and I would see them to a place that might be easier to hold. Besides, we cannot count on the help of mercenaries for all time."

"I suppose that makes sense. Where do you plan to stay in the meantime?"

"There is a fortress near Draug's Hill. It's older but more or less intact and it has enough space for all of us. It will be rough at first, but it will be the finest location for us to be in, I think."

Cassandra smiled. "It is important for your people to have a home."

"And we are lucky that my ancestor was as ambitious as he was, I suppose. Do you know where you will go?"

"Not yet but we'll know before too long. If you don't mind, we might move with you for a while until we have a better idea of our course for the future."

"You will always be welcome among the people of Torsburch and I think you know that." The chieftain laughed, finished inspecting his horse, and moved to the gate. "I'll talk to you later."

"Look out for yourself. There's no telling if there are still dangers in that fortress for us to deal with."

"I'll keep that in mind."

If the truth be told, she didn't know what kind of power had been used to level the stronghold but she did know that power like that tended to have consequences that extended beyond a quick and easy death.

If they left soon enough, perhaps they would be spared whatever those might be.

She heard the gate open again and frowned as a donkey was led in.

"I don't think we have enough space for more beasts in this area," Cassandra said and shook her head. "You might have to build another paddock. I guess you folk can't stand to leave any of the beasts the Herald's mercenaries left behind."

"True, but this one and I have traveled the continent together and I would see him to some hay at least before night falls."

The brush fell from her hand and she spun toward the familiar sight of an old man and his donkey. He had a particular kind of gleam in his eyes that was enough warning to any and all who encountered him that he was far from ordinary.

"I suppose asking you to introduce yourself like a normal

fucking person is too much even for you." She growled her displeasure and ducked to collect the brush from where it had fallen.

"It has been many years since I have been within the same league as a normal fucking person," Theros answered with a chuckle. "Then again, are normal people not known to play the occasional joke on their friends?"

"You and I are not friends," she snapped quickly, having almost anticipated that this was where he wanted the conversation to go.

"We aren't?" The god sat on a stool she was sure had not been there before and he produced an apple from his pocket and fed it to his donkey. "Now that is certainly odd. I could have sworn that friends are those who look out for you and help you when you need it. That kind of thing. Is that wrong?"

She turned and realized that she had no real answer for him.

"I wouldn't say you led me anyplace safe."

"Safe was not where you wanted to be. You wanted an adventure and for the Barbarian Princess to help those in need. The gentle nudges I provided brought you there."

"Against impossible odds."

"Odds you make a habit of challenging, as you showed. Now, I don't expect thanks for my efforts or even gratitude. I am well aware that you performed most of the work—along with some help—and even helped me as I needed it as well. But all things considered, I would say ours is a partnership that has been more than profitable to both of us. I understand if you would prefer to avoid the term of friendship to describe it, however."

It was annoying for her to be angry when he presented these entirely reasonable points. She would ordinarily be a little more argumentative—as she expected he wanted from her—but it had been a long day at the tail end of a long week, and a long journey besides that. She needed rest far more than she needed to banter with a god.

"Fair enough," she stated, shook her head, and finally put the brush away. "I don't suppose you knew anything about this Belladonna before she made an appearance? Or maybe the person she was heralding for?"

"Grimm the Cruel?" Theros sighed and scratched his beard. "I must say that I knew something of them before they attacked, although even I did not expect them to possess such powers. It means there are those in my realm intent on hiding who they are and what they are. I will need to study them a little closer now that they have been brought to my attention."

"So what do you know about them?"

"I know that what Belladonna said of them is not merely pageantry, and both Grimm and his father Karthelon are...well, real. I cannot say whether the rumors about them are true but I can say their reputation for power and cruelty are more than earned by this point. Legend says that Grimm took power and presented his father with the option of single combat to decide who would hold the throne. Karthelon took the option, lost, and spent nigh on a decade being killed as a result. And I can assure you that it was not a pleasant death and its duration was extended by magic to make it more painful."

Cassandra raised an eyebrow. "That is how the story goes. When it comes to folk with that kind of power, they have a habit of elevating their tales for their benefit."

"And yet I have a feeling that these tales will prove only too true," he answered. "And if you continue down this contentious road, I would say that they will begin to take notice of you and your efforts."

She tilted her head and sat beside him. "Now that sounded suspiciously like a warning. Possibly even a threat. Do you want me to stop or is it merely friendly consideration to let me know who and what I have on my hands?"

"You thought I would be able to dissuade you once started down this path?" Theros laughed. "I cannot tell if I should be insulted that you would think so little of me or honored that you consider me to be that persuasive."

"Neither," she retorted. "So you want me to go, then? I suppose I would want to travel a little farther north if only to spite you and get out of this fucking heat."

The god laughed again. "I want you to do what you know to be right. Of course, the fact that such a decision is so damn predictable is your fault. I had a feeling you were already planning to find out more about this Grimm and why he sent a herald out with an army so I thought it was only fair that I provide you with good intelligence regarding who he is and what to expect from him."

"That is fair, I suppose."

"Yes, well. You are on a road you've set for yourself and I have no intention of changing its course."

"Do you know anything else about this Grimm?" Cassandra asked. "I haven't even heard the name, much less any rumors of what he did to his father."

"I've learned little but I plan to learn more. It can be inferred that he is powerful, given the power held by those who fear him. It stands to reason that he does not wish for his reputation to be spread and too much attention drawn to him before a time of his choosing. And I suppose he chose now."

"What kind of power was the Herald able to call on to level the fortress?"

"Dark magic. Literally, taking hold of the shadows and turning them into agents of chaos in their own right. It has been many years since I've seen it used and even longer since I've seen someone powerful enough to wield it in full daylight. And I do not like the precedent."

"Now that is interesting." She leaned forward. "You almost sound...afraid."

"Fear is...not the word I would use. Sound knowledge of the consequences is preferable."

"That is called fear. A very human emotion for a god to feel, wouldn't you say?"

Theros tilted his head and nodded. "Fair enough."

There was something to be said for his father's tastes. Grimm was never partial to them but there was no denying the sheer amount of awe they inflicted on all those present. And fear was most definitely the most powerful tool to be used.

He had tried love, loyalty, and even—on occasions—tried to stimulate the feelings of guilt and jealousy in others, merely to see how they would react.

The results were less than satisfactory.

Fear made people predictable. It either cowed them or made them violent. They were useful as the former and if they proved to be the latter kind, they could always be an addition to the skulls that bedecked his throne room.

Yes, his father had something of an obsession with skulls. Human, orc, dwarf, nymph, and even a couple of dragon skulls were scattered around the keep. The walls themselves glimmered with a dull green light that did not come from the torches suspended on them. The cavernous stone hall had also been the old man's ideal representation, the concept meant to instill awe in those who were present in it.

The glowing braziers led any who approached to the throne itself, and each one was flanked by two of his men. They were silent guardians, sworn to never make a sound except with the intention to inflict violence, and none of that would be required this night.

Their skull-shaped helms glittered black in the firelight and further intensified their inhuman appearance.

By contrast, Grimm did not appear quite as much a threat. He was a young man with boyish looks, a gleaming smile, and a tussle of silver hair that proved to be impossible to tame. Even with the dark robes he wore, there was little to indicate that he was not merely another spoiled brat with a little power.

Two figures flanked the throne, which was where most eyes were cast. One was a young man with long black hair and crimson robes, and to the right, a dark figure towered over both of them, seemingly made of pure shadow and showing no reflection from the odd and unsettling lights that filled the whole chamber.

No gazes would be cast at the boy on the throne and that was by design. Grimm had a great deal to thank his father for. The old man had gone through all the work so his son wouldn't have to. Of course, he hadn't expected to give the position up quite so soon, but the world they lived in was a chaotic one. Why make the succession any different?

He could tell that the bedraggled warrior suffered the full effects intended by the throne room. His eyes were wide and his fingers itched for a sword that was no longer at his hip. He displayed all the instincts of a frightened bunny hoping that if it remained still enough, the fox wouldn't see it.

Perhaps this one was a little too cowed.

Grimm sighed and gestured for the man to approach. There was no reaction and the warrior looked like he might run instead.

"Bring him to me." He hissed annoyance, rolled his eyes, and drew a deep breath. It was too early in the evening for him to be this aggravated but all his evening plans had come to a grinding halt, all because a mercenary sent with his Herald had returned and looked like he hadn't stopped for rest, food, or drink in days.

And he smelled too. Grimm wondered what details of the horse he could divine merely from the stench the man emitted.

His order was heard by two of the Silent Ones, who immediately grasped the mercenary by the shoulders and dragged him to the base of the seven steps leading to the throne, all carved from the base of a jagged, obsidian pillar.

"Oh, maybe not," Grimm muttered and covered his nose as the smell grew worse. "I suppose it would have killed those shits at the front gate to fling some water on this animal before they brought him before me."

Neither of the Silent Ones answered and instead, looked stoically ahead.

"I was talking to you, little one." Grimm growled and nodded to the mercenary, who jumped like he had been struck by lightning. "There must have been a reason that drove you to the condition you are in and more importantly, to demand an audience this late in the night. I would rather you get on with it while we are still young and of this world."

"Ye…yes, your majesty." The mercenary had the good sense to finally drop to one knee and bow his head in deference to the man whose presence he was in. "I was…I was sent with a message for the Lord of Silence, Grimm the Cruel."

"And you knew better than to keep me waiting." He chuckled and clapped slowly. "Of course, I wouldn't know I was waiting for you given that no word was sent of your arrival, but something tells me you will explain that as well. Why has Belladonna not answered my summons?"

"My lord… Your Herald has fallen in battle."

His clapping stopped and the amused expression left his face. Maybe the fear the man felt had less to do with his surroundings and more a dread omen of being the bearer of bad tidings.

"I would assume you have more to tell me than only that."

"There was a woman—the Barbarian Princess—who stood against her. She was a powerful magic wielder and she rallied and organized a city we had taken. We moved to counter the insurrection and your Herald fought her, but she was killed in battle."

"Odd," Grimm muttered and toyed idly with an amethyst that had been embedded in his throne as he stood slowly. "You watched this fight yourself, yes? You are not merely telling me what others told you?"

"Of course."

"And yet you put in no effort to save my Herald? The one woman you were sworn to serve and to kill for, no matter what threats might have stood in your way? I can see that such oaths mean little to men like you."

The warrior's eyes widened and he realized the danger he was in. There was no escape, however. Even as he stood and tried to move back, the Silent Ones held him in place.

"I am but a man," he whispered. "What difference would I have made by standing against the Barbarian Princess? She struck with the power and fury of a god."

Something hot filled Grimm's body. He'd learned to embrace the rage when it came to him and let it flood through his body. It made him powerful as he flicked down the steps in the blink of an eye. His hand grasped the warrior's throat and lifted him completely off his feet, his other hand still holding the amethyst.

"Barbarians have no concept of royalty." He hissed an irate breath and tightened his hold around the man's throat. "It is the only redeeming feature to that mongrel race. And there should only be room in your heart for fear of one god—he with his hand closing around your throat."

There was nothing but a choked reply and he flung the man aside and smiled coldly as he landed five paces away from where he had knelt not seconds before.

Panicked, the warrior stood, looked around, and finally turned to run as Grimm raised the hand that held the amethyst. He relaxed his mind and watched as the flames poured out of it. They were colorful flames, almost like a rainbow, but they lashed out at the man until they were buried in his back.

The fire did not burn him. Something else happened and he screamed and fell to his knees as the life fled from his bones and his body desiccated in seconds. His eyes dried first, followed by the rest of his body. Everything drained from him before he could move until he settled on the floor, nothing but a pile of ash and bleached bones.

Grimm looked at the amethyst in his hands and smirked when he saw a hint of a gleam of light in there that had been absent before.

"You have been foolish, boy."

It truly was annoying how that voice made his hairs stand on end. He gritted his teeth and looked at the throne as the figure of pure shadow descended the steps slowly, one by one.

"How?" he snapped and took a step forward. "I sent my Herald out. Fear of my name will rip through the world, even in her failure."

"And yet a god does not let himself become angered or goaded into such hasty and wasteful action. Information is now forever lost to you because you chose to kill instead of listen."

"I did what had to be done!" His voice echoed through the chambers. The only other sound that could be heard was that of the Silent Ones returning to their post. "His death served a purpose. All their deaths serve my purpose."

The figure stopped in front of him, and Grimm felt the rage leeching from his body. Yelling like a child only proved Karthelon's point and made it so that there was nothing to shout about in the first place. He wouldn't tell his father that he simply wanted to kill the man. What purpose did it serve?

"Patience is a virtue," the darkened visage answered him and his voice never rose above a whisper. "If you cannot learn this, you will never truly rise above petty mortality and my time spent in siring you has been utterly, truly wasted."

The truest sting to those words was that there was no emotion attached to them. His father appeared to be uninterested and unconcerned about the outcome either way, no matter what happened.

"Ten years," Grimm retorted. "For ten fucking years I proved my worth to you above all your other whelps. I killed them all, murdered them all, and I bound you for ten years to show you the truest depth of my rage and hatred."

"Yes." The voice sounded almost like it was laughing. "And now your real challenge lies before you."

The shadow figure seemed to lose all its menace and its power as his father's consciousness left it with nothing to do but to march up the steps to where it had stood before, watching silently and patiently.

"Son of a fucking whore," Grimm whispered and clenched his hands around the amethyst. He felt its warmth and wanted to crush it between his fingers.

There would be no time to stop and think about how he had called himself the grandson of a whore, but there was also no point in pondering the truest aspects of his insults.

"You," Grimm snapped at the nearest Silent One to him. "Send word out. I want my scouts to scour the fucking continent. I want them to tell me exactly who this barbarian bitch is and what I can do to end her."

The Silent One bowed his head and moved away at a decent pace.

Of all the fucking things to go wrong. Now, he didn't even feel like indulging in his evening routine.

AUTHOR NOTES - MICHAEL ANDERLE
OCTOBER 13, 2021

First, thank you for not only reading this story but these author notes in the back as well.

For those who don't know me, I'll add an "About Me" at the bottom of these author notes. For those who do, I'll get right into it.

Why a barbarian princess? Because this character needed more book time than I could give her in the *Skharr DeathEater series*.

When I created Cassandra, I didn't realize she would take on a life of her own. She has problem(s) created decades ago as a little girl, and due to Skharr's influence, she is figuring out who she wants to be.

Plus, she loves acting like a barbarian. Wearing her god-provided armor, she is a tank. Perhaps that is what she will go back to, but perhaps she will stay with this other persona. We will have to see!

If you haven't read anything before this book, do go back and read the *Skharr DeathEater* series where Cassandra is first introduced (*The GodKiller*, Book 04).

Now, for those who have never read one of my books (or one where I didn't introduce myself), here is the obligatory "About me" section ;-)

I wrote my first book *Death Becomes Her* (*The Kurtherian Gambit*) in September/October of 2015 and released it November 2, 2015. I wrote and released the next two books that same month and had three released by the end of November 2015.

So, just under six years ago.

Since then, I've written, collaborated, concepted, and/or created hundreds more in all sorts of genres.

My most successful genre is still my first, Paranormal Sci-Fi, followed quickly by Urban Fantasy. I have multiple pen names I produce under.

Some because I can be a bit crude in my humor at times or raw in my cynicism (Michael Todd). I have one I share with Martha Carr (Judith Berens, and another (not disclosed) that we use as a marketing test pen name.

In general, I just love to tell stories, and with success comes the opportunity to mix two things I love in my life.

Business and stories.

I've wanted to be an entrepreneur since I was a teenager. I was a very *unsuccessful* entrepreneur (I tried many times) until my publishing company LMBPN signed one author in 2015.

Me.

I was the president of the company, and I was the first author published. Funny how it worked out that way.

It was late 2016 before we had additional authors join me for publishing. Now we have a few dozen authors, a few hundred audiobooks by LMBPN published, a few hundred more licensed by six audio companies, and about a thousand titles in our company.

It's been a busy five plus years.

Have a great week or weekend, and talk to you in the next book!

Ad Aeternitatem,

Michael Anderle

CONNECT WITH THE AUTHOR

Connect with Michael Anderle

Website: http://lmbpn.com

Email List: http://lmbpn.com/email/

https://www.facebook.com/LMBPNPublishing

https://twitter.com/MichaelAnderle

https://www.instagram.com/lmbpn_publishing/

https://www.bookbub.com/authors/michael-anderle

BOOKS BY MICHAEL ANDERLE

Sign up for the LMBPN email list to be notified of new releases and special deals!

https://lmbpn.com/email/

For a complete list of books by Michael Anderle, please visit:

www.lmbpn.com/ma-books/